Virgin in the Gym
and Other Stories

Virgin in the Gym

and Other Stories

Wendy Perriam

ROBERT HALE · LONDON

ISBN 0 7090 7523 5

Robert Hale Limited
Clerkenwell House
Clerkenwell Green
London EC1R 0HT

2 4 6 8 10 9 7 5 3 1

Typeset in 10½/13pt Sabon by
Derek Doyle & Associates, Liverpool.
Printed in Great Britain by
St Edmundsbury Press, Bury St Edmunds, Suffolk.
Bound by Woolnough Bookbinding Ltd

For Ginny and Saxon Tate
– most dear and generous of friends

Contents

Hols

'Where are you going for your hols this year?'

Rowan played for time, arranging the neatly labelled envelopes into a pile. 'I'm . . . not sure.'

'Tom and I are wondering about Tangier. We spent a day there once when we were cruising on the *Oriana*, and we've often talked about going back.'

Rowan fiddled with a paperclip, trying to place Tangier – Morocco, wasn't it?

'On the other hand, we do love Spain. We had a great time in Segovia last year.'

Rowan nodded, anxious to convey her familiarity with major foreign cities. But *was* Segovia major? The only Segovia she knew was a classical guitarist. 'Goodness!' she exclaimed, pretending to notice the time. 'I'd better get off. I'm meeting someone for lunch.' Picking up her damp raincoat, she used it as cover to smuggle the cheese sandwich out of her desk drawer into her bag.

'Ta-ra!' said Cathy. 'Don't get wet.'

Some hope. By the time she reached the travel agents the rain had plastered her hair to her head, and her pale suede shoes had turned black.

Inside she felt little safer. The glaring lights and oppressively low ceiling made her shrivel like an uprooted plant. Nor had she expected such a crush of people: every desk occupied, mainly by customers in pairs. Of course, before you planned a trip, you really needed somebody to go with. There were probably special tours for singles, but the word drooped and sagged with failure. Being divorced or widowed wasn't such a cause for shame because already you'd been half of a couple, whereas she had only been a threesome, with her parents.

9

She remained hovering by the door. All the customers looked solemn and intent, as if they were consulting a doctor about a terminal disease, not booking a holiday. And the assistants (agents?) were positively intimidating, oozing self-assurance in their smart uniform of blue jackets and white shirts.

She finally plucked up courage and positioned herself behind the nearest couple, who sat side by side, holding hands.

'We're toying with the idea of Riga,' she heard the woman say.

Riga? She wasn't even sure what country it was in. She moved a little closer. Any facts she gleaned here would be useful when she talked to Cathy – not that Cathy often let her get a word in.

'Just for a brief stay. What do you recommend?'

The man behind the desk produced an illustrated brochure and opened it with a flourish. 'Well, there's a special weekend package, flights and meals included. It starts at four hundred and fifty, staying at the Radisson, or five hundred at the Metropole.'

Five hundred pounds for a weekend? Her annual fortnight with her parents at Bexhill cost her only the price of the odd ice-cream. They were expecting her this August again, of course. What could be more natural than spending all the major holidays – Christmas, Easter, summer – with their one and only child?

The woman was studying the details of the two hotels. 'I can't say I'm struck with either of them,' she observed.

'How about Stockholm then?' her partner (husband?) suggested.

'No, I've changed my mind. Let's go to Venice again.'

Rowan drew in her breath. Venice she *did* know: the one place she longed to see in all the world.

'Oh, darling, it's ghastly in the summer – hot and smelly and heaving with loathsome tourists.'

The woman grinned. 'Two of the loathsome tourists would be us! Look, let's go and have some lunch and talk it over. I don't want to be rushed.'

Rowan sat in one of the chairs they'd vacated, miserably conscious of her bedraggled appearance. Would the man even take her seriously? Despite his youth, he seemed authoritative, meeting her eyes directly and raising a quizzical eyebrow.

'Yes, madam, how can I help?'

'I . . . just wanted some brochures.' She looked down in confusion. Cathy would have flirted with him.

'Help yourself.' He gestured to the racks lining every wall. How could she have missed them? 'Anywhere particular in mind?'

'Venice,' she said, blushing like a schoolgirl.

'And do you want a package tour?'

'I'm not sure. I'm very . . . open. I'm keen on Italy in general.'

'Well, have a little rummage over there. The *Citalia* brochure's good. And try *Italian Escapades*. They're both fairly comprehensive.'

A clutch of booklets under her arm, she emerged into the street again, picking a zigzag course between the puddles. To her surprise, the rain had stopped – the wettest June since records had begun.

She found an empty bench in the park and sat gingerly on the damp, broken slats. After sharing her lunch with a few voracious pigeons, she turned her attention to Italy. Everyone was smiling – smiling as they swam, smiling as they lounged on beaches, smiling as they munched their *fettuccine* or strolled arm in arm along picturesque cobbled streets.

Smiling was a skill she hadn't mastered, like swimming, flirting, driving a car. In her parents' photo albums, from babyhood to the present day, she stared at the camera with the same impassive gaze. But if she could only escape, there would be a chance to learn. What she ought to do was pick a place and stick to it; not agonize, just go for the first letter of the alphabet.

Amalfi.

The towering cliff gave her instant vertigo. It plunged terrifyingly down to the sea, and some of the villas built into its face were clinging on for their very life. Indeed, as she watched, they became dislodged and began slithering into the hungry waves below.

No, not Amalfi.

Venice would be safer – no cliffs there, at least. And nobody was smiling. In fact, there were no people in the pictures at all, only domes and gondolas. 'Special honeymoon offer,' one hotel announced. 'A free bottle of Chianti awaits the happy couple in their room.' Her parents had spent their honeymoon in Scarborough. Not a success, her mother had once confided, and certainly no free wine. Her parents were teetotal anyway.

Turning the page, she came upon a treacherous canal, where a gondolier was approaching a low bridge. The crash of splintering wood shook the bench and echoed through the park, then, with a sickening eructation, gloating, gurgling water consumed the hapless boat.

There was no escape from water – it blighted every page: Como, the deepest lake in Europe, already closing above her head; Garda, with its horrific mountainous backdrop; Ischia, pea-size on the map, yet harbouring an extinct volcano. No, not extinct. It was erupting in her stomach, lumps of hot black lava choking up into her throat.

White-knuckled, she gripped the bench. Other people weren't beset by fears, except of normal things like snakes or flying. Cathy was so brave she'd been on the London Eye. For *her*, though, even words could induce alarm: the tumble of intimidating vowels in Santa Margarita di Pula glaring at her in defiant print, and every adjective making her more dizzy: breathtaking, spectacular, panoramic, precipitous. . . .

The pictures were appalling: another ominous sea with no warning-flags or lifeguards, and skies so unnaturally blue they must be laden with poisonous chemicals. It was a relief to bundle them into her bag and return to the haven of the office.

'Nice lunch?' Cathy glanced up momentarily.

'Not bad.'

'Where did you go?'

'Oh . . . only Pizza Hut.'

'And how was your friend?'

'Friend?'

'The one you met.'

'Oh, yes, she . . . *he*'s fine. In fact we went to Thomas Cook's and booked a holiday.'

'Really? Where?'

'Italy. We're touring. Amalfi, Venice, Ischia . . . oh, and Santa Margarita di Pula.'

She finished the last mouthful of baked beans. Breakfast with her parents invariably featured beans. Sausage and beans on Monday, beans and bacon Tuesday, beans on toast Wednesday. Her father needed the fibre for his bowels.

Shading her eyes against the effusive Venice sun, she gazed out across the canal, admiring the mosaics shimmering on ancient palazzos. She was reclining on the terrace of the Hotel San Luigi, eating not baked beans but pomegranates. There had been a picture of the hotel restaurant with an extraordinary six-tier platter as its centrepiece. On the top sat a pineapple, complete with its crown of leaves; clusters of black grapes dangled down several tiers, past voluptuous figs and sun-kissed nectarines. She had sampled all the fruits in turn, but kept returning to the pomegranates, which seemed the very essence of foreignness: menacing, exotic and posing a head-on challenge. You couldn't pop one into your mouth like a grape, or bite into that hard leathery skin. Instead, they must be sliced in half and attacked with a spoon and courage. Blood-red juice spurted into your face from the gelatinous, glossy flesh, and cunning pips lodged between your teeth, or shot on to your lap.

She took another, its skin a hectic red on one side, as deep-dyed as her blushes. A waiter bustled up to slice it deftly in two and provide her with a finger-bowl. Smiling her thanks, she crunched the sweet-sharp pips, then smiled again, despite their curious taste. Smiling was what you had to do abroad. Having practised long and hard, she had nearly got the hang of it.

'What's funny?' asked her mother.

'Nothing.'

'Well, you certainly seem brighter than you were at Easter. We were quite concerned about you, weren't we, Frank?'

'Mm,' said her father absently. He was busy picking pieces of peel out of the marmalade and arranging them on his toast in careful lines.

'I'm sorry,' she murmured, dabbling her hands in the finger-bowl before settling back luxuriously beneath a pink-fringed parasol.

'No need to be sorry. You just seemed a bit down, that's all.'

Hardly surprising. She'd been thirty-eight in April and every birth-day seeded a new crop of fears, as many now as all the pips in a pome-granate. These last few months she'd had to sleep with the light on, and she'd avoided writing letters for almost a year. To put her bare hand into the cavernous mouth of the postbox required a courage beyond her powers.

'Well, what shall we do this morning, dear? It's too cold for the beach. How about a nice brisk walk up to the Pavilion and back?'

'Mum, would you mind awfully if I spent today on my own? I've got some . . . things to do.'

'What sort of things?'

'Shopping – you know, clothes and stuff.'

'Well, I'll come too. In fact it would suit me fine. Dad needs a new pair of slippers.'

'No, I don't,' her father grumbled. 'There's nothing wrong with these.'

'Don't be silly, Frank. They're covered in coffee stains.'

'It wasn't coffee.'

'Of course it was.'

Rowan descended the grand staircase to the foyer. The tall, black-eyed doorman bowed to her respectfully as she stepped into the waiting gondola.

'It was *tea*, Peggy. I remember distinctly. You'd just poured me a second cup and—'

'Tea, coffee, whatever. They're ruined, anyway. I mean, look at them! What will people think?'

'People? We never see any people. Except for Rowan.'

'Yes, and now she wants to go out on her own.'

'I don't, Mum. It's just that—'

'I expect you've arranged to meet someone. Maybe *that*'s why you're so cheerful today. There's a man involved, I'll bet. Don't trust him, Rowan. Men are all the same. They're only after one thing – I should know.'

Frank banged his cup down and disappeared upstairs, muttering to himself.

'Now you've driven your father away.'

Rowan tipped the handsome gondolier as he helped her step ashore at the Lido. Of course there was a man involved – Alfredo. He was approaching this very minute, his black hair a delicious contrast to the milk whiteness of his suit. '*Bellissima*!' he whispered, pressing his lips to hers.

'Have you seen the rubber gloves, Rowan?'

'Yes, I put them under the sink.'

'That's not where they live. I've told you enough times.'

Guanto. Glove sounded so romantic in Italian. She had set herself a task to learn ten new words each day from her pocket dictionary – starting with the A's again: *amore, adorare, avventura*. Alfredo used *amore* all the time.

'*Ti amo*,' he breathed once more, spreading his jacket on the sand and pulling her gently down towards him.

'Are you going to help me dry?'

Rowan picked up the tea towel and stood running it through her fingers, enjoying the silky feel of Alfredo's shirt. And even more enticing were the whorls of springy hair that furred his broad, bronzed chest and crept tantalizingly lower down, to . . .

'Careful, Rowan! Those are the best cups, I'll have you know.' Her mother fished a last knife from the sink and rinsed it under the tap. 'Now,' she said, drying her hands, 'who's this man you're meeting?'

'Don't be silly, Mum! You're imagining things.'

'In that case, why can't we go shopping together?'

'We can, if you want.'

'Well, of course I want. I miss you, dear, you know. We hardly see anything of you these days. It was different when you lived here, but now you seem to keep away on purpose. I suppose you find us dull? That's the trouble, isn't it? Once you got that exciting new job, you consigned your poor old Mum and Dad to the scrap-heap.'

'It's not an exciting job, Mum. I'm just a glorified typist.'

'Well, why stay there, pray? There's plenty of jobs in Bexhill. And it would be much cheaper living with us than paying rent for that fleapit of a flat.'

True, the flat was not ideal. The keyhole in the front door seemed to have a hostile eye behind it, spying on her day and night. And the radiator wheezed like an asthmatic. 'I suppose I could see what's going locally,' she said without conviction. 'I seem to remember an employment agency just along from Boots.'

'That's my girl! Shall we set off straight away?'

'But what about Dad?'

'Oh, he can stay at home and sulk.'

'Alfredo!' Rowan hissed, wishing he wouldn't lag behind. It was harder to keep him close to her outdoors. There were so many real fears to contend with: the steeply shelving beach, the blurred uncertainty of the horizon stretching away in mist. And even in the centre of the town, she could hear the relentless booming of the waves. Like shellfire. Her parents had been born in the War, but she had arrived (undersized and squalling) in 1964, the era of Peace and Love, miniskirts, the Pill – although such things remained alien to her as well as them.

Her mother pulled her coat more closely round her. 'If this is what they call summer, they can keep it!'

'Yes, it is a bit on the cold side.' Cathy would expect her to return with a tan. There were sun-beds, of course, but the very thought made her claustrophobic. And what about holiday photos? Cathy was bound to have dozens to show her of Tangier.

Stopping outside Federico's, she peered in at the pink linen table-cloths and Chianti-bottle lamps. 'Mum, d'you fancy something Italian for lunch? My treat.'

'Oh, I don't think so, dear, thank you all the same.'

'Come on, just this once.' Rowan ran her eye down the menu in the window, savouring more new words: *crespoline Fiorentina, osso bucco* . . .

'I don't trust these foreign places, Rowan. You never know what sort of meat they use. I mean, they can get away with murder, smothering everything in sauces.'

'You could have pasta, though, or fish. They do grilled lemon sole—'

'Yes, and look at the price! It's wicked! Anyway, I've already planned lunch. We're having Lancashire hotpot and rhubarb pie and custard. Now come along, we haven't bought a thing yet. If I don't get your father's slippers, he'll be wearing those old stained ones when he's carried out feet first.'

Rowan shuddered. Death was the greatest terror – that girl she'd read about last month, nailed in her coffin still alive . . .

'I think I'll get him some vests as well. We'll go to Austin's, shall we? Is there anything *you* want?'

Souvenirs, she thought – booty as proof of her travels. And a little present for Cathy. Vests would hardly do, or a stick of Bexhill rock. She might find a delicatessen selling Italian cheeses . . .

'Oh, look – a closing-down sale! And that nightie's just my size. Can you read the ticket, dear?'

Rowan peered through the window. 'Yes, eleven ninety-nine.'

'Well, that's not bad, is it? What do you think? Do you like it?'

'Mm, it's nice.' Baby-blue brushed nylon with long sleeves and a high neck. 'I'll buy it for you if you want.'

'No, you keep your money, Rowan. You'll need it when we're dead and gone. And it might be an idea to get yourself a decent slip. That one I saw in the wash last week looks as if it's seen better days.'

Rowan blushed. The only slips on display were dreary unglamorous things. And the knickers were worse still – nothing black or slinky, but capacious bloomers that came up above the waist. In her mother's opinion, wearing sexy underwear meant you were 'asking for it'. And yes, indeed she was – not just asking but begging. 'Alfredo,' she implored, 'Come to me. Tonight.'

'Wow! That tan! You've really caught the sun.'

Rowan smiled – an art she had finally mastered. She had even survived the sun-bed, in spite of the initial horror of the goggles. 'Yes, we had a fantastic time. And the food was wonderful – *crespoline Fiorentina, osso bucco* . . .'

'I hope you've got some pictures.'

'Hundreds,' said Rowan airily. 'They should be back any day.' (How unfortunate that they would be mislaid in transit.) 'Oh, and I bought you something – just a tiny present.'

'Rowan, you shouldn't have!' Cathy unfolded layers of tissue to reveal a dainty turquoise necklet. 'Oh, it's gorgeous! And real Venetian glass, I take it?'

'That's right.' It had come from the charity shop two doors from her flat. 'And a bottle of wine for Tom.' Tuscan *Sangiovese*, courtesy of Oddbins.

Cathy was surveying herself in the mirror, holding the necklet against her throat. 'Gosh, thanks, Rowan. It looks great. Tell me, what did you think of Venice?'

'Out of this world.'

'I'd love to hear all about it. Are you free for lunch?'

Rowan returned to her desk. 'Sorry. Not today.' She had to use the lunch-hour to go back to Thomas Cook's. There were more holidays to book: Christmas in the Arctic Circle, Easter in Vladivostock, August crossing the Gobi Desert . . .

She smoothed her prim grey skirt across her knees, exquisitely conscious of the black G-string underneath. Alfredo had worked wonders for her.

And she had even managed to stop blushing.

Best Friends

'Come in!' Louise extended her arms in a hug. 'Great to see you after all this time.'

Pam tried to hide her shock. Louise was different. *Fat*. She felt herself squeezed against voluptuous breasts, lost in folds of ample flesh. Pregnant again? Surely not. Oliver was barely three months old . . .

'You *do* look well,' Louise said, standing back to appraise her. 'Come on through. And please forgive the mess. Adam says he can't believe how much clutter one tiny baby makes!'

Dead right, thought Pam, as she skirted the pram in the hall, only to tread on a rubber duck, which squawked in protest.

'In fact, I hope His Lordship doesn't wake up too soon. It'd be nice to have lunch in peace. We've masses to catch up on.'

'Oh, by the way, I've brought something for him.' Pam handed over a carrier bag containing a teddy bear. She wasn't one for wrapping gifts. 'Not very original, I'm afraid.' She had just noticed the two larger teddies already ensconced on a chair.

'Oh, he'll absolutely adore it! Thank you so much.'

'Don't mention it.' They were strangers to each other, reduced to banalities.

'Now, while it's quiet, how about a drink? I've got some Chardonnay chilling in the fridge.'

Pam would have preferred a gin, but she accepted gracefully. 'Aren't you having one?'

'No, it affects the milk. *Breast* milk,' she added, seeing Pam's puzzled frown. She moved a box of baby-wipes from the sofa and gingerly seated herself, as if still uncomfortable after the birth. 'What I'm dying to know is why you're back in Devon. Last time we spoke you said wild horses wouldn't drag you away from London.'

'Last time we spoke, Louise, was at your wedding.'

'It can't be! I don't believe it. That was over two years ago.'

It might as well be twenty years, such was the gulf between them now. Hadn't they sworn an oath at the age of ten never to grow up, never to have boyfriends, never to wear hateful things like petticoats or dresses. Yet here was Louise, not only married with a baby but wearing an unspeakable pink gingham frock with pearl buttons down the front.

'I did write, though, I remember – and more than once, I'm sure. But I don't think you ever replied.'

Of course she hadn't replied: she'd been too hurt by the betrayal.

'Never mind,' Louise smiled. 'Today we'll make up for lost time! Tell me first what happened to that job you had in Southwark. You were working for a Polish woman, weren't you?'

'Yes. Irena. It didn't . . . work out.'

'Oh, I'm sorry, Pam.'

'Don't be. I'm freelance now, which suits me fine. And I've bought an old mill on the River Teign. It's a bit of a wreck, to be honest, but I'm in the process of doing it up.'

'That sounds fun.'

'It's bloody hard work, actually. Look at the state of my hands.' Pam presented them for inspection: dirt-ingrained fingers and callused thumbs. Louise's hands, in contrast, were soft and absurdly manicured, the wedding finger shackled with a wide gold band and diamond solitaire. Wedlock – aptly named.

'And do you intend to—?' The question was truncated by a piercing wail from upstairs. 'Goodbye to peace!' said Louise, sounding more doting than cross. 'He's got a fantastic pair of lungs on him. I'll feed him down here, shall I? Then we can chat.'

An unlikely prospect in view of the yells, which increased steadily in volume until Louise reappeared with a flailing, squalling bundle in her arms.

'Ollie, say hello to your Auntie Pam.' She had to raise her voice above the commotion.

Pam proffered a nervous finger. Could the creature even see her? Its face was contorted in crimson rage; its eyes lost in the furious grimace as it let out another bellow.

'He'll be OK as soon as he's feeding. He's a real piggie-porker, aren't you, Ollie darling! I'm up every two hours at night.'

Again, that note of pride. Once, she and Louise had taken pride in sensible things: catching newts, breeding white mice, cycling with no hands.

Louise unbuttoned the top of her dress. 'Are you sure you don't mind this, Pam? I mean, I can go upstairs if—'

'No, it's fine.' How could she object? Women breast-fed babies all over the place these days – in shops, restaurants, buses, even the House of Commons. She took a sip of wine, wondering when *she'd* be fed. Or was it to be liquid lunch only, for her as well as Oliver? At least the screams had now given way to faint suckling, snuffling noises.

However, she averted her eyes from the process, preferring to picture Louise dressed in an old jersey and jeans and galloping along muddy lanes full-pelt. They were Thunderhead and Black Beauty, horses that could talk, as well as whinny and jump fences and crunch their way through tons of sugar lumps. When she stayed at Louise's house, they would lie awake into the early hours, discussing weighty matters such as whether animals had souls, or if sherbet lemons were superior to humbugs.

A sudden gasp from Louise jolted her back to the present. Glancing up, she was confronted by the unnerving sight of a vast naked breast, engorged with milk. The baby's face was half-smothered by it – how on earth did he manage to breathe? 'What's wrong, Louise? Are you OK?'

'Yes, sorry. I didn't mean to alarm you, but it's painful when he latches on. I'm having a bit of a problem with cracked nipples. And last month I had a blocked duct. I seem to live at the doctor's these days.'

'Poor you.'

'Oh, no, I'm not complaining. I've never been happier, in fact. I can't tell you, Pam, how amazing it feels to . . . well, create a new life. Adam and I are so lucky. Ollie's just perfect, aren't you, cutesie-pie?'

Louise was gazing at the child with unalloyed devotion. Devotion was what you felt for your best friend. You would protect her from sneaks and bullies, defend her against loathsome teachers, share your only piece of chocolate with her, give her your last penny, die for her, if need be.

'Actually our GP's not much use. All he does is dole out antibiotics.

But I've got this marvellous baby book Adam's mother gave me. It may be old-fashioned but it's full of good ideas. For instance, a tea-strainer for cracked nipples.'

'A *tea*-strainer?'

'Yes, you detach the handle and slip it inside your bra, and it works like a nipple shield.'

Pam took a gulp of wine. If she was offered a cup of tea, she could only hope it was made with teabags.

'Oh, Ollie, poppet, wake up! He does that sometimes, you know – screams the house down to be fed, then promptly dozes off.'

Louise gave him a little jiggle and the suckling noises resumed. Pam tried to imagine the taste of warm breast milk and found herself almost gagging. Booze would be infinitely better, ready-mixed gin and tonic gushing from a nipple.

'Now, where were we, Pam? Oh yes, you were telling me about your house.'

'*Mill.* I got it dirt cheap, although it's cost me a hell of a lot in—'

'Ollie, what's the matter, precious? Sorry to interrupt you, Pam – he's not normally like this.'

'I hope it's not me that's upset him.'

'Don't be silly. Of course it's not you. He can probably sense that I'm in pain. Even at this age they're incredibly sensitive.'

'Why not change to a bottle, then? Wouldn't it be easier for you both?'

'Oh, no. I'm a firm believer in "breast is best". It gives them important antibodies, and it's natural, isn't it?'

Is it? Pam wondered, her eye drawn anew to the grossly distended udder. At school, she and Louise used to despise the girls with breasts. They, thank God, were both late developers and had succeeded in fending off their periods through sheer willpower.

'Ah, *that*'s the trouble, is it?' Louise was sniffing Oliver's crotch. 'You need changing, don't you, sweetheart? You've done lovely poo-poos for Mummy.'

Couldn't parents use the proper words? Not bow-wow – dog; not lovely poo-poos – shit.

'Come up with me, Pam, and you can see his room. We're really rather proud of it. We decorated it ourselves.'

The wallpaper teemed with gambolling bunnies, pink and blue, and dressed in frilly bonnets. She and Louise had once kept rabbits – live ones. Animals were serious creatures, with deep-seated feelings and distinctive personalities. 'Pets' was another inadequate word.

As Louise laid the baby on the changing-table, the yelling started again. Pam watched, appalled, as his nappy was unpinned. Not innocuous rabbit-droppings but a curdled mass of yellowish sludge. 'Just, er, going for a pee,' she said, seeking refuge in the bathroom.

But there was no escape from babies. A baby-bath occupied one corner, a nappy-pail another, and every ledge and shelf was crowded with jars and bottles, duplicates of those in his room: baby oil, baby cream, baby powder, baby shampoo. Even a box of what she took for innocent tissues turned out on closer scrutiny to be nursing mothers' breast pads. And beside them was a bulky packet of super-size sanitary towels. Poor Louise must be leaking both ends.

Returning to the nursery she found her anointing Ollie's bottom with a viscous white cream, which she then spread on his genitals. His penis was little more than a bud, yet looked red and angry, like his face. Penises were the cause of all the trouble. Adam's had seeded this interloper.

'We may as well stay up here while I finish his feed, if that's OK with you, Pam?'

'Oh, I thought you *had* finished.'

Her irritation was lost on Louise, who was planting butterfly kisses on Oliver's bare tummy as she put on a clean nappy and manoeuvred his wriggling limbs into a duckling-patterned stretch-suit. 'Park your bones,' she smiled, patting the seat of the upright chair before settling herself in the rocker. 'Adam usually sits there when I'm feeding. He loves to be part of it. In fact, he's such a doting father, I think he'd breastfeed Ollie himself if he could!'

Pam shuddered. Being reminded of Adam was vile enough, but Adam with milk-filled breasts . . .

'Ollie, treasure, what's wrong? You just don't seem hungry, do you, pet?'

Well, if he's not, I am, Pam muttered, as her stomach rumbled audibly. Given the chance of food, she wouldn't fiddle-faddle around like this pampered little fusspot.

'Oh, *what* a big yawn! Who's a sleepy baby, then?' Louise turned to Pam. 'You know, he seems more tired than hungry. I think I'll put him down for a nap.'

Now they could have lunch, perhaps.

23

'Or shall we have one last try? Come on, snookums, show your Auntie Pam what a big appetite you've got. No? You want your beddy-byes? All right. Let's get that nasty wind up . . .' Louise hoisted him on to her shoulder and gently rubbed his back. There was a sizeable belch, and a gobbet of milky liquid spewed down the back of her dress. 'Clever boy!' she purred.

A veritable Einstein. He could not only shit, he could vomit too. Pam watched impatiently as he was cleaned up and laid in his cot, the covers tucked round him and his forehead tenderly kissed. All at once a memory surfaced: she and Louise sharing a double bed when they were staying with Aunt Ella in her spooky house in York. They had clung together in the dark for fear of ghosts and monsters, and when they woke the next morning their arms and legs were still entwined. To this day she could recall the shock of it, the wonder.

'Now my little chickabiddy, you have a nice long nap. And Auntie Pam says goodnight, too.'

'Goodnight,' Pam repeated dutifully. Were nights ever good for Louise, or just an endless round of screams and pain and drudgery?

After further cooings and gurglings, Louise dragged herself away at last and tiptoed to the door. 'Now for that lunch,' she said, ushering Pam downstairs. 'It's only cold, I'm afraid. I don't seem to have time to cook these days.'

Hardly surprising, when Oliver filled her every waking moment. For children, though, time was boundless, like the sea. Not that they'd waste it on stupid things like cooking. She and Louise had decided that when *they* were in charge of domestic arrangements it would be picnics for every meal – no cutlery, no washing-up, and no tablecloth except the grass, or sand. 'Remember our picnics on the beach?'

'Oh, yes! Those ghastly doorstep sandwiches. And always peanut butter.'

'There's nothing wrong with peanut butter.'

'Oh, Pam, it's frightfully unhealthy! – full of salt and sugar and E-numbers. When I wean Ollie I intend to be really strict. Not a gram of salt, and nothing sweet except fruit in its natural state.'

And he'd probably grow up to be a raving chocoholic.

She followed Louise into the kitchen – another shrine to infant-dom, with its 'Baby's First Year' wall-chart, its Mickey Mouse mobile dangling from the dresser and a daunting array of nappies on the airing rack.

'I thought everyone used disposable nappies these days. Aren't they meant to be less work?'

'Ollie prefers the terry ones.'

Oh, he told you, did he, Pam refrained from saying as she seated herself at the table. Lunch was already laid out – everything natural, of course: feta cheese, wholemeal bread, a variety of salads and a bowl of fresh fruit. Louise's mother used to make them toad in the hole and steamed puddings glistening with syrup.

'Do help yourself. The green stuff's all organic.' Louise was busy mixing the dressing and slicing bread. 'Now, this mill of yours – it must be pretty sizeable. Do you live there on your own?'

She nodded. After you left school, best friends were near impossible to find. It was a unique relationship, requiring a total focus on each other, like lovers without the sex.

'We'd love to come and see it, if you'll have us.'

'Us' meant Oliver, presumably, and Adam. She had only met Adam at the wedding and they had loathed each other on sight.

'It'll be nice to see more of each other.' Louise leaned forward eagerly. 'In fact I was going to ask you a favour.'

Would she babysit? Well, OK, occasionally, so long as earplugs were provided and a decent supply of booze.

'We're having Ollie christened later this year, and we'd love you to be the godmother.'

'What?' Pam almost choked on her tomato.

'Oh, I know you're not the churchy type. Nor am I, to be honest. But the ceremony's so lovely. And it would make it extra special, Pam, if you were there, and part of it – you know, for old times' sake. I mean, we were so close as children, weren't we? Soul mates and blood brothers.'

So Louise hadn't forgotten. She had even used the correct word: brothers. Who in their right mind would choose to be a girl?

'Remember that summer in York? We were hardly apart for a minute, and I used to think I'd never love anyone as much as you.'

I still feel the same, Pam longed to say. But was it even true? Could she love the leaking breasts, the fleshy thighs, the goo-goo baby talk? Yes, she could, because underneath was the real Louise. People didn't change so radically. Poor Louise had been duped by Adam's romantic

25

promises and by the spurious happy-families beaming from every magazine and hoarding, those cute gap-toothed kids from never-never land. But now that her blood brother had returned, the old Louise would come cantering, whinnying back. 'Thunderhead,' she whispered.

'Black Beauty,' Louise echoed, looking into her eyes.

They held each other's gaze. Then slowly, very slowly, Pam got up and put her arms around her – a quite different embrace from their earlier hug of greeting. This was a solemn gesture of commitment, a formal restatement of love.

'Oh, Pam, I've missed you so much . . .' Louise drew back a little, but took Pam's hand in hers. 'I'm so glad we're in touch again. You're my oldest friend, you know. And when I think of all the things we've shared, everything we've done together . . .'

Pam smiled in silent pleasure. Speaking might break the spell, disrupt this sacred moment. She knew she must learn to be patient, simply wait for as long as it took. Oliver wouldn't scream for ever, nor be breastfed for ever. Breasts could shrink, Louise be unshackled. They would gallop side by side again one day.

Louise finally let go her hand. 'But listen, you haven't told me yet what you think about being godmother.'

Pam drained her wine in a single angry gulp. Must they return to the brat so soon? She despised christenings as much as weddings: the hypocrisy, the hats, the smug society vicars . . . 'Well, to be honest, I'm not keen. I haven't set foot in a church for years.'

'Yes, but what matters is Ollie, surely you agree? I want his godmother to be someone I know and trust, someone he can relate to as he's growing up. The friends I've made here are really only acquaintances, and anyway—' Her words were lost in a bellow from upstairs. 'Oh, dear.' She looked anxiously at the ceiling. 'I was afraid this might happen. He took so little at his feed, he's starving hungry again. Excuse me, Pam, won't you?'

As soon as she'd gone, Pam crept out of the kitchen and stood listening at the foot of the stairs. The noise was barbarous, malevolent. Oliver must have heard their conversation and was now reclaiming his mother for himself. The shrieks were easy to translate: 'No rivals.' 'No intruders.' 'Mummy's *mine*, and mine alone.' Pam shut her eyes, tried to stop her ears.

'Oh, Ollie, precious, have we got a nasty pain, then?' Louise was already on her way downstairs, cuddling the bawling infant, trying to comfort him.

But that was impossible, Pam realized, so long as *she* was here. Like his father, the child detested her. 'Look, I'll go, Louise. I can see you have your hands full.'

'*Go*? What on earth do you mean? We haven't finished lunch yet.'

'It's OK. I'm not hungry. Oliver is.'

'No, I was wrong. I found him doubled up with pain, poor lamb, so I think it must be colic. Come on, angel, Mummy kiss it better.'

The screams redoubled – primitive, implacable. This wasn't colic, it was sheer unadulterated loathing. There was no way she could fight it. Oliver was too powerful, through his very vulnerability and the closest of close ties. A blood brother was no match for a blood son.

'Ollie, darling, don't cry. My poor, poor poppet, what can Mummy do to take the nasty pain away?'

Pam could answer that question. The baby's rage, she knew, was directed at her alone. The clenched fists and thrashing feet were saying, 'Go away! Go home!'

Except home was still too close. She would still be Louise's neighbour, within range of friendly visits, christening parties, birthdays, invitations to school plays – their entire lives ruled by Oliver. She must uproot herself altogether; move abroad, somewhere remote, far enough from his tyrannical demands. She would have to give up her freelance work, abandon her beloved mill, despite the time and money she had already lavished on it . . .

But there wasn't any choice. She was being forced into exile and must go in silence, without complaint.

She rose from the table with a final glance at Louise, who was completely engrossed in Oliver once more: rubbing his stomach, murmuring endearments to him, staunching his tears with kisses.

Slipping quietly into the hall, she closed the door on mother and child, and cantered miserably away.

Thunderhead and Black Beauty would never see each other again.

William

'Excuse me, madam, could I take up a few minutes of your time?'

Vera stopped. The man looked safe enough. Respectably dressed in a decent suit and raincoat, not one of those dreadful anoraks. 'Yes, gladly.'

'Are you a dog-owner, madam?'

Vera hesitated. If she said no, that might be the end of it – the conversation over before it had begun. And conversations were rare, especially with men.

'Do you own a dog?'

Evidently he thought she hadn't understood. She might be old but she wasn't daft or deaf. 'Yes,' she said, 'I do.'

'May I ask what breed it is?'

Only a few breeds came to mind. The Queen had corgis, but weren't they rather snappy? Labradors were good with children – not much use in her case. 'A . . . a golden retriever,' she said.

'Ah, lovely!' The man smiled – a genuine smile that lit his eyes. 'Male or female?'

'Male.' She had never had a male. Not of any kind.

The man was writing her answers on his clipboard. Which meant she must be important, someone whose opinions mattered. Waking this morning she had felt shadowy, unreal.

'And how old is he?'

Ninety-three, she nearly said. She liked seeing people's look of incredulity when she revealed her age. Most ninety-three-year-olds did little more than sit and stare, and had long ago succumbed to Meals on Wheels. She still shopped and cooked for herself, and took a daily walk to the war memorial, regardless of the weather. 'Er, three.'

'Quite a youngster, then. And what's his name?'

While a bus rumbled past, she ran through various names in her head. Rex was hardly original. Barney lacked style. Major sounded boastful. 'William,' she replied at last – her father's name. William, never Bill. If her father had been a dog, he would probably have been an Alsatian or a Dobermann: fierce and unpredictable. She put her shopping basket down, pleased – indeed surprised – that the man hadn't yet lost interest. Sometimes she worried about her voice drying up, from lack of use.

He sneezed, and begged her pardon. She could see he had nice manners, although his eyes were rather sad. Perhaps his wife had passed away.

'And what do you feed him on, madam?'

Did people *cook* for dogs these days? She remembered her Aunt Annie stewing tripe for her three spaniels, and even making dog-cakes with oatmeal and grated carrot. But Annie was an eccentric. She practically starved herself so she could spoil her beloved dogs.

Pencil poised, the man seemed about to repeat his question. If she didn't answer correctly he'd find someone else to ask. 'Bounce!' she said triumphantly, suddenly remembering the name from the television.

He jotted down her reply. Every word she said was noted with near reverence. And some of the people going in and out of Debenham's glanced at her, and the clipboard. She stored the glances in the larder of her mind, as she had stored corned beef and condensed milk during the war. Most days she was invisible.

'What flavour?' he asked next.

That was easy. 'Chicken.' She had just bought a piece for tea. Not that you could trust it. Or eggs, for that matter. E.coli, salmonella – nothing about poultry was very safe just now.

'Chicken every day, madam, or do you ring the changes?'

Chicken every day? Whatever was he thinking of? Yesterday it had been macaroni cheese with grilled tomatoes, and the day before a nice Sunday roast. 'Beef on Sundays.'

'Would that be the Super-Chunks or the Mince?'

'Topside.'

'I beg your pardon?'

'Er, Super-Chunks.'

'And have you ever tried the Liver and Heart?'

30

'No. I don't like offal.'

'You mean William doesn't,' the man smiled.

Her father hadn't liked anything. He would glower through meals, complaining about non-existent gristle on meat, and skin on skinless custard. And he particularly disliked dogs, doubtless because they enjoyed their food – enjoyed everything in life: walks, sticks, woods, children. When she visited Aunt Annie, the spaniels went delirious with excitement, skidding along the hall, their claws scrabbling on the parquet, barking, yelping, rushing round in circles. Returning home, she used to pray for a miracle – that her father would do the same: bound from his study to greet her, skidding along the parquet in an ecstasy of joy. Instead he avoided his children. 'Yes, that's right – William doesn't like it.'

'And what about the Turkey? Is he partial to that?'

'No.' She grimaced. Her father loathed Christmas and everything to do with it. Turkeys were a bother to carve, and had little flavour anyway; Christmas trees were a fire-risk and, worst of all, the children were home from school.

'So it's just the Chicken and Beef you buy?'

'Yes.'

'And do you ever use other brands than Bounce?'

She shook her head. Once, she'd been full of bounce. (Before the move, and the bronchitis.) 'Chum' and 'Pal' were different words entirely – common, and somehow false. You didn't have chums in your nineties; no one was left.

'How about dry food? Dog biscuits or meal?'

'I make my own,' she said airily. Aunt Annie always had. And she'd also made special doggy sausages, out of rabbit and pigs' trotters.

Another bus rumbled past, empty, by the looks of it. She hated empty buses. Even with just a few passengers you could imagine conversations. 'Well, we're lucky the rain's held off.' 'Yes, honestly, ninety-three. I remember seeing a Zeppelin over Dulwich when I was a little girl.' Perhaps this nice man would need her again, for a survey on something else. Gardens, for example. She knew a lot about gardens; she could tell him how to get rid of slugs and what to plant in acid soil. 'Are you keen on gardening?' she asked.

He looked startled for a moment, as if he'd been thrown off-course.

She flushed. Clearly *he* was the one who asked the questions. Like her father. 'I feed William in the garden,' she said, by way of explanation. 'On warmer days, anyway.'

'Oh, er, yes, I see.' He cleared his throat, before returning to the matter in hand. 'Could you tell me roughly how many tins of Bounce you buy a week?'

'Three dozen at least.' She needed all the bounce she could get. Since the winter her knees had stiffened worryingly.

'That's a lot,' he observed.

'Yes, William's rather a greedy-guts.' Her father's name for her, when it wasn't Clumsy Clogs or Lazybones.

'And would they be the standard size tins or the large?'

'The large.' She wished he'd give his lovely smile again. Perhaps she had offended him. Men took offence so easily.

'Right, we're almost done.'

Disappointment seared through her mind. She had imagined spending all day with him – the shops closing and twilight falling while the two of them still stood beneath the stars together, deep in conversation.

'Just a couple more questions – about you, this time. May I ask your marital status, if you have no objection? Married, single, widowed, or divorced?'

'Married,' she said, beaming. If she had been lucky enough to marry, she would have chosen a man like him – someone with beautiful sad eyes who looked at you intently when you spoke. She had never got to choose, though. In her day it wasn't done. And anyway, most of the men had been killed off in the war.

'And do you live in your own home, or in rented accommodation?'

'I live in Cedar View.' Sheltered housing they called it, but there was nothing very sheltered about it. The main road thundered past outside, and when you rang for assistance the warden didn't hear. Her father would have approved, though – children and pets were forbidden.

'Is that a block of flats, madam?'

'No, my own private house. I told you – the one with the big garden.'

'Yes, of course. You feed William in the garden.'

'Only on warm days.' It was warm today. He didn't need the raincoat. Perhaps, like her, he suffered with his chest.

'Well, that's it, madam. Thank you so much for your time.'

'Just a moment . . .' Dare she suggest a cup of tea in Debenham's? The restaurant was very nice there. They could order hot buttered scones with those tiny individual pots of jam. Her treat, of course.

'Yes?'

'W. . .will you be doing any more surveys?'

'How do you mean?'

'I have a cat as well, you see. A beautiful grey Persian. *And* a budgerigar. Perhaps you could drop me a line if . . .'

'I'm afraid we're not allowed to record names and addresses, madam. But thank you all the same.'

He had already turned away. She stared after his departing back, storing up the details for her scrap-book of what might have been: smart beige coat, broad shoulders, mid-brown hair with just a hint of grey . . .

Briskly she picked up her bag and set off again for Sainsbury's. There were things she had forgotten: Bounce, of course – Beef Super-Chunks and Chicken – and oatmeal for the dog-cake, and an extra large baking tin.

She approached an assistant, a young lad stacking tubs of margarine. 'Excuse me, please – could you tell me where pet foods are?' There were whole areas of the shop she had never penetrated: wines and spirits, baby foods . . .

Having been ushered to aisle seven, she stood open-mouthed before shelf after shelf of treasures: dog toys, dog chews, dog chocolate drops, dog vitamins. And food she would never have dreamed of – a 'High Society' Gourmet Selection, including pork fillet, duck breast and venison terrine, and an organic range, with fresh vegetables and no additives, and even fish for dogs, in fancy cartons with a leaping salmon on the front. Would William care for salmon? Most definitely he would.

She exchanged her basket for a trolley and scanned the various products, peering at the labels and trying to decide between Organic Chicken Chunks in Jelly and Luxury Lamb for Discerning Dogs. Except why decide? She'd take them both, *and* the Tripe and the Rabbit, in memory of Aunt Annie. And how about a packet of Beef Schmackos, and a Chocolate Mega-Bone? And she couldn't resist the Dental Chews with Fluoride, or the scarlet leather collar with TOP DOG spelt out in silver studs.

She could hardly wait to get them home, although it hurt her knees terribly, lugging all the shopping from the bus stop. The Cedar View lift was working, thank the Lord. (It had off-days, like the warden.)

Standing amidst a cluster of Sainsbury's carrier bags, she fumbled for her key. 'William!' she called. 'William?'

And with a joyous bark he was there, skidding along the hall to greet her, rushing round in excited circles, jumping up to lick her face.

She stooped to fondle him, gazing into his eyes – beautiful sad eyes. She had never been close enough to notice them before. William hated children; William kept people at bay.

No, she was mistaken. He was shy, that's all, and had been waiting for her to approach him. Waiting all these years for her to make the first move.

In trepidation she put her arms around him. He didn't growl or bare his teeth, not even when she held him close. 'Daddy,' she whispered, 'I love you.'

It wasn't too late.

The Eighth Wonder
of the World

Miss Orange-Legs holds up her hand for silence. 'Today,' she announces, showing her big horse-teeth, 'we're going to see the Eighth Wonder of the World.'

I stop fiddling with my hair. 'What is it?' I ask. My voice comes out in a nervous squeak. It's the first time I've dared to speak to her. I'm not supposed to be here. The others are all old – except Mum.

'Wait and see.'

I hate it when grown-ups say that. And other stupid things like 'Because I say so.'

'And it'll be a long wait, Tilly. It's right on the top of the Downs, so it'll take a good hour to get there.'

'My name's Natalie,' I mutter.

'Shh,' Mum hisses. 'Don't be cheeky.'

It's not cheeky; it's a fact. I was christened Natalie Teresa. It was Dad who thought up Tilly, and Dad's disappeared. When strangers use his special name for me, it makes me feel horrible inside, like seeing his half of the wardrobe empty, and his 'Best Dad in the World' mug hanging on its hook.

'Well now, if everybody's ready, let's make a start, shall we?' Miss O-L ambles along the path in her bright orange knee-socks and great clomping leather boots. They all wear walking-boots except Mum and me. I can't see why – it's not proper walking because we have to go so slowly and every time we see a flower she makes us stop and look at it. (I mean yesterday we stood for ages round a boring thing called toothwort, even though it was brown and shrivelled up.) And they're all loaded down with so much gear they couldn't go fast if they tried. Kenneth is the worst. He's got a huge rucksack on his back, and a pair of binoculars dangling round his neck, and two cameras and three wild-flower books, and a sort of metal stick thing that turns into a seat, and fold-up yellow waterproofs in a poncy little bag, and a specimen box and a notebook. He keeps getting out the notebook and writing down what Miss O-L says, like he's trying to be teacher's pet. When he walks close to Mum I can't bear to look, and if he holds her hand I feel sick. I keep away from them, trailing behind the others and wishing there'd be an eclipse of the sun, so it would suddenly get dark and the weekend would be over and Mum and I could go home on our own. Kenneth hasn't stayed the night yet. If he does, I'll kill him.

Miss O-L stops again to point at a plant that hasn't even got a flower on it. 'Round-headed rampion,' she says. 'It's one of the campanula family – the bell-flowers.'

Mr and Mrs Bell-Flower. They've stayed married and still love each other. I can see them lying side by side in bed.

'The harebell's in the same family. And so are sheep's-bit and heath lobelia. But the only other rampion that grows in Britain is the spiked – *Phyteuma spicatum*.'

Scribble, scribble, scribble, goes Kenneth. He thinks he's clever because he knows the Latin names of flowers. He'd talk to Mum in Latin, given half a chance, so I couldn't understand.

Everybody peers at the plant. It's nothing special – a few green leaves, that's all. It'd be worth stopping for if the leaves were bright blue or something.

'When it flowers in July, each floret has five linear petals that form a sheath around the style and stamens. As the floret matures . . .'

Miss O-L drones on. The rucksack's hurting my shoulder. I feel silly with a rucksack, but Mum wanted us to look the same as the others, so she bought us one each in Oxfam. Theirs are made of thick khaki stuff with loads of straps and pockets, and ours are only nylon. Mum's is red and mine's yukky pink.

We move off at last, but shuffle to a stop again when the lady in the glasses goes, 'Oh, look! White campion – almost hidden behind the bur chervil.'

Rampion. Campion. Perhaps I'll be a poet. Dad used to read me poems but I don't know where he's gone.

'Well spotted,' Miss O-L says. Her real name's Muriel but she ought to have a flower name like Violet or Lily. Flowers are her whole life. She's never married or anything.

'We should see red campion, too. The red goes on flowering much longer – right through to November.' She turns to me and smiles, 'Feel the stem, Tilly – it's sticky, isn't it?' (She's always trying to teach me things.) 'And look at the tiny hairs on the leaves.'

She has hairs, on her chin. Not small and pale, like on the plant, but two long dark ones, sticking out of a mole.

Now Duncan's asking her something. Duncan mumbles, so I can't hear what he's saying.

'Yes, that's right,' she nods. 'The male fern's more upright and the female fern's more graceful.'

Mum and Kenneth aren't like that. Kenneth's forever stooping to look at some plant or other. And Mum's not what you'd call graceful. She's always been a bit clumsy and she's got worse since Kenneth appeared. Kenneth isn't right for her. She just wants a man around again, so she started going out with him after they met at the singles club. They haven't really got anything in common, not even flowers. Mum wouldn't know a daffodil from a dandelion. She only joined the Wildlife Trust to please him.

We dawdle on again. Yesterday I ran ahead, then Miss O-L said I'd missed the stinking iris and dragged me back to look at it. It didn't stink at all and it was a sort of dreary brown, not blue like normal irises. Stinking Kenneth smells of peppermints. He keeps a tube of Polos in his pocket and he's always sucking and crunching. Mum says he's given up smoking and the Polos are a crutch. This morning he bought me a bag of Maltesers, but that was just to get in with Mum. I know he hates me really. Sometimes I see him looking at me like I'm an insect he wants to swat. He's even more ancient than Miss O-L but he's never been married, either. I wish he'd fallen in love with *her* and not with Mum. Or perhaps they're not in love. I don't know how you tell.

I lag behind again. There's lots of trees I'd like to climb, but they'd probably say it's Cruelty to Trees. They care more about plants than people. I mean, the whole point about flowers is to pick them, isn't it? But yesterday when I picked a bunch of bluebells, they all went ballistic, even Mum. And then I trod on something

called spotted medick, and Duncan did his nut. He said it was a
flower that grew under the cross when Jesus was crucified, and the
little black dots on the leaves were spots of blood. That's just stupid.
The spots didn't look a bit like blood, and anyway, it would have
dried by now. He was just trying to make me feel bad. I *did* feel bad
and I said sorry about twenty times, but he kept muttering about
how children had no business coming on serious botanical walks.
Well, I didn't ask to come; Mum wouldn't let me stay at home on
my own.

Today I stick to the path. I don't want to make trouble for Mum. I
still love her. It's only her-and-Kenneth I can't stand.

'Imagine!' says the woman in the glasses, 'our ancestors walking
these hills fifty thousand years ago.'

I shiver. History's my worst subject. I hate everyone being dead.
Sometimes I wonder if Dad's dead, too. I keep asking if I can see him,
but Mum says give her time.

I whistle to my imaginary dog. I'm out for a walk on my own, and
Charlie's rushing around in circles, wagging his tail. I'm walking to
Dad's. He's not dead – he's expecting us. He's bought Jelly Pots for
tea because he knows they're my favourites, and a meaty chew for
Charlie.

'Yes, that's betony,' Miss O-L is saying. '*Stachys officinalis*. It's been
used by herbalists since Roman times for liver complaints and bronchitis. It's a member of the *Labiatae* family, of course.'

Plants are lucky to have families. I don't think two people on their
own's enough. I asked Mum once why I didn't have a sister or
brother, and she went red and changed the subject. Betony's a pretty
name, so she can be my sister, and herb Robert my brother. I'm beginning to feel better now. Five is definitely a family, and by the time we
reach the top of the Downs I have lots of cousins – Daisy, Bryony,
Hazel, Rose and Ivy, and a best friend, Germander Speedwell.

'And *now*,' says Miss O-L, motioning us all to stop, 'we've reached
the high point of our walk. Indeed, I might even go so far as to call
today a pilgrimage. You're about to see the Eighth Wonder of the
World.'

I gaze around. All I can see is the slope of the hill and the stony
path going up it and a great blue lid of sky, and some hazy trees and
bushes in the distance. There's no pyramids or temples, nothing you'd
call a Wonder.

'Normally I'd hesitate to show it to a group. But most of us have been together so long, I know I can trust you not to reveal its where-abouts to anyone.' She gives a little giggle. 'Let's just keep it as our secret.'

I still don't know what she's talking about, but I like the thought of a secret. Secrets mean you're special. Best friends tell you secrets. I haven't got a best friend – well, apart from Germander Speedwell.

'What you're going to see' – Miss O-L pauses and her voice goes all deep and breathy – 'has never, ever, been seen before in Sussex. The Botanical Recording Society are tremendously excited and a taxonomist from Kew has already been down here to visit. So I'm sure you'll realize how privileged you are today. Most people would give their eye-teeth to witness a sight like this.'

Although it's hot, I feel goose-bumps on my skin. I don't know what eye-teeth are, but I'd give all my teeth and both my eyes in return for Dad walking in the door.

Miss O-L falls to her knees. It reminds me of church – the hush, the circle of unsmiling Sunday faces. If she doesn't show us the Wonder soon, I think I'll burst.

She bends forward and moves aside a clump of grass. Behind it is a small, skinny plant – just a spike really, with no leaves to speak of and a few weird-looking flowers near the top. 'This,' she breathes, 'is a most extraordinary hybrid.' She pauses again and looks round at us – her eyes are bulgy anyway but now they're almost popping out of her head. 'It's a cross between a bee orchid and a fly orchid.'

There's a little gasp from the group, followed by some oohs and aahs.

'A hybrid like this was produced artificially in East Germany, in 1962. The first sighting of a *natural* specimen was in Leigh Woods, near Bristol, in 1968, but it hasn't been spotted in Sussex until now. This is unique for us, a one-off. Isn't it thrilling?'

No, it's not. It's a cheat. I stand there, trying not to cry. I was expecting something fantastic that would change Mum's life and mine. And instead it's just another boring plant.

'Be very careful where you kneel,' Miss O-L warns as they cluster round to examine it. 'There might be seedlings of other orchids nearby.'

Kenneth's big blue backside is sticking up in the air. He's on his hands and knees in front of the orchid, gazing at every detail through his lens. 'Incredible!' he goes, and he gives this silly laugh, like he's overjoyed to be kneeling in the dirt.

And Miss O-L puts her face so close to the flowers, I think she's going to bite them off, but she starts on one of her lectures again. 'You'll notice that the outer perianth segments are characteristic of the fly orchid, and the upper inner segments more akin to the bee orchid. Can you see the small furry humps on either side of the base of the lip, and the broad blue band across the middle. . . ?'

I look at Mum. Like me, she hasn't a clue what the old bat is on about. I know she feels embarrassed and left out, but she's put on her fake face, pretending to be pleased like all the others.

Kenneth's taking photos now, millions of them – click, click, click, click, click. He'll never love *you* that much, I want to yell at Mum. You'll always come second to some rotten plant or flower. He'll never go down on his knees to you, or lie on his fat stomach and photograph you from every angle.

But I stand in silence, watching Ruth take over from Kenneth, then the woman with the glasses, then Duncan, then Elaine. All of them goggle-eyed, and whispering words like 'phenomenal' and 'fascinating'. All taking photos or making little sketches. When it's her turn, Mum says nothing. She hasn't got a camera and she can't draw to save her life. She does borrow Kenneth's lens, though, and peers through it for some time, while he shows off, pointing out the bee-like lip and the sepals. I can't bear to see his thick, fat, fleshy finger and imagine it touching Mum.

Miss O-L can hardly get a word in. Then she swivels round to look at me. 'Don't you want to see it, Tilly?'

I shake my head, still scared I'll cry. I hate crying in front of people.

'Silly girl,' Duncan tuts. 'You don't know what you're missing. This is something you can tell your children.'

'I'm not *having* any children,' I mumble. 'And I'm never getting married.'

Mum reaches across and takes my hand, but I shake it off. She held Kenneth's hand yesterday and there's probably traces of him there still.

'Now, Tilly, let me explain,' Miss O-L gurgles. 'If you understand how nature works, you'll be interested, I'm sure. Do you see this little lip? It's shaped like the back of a bumble bee, and that's to tempt a

real bee to land on it and try to mate with the flower. Then pollination can . . .'

Mate's a disgusting word. I close my eyes and see Mum and
Kenneth mating in Mum and Dad's big bed. There are hairs all over
his body like on the campion leaves, and little black spots of blood all
over Mum. 'I feel sick,' I say, but no one hears.

'I thought the bee orchid was self-pollinating,' Kenneth says. 'I
mean, despite all that fancy bee mimicry.' I don't get what he's saying,
but I can tell he's showing off, as usual.

Miss O-L beams at him like he's the cleverest boy in the class. 'Yes,
normally it is – in Britain anyway. But this hybrid must be the result
of pollination by an insect. You see, bee orchids and fly orchids don't
grow close together as a rule, and even when they do, their flowering
times rarely overlap.'

Elaine squats down again. 'Gosh!' she goes, 'the markings on the
flowers are just amazing.' She's wedged herself between Duncan and
Ruth and their three fat bottoms stick up in a row. Mum said to me
last night they ought to call it bottomizing, not botanizing. That gave
us a fit of the giggles. It was a good job Kenneth had gone home
because I don't think he likes jokes.

'It must be priceless,' Ruth sighs, as she focuses her camera. She's
another one who can't stand children. Every time I'm anywhere near
her, she sort of edges away, like I've got mumps or measles or something.

'Yes,' Miss O-L agrees. 'One can't value it in cash terms. It's just a
wonder of nature, to be admired in its natural habitat.'

'It's the imported tropical varieties that fetch big money,' someone
else chips in. 'I've seen them in growers' catalogues for hundreds of
pounds apiece.'

'And did you hear about that new hybrid, *Paphiopedilum* Princess
Sophia? – it fetched *thousands*!'

I still don't know what a hybrid is, but I'm too shy to ask in case
it's something rude. Miss O-L loves questions, though. She sort of
dribbles with excitement if she thinks you're interested.

At last she gets up from her knees, creaking a bit and nearly
overbalancing. Her skirt's all creased and there's a smear of earth
on her cheek. 'I think this would be a good point to break for
lunch,' she says. 'There's a picnic area round the other side of the
hill.'

I drag myself up the path, listening to them still twittering on, and eventually we reach the benches and tables. 'I'd rather sit in the shade,' I whisper to Mum. 'I don't want any more freckles.' I already get teased about them at school. Some of my class are really vile. I heard Sharon telling Rick the other day that her Mum said we were well shot of my Dad, because he was a sponger and a slob.

Mum offers to sit with me but I know she'd rather be with Kenneth, so I say I'm OK on my own. I watch him unpack his rucksack. It was his turn to bring the picnic today, so it's yuk like pongy cheese and chunks of sweaty liver sausage and stale brown bread with a smear of margarine.

Mum brings me over my lunchbox and a plastic cup of orange juice with horrid little shreddy bits floating on the top. 'I'm not hungry.'

'Well, try and eat something, pet.'

OK, I think – for your sake, Mum. I bite into the bread. The crust is rough and hard. When Dad was around he used to take me roller-skating and afterwards we'd go to McDonald's and have Coke and Mega Macs. I can taste the soft whiteness of the bap all jumbled up with the dark sweetness of the Coke, and feel the melted cheese gooey on my tongue.

I glance at Mum. She has her hand on Kenneth's knee while he stuffs his face with liver sausage. I ram the lid on my lunchbox and bung it into my rucksack, then I march over to where they're sitting. 'I'm going for a walk,' I tell her.

'Aren't you tired?'

'No.' I point down the hill, the way we've come. 'I saw a fallen tree and I want to climb along it.'

'Well, be careful, love, and don't go far.'

As soon as I'm out of their sight, I race back towards the orchid. An idea's been forming in my mind. Whatever hybrids are, they're obviously worth a lot, and if this one's meant to be so special, it could sell for thousands of pounds. Dad's always broke. That's why Mum kicked him out. She said as fast as she earned money, he chucked it down the drain. But if I could *give* them money, things might be all right.

I look up and down the hill. I can't see anybody. Quick as a flash I get my lunchbox out and dump Kenneth's rotten picnic in the middle of a bush. Then I scrabble at the soil around the orchid. I mustn't damage the roots. Roots are important, Miss O-L says. But my hands aren't strong enough to loosen them, so I hunt around for a pointed stone and use it as a digger. At last the roots come free and they're even weirder than the flowers. There's two round bits like little new potatoes (one of them sort of old and shrivelled), and above them, growing from the stem, some pale, damp, creepy things that remind me of Kenneth's fingers. I keep looking up to make sure no one's watching as I wrap the plant in my paper serviette and put it in the lunchbox. And once I've smoothed the patch of soil, you can hardly tell the orchid's gone. It isn't very big and it was hidden by the clump of grass. And anyway we're not coming back along this path. Miss O-L's already said we're going down the other side of the hill so she can show us some common twayblades – whatever *they* are.

I stuff the lunchbox in my rucksack, right down at the bottom under Panda and my sweatshirt. Mum doesn't know I take Panda everywhere – out of sight, of course. Dad gave him to me the day I was born. He said he was my birth-day present.

I have one last look round, then I walk across to the fallen tree, like I've just finished my lunch and I'm going exploring. I won't climb along the trunk, though. It's too risky with the rucksack – I don't want to bang the lunchbox. *Dad's* lunchbox. I imagine him munching the orchid, and little gold coins spilling from his mouth like crumbs. Charlie's excited too. He's barking like mad and leaping over the tree trunk, and then he licks my hand because he knows my insides are all fluttery.

'Tilly! Tilly!'

I jump up in a fright. Mum must be coming to find me. The pale pink of my rucksack seems to be blushing deep, deep red as I try to hide it behind my back.

'Are you OK?' Mum asks.

'Mm.'

'Eaten your lunch?'

'Yes. Some.'

I let her squeeze my hand this time. I love her ever so much.

We walk back together to the others. They're packing up their things. Elaine is putting sun-cream on, but she hasn't got a mirror so her face is white and smeary. Duncan is eating chocolate. He doesn't offer *me* any. He just breaks off the squares and gobbles them up without stopping, one after another. Ruth pounces on the wrapper and puts it in the rubbish bin, along with every tiny scrap of paper she can find. She'd put me in, too, if I'd fit. They're complaining about litter and transistor radios and people who leave gates open and don't control their dogs. I know they'd complain about Charlie, because he's noisy and messy and bounces about all over the place.

'Ready?' Miss O-L says. Some of her hair has come out of its clip and there's a bit of lettuce caught in her front teeth.

They all answer 'Yes,' except Ruth, who says 'I'll catch you up, if you don't mind. I want to take a few more pictures of the orchid.'

My heart stops beating, honestly it does. And the little piece of bread I ate starts swelling in my stomach, and soon it's as big as a whole knobbly loaf and fills up my insides. Ruth is getting bigger, too. She's tall anyway, and as I watch her walk away her head seems to touch the sky. *Stop* her, Miss O-L, I want to shout. Tell her she's not allowed to go off on her own. Tell her you're in a hurry. Tell her . . .

But I can't say a single word. I can't even grunt or croak. The loaf of bread is still growing and growing and now it's blocked my throat. And there's great lumps of concrete stuck to my feet, so when the group sets off in the other direction I'm left stranded on my own.

Mum comes back for me. 'Tired, love?' she asks. She looks tired herself.

I make a sort of choking noise and she links her arm through mine. My legs won't work but somehow we catch up because *her* legs shunt us along.

'Now, if we're lucky,' Miss O-L is saying, 'we may see a common twayblade with a third leaf. My colleague spotted one last week in West Dean Woods.'

I pull my arm out from Mum's and look back over my shoulder. Ruth has disappeared. Any minute she'll find that the orchid's gone.

'Yes, Duncan, that's correct – the common twayblade grows in every part of Britain except Shetland. And it's pollinated by beetles and ichneumon flies. They're attracted to the nectar secreted in a groove in the centre of the lip—'

All at once there's a shout behind us. 'Stop! Stop! Something terrible's happened!'

Everyone turns round. Ruth is stumbling over the grass towards us. She's out of breath and flapping her arms about. 'It's *gone*!' she cries.

'The orchid's gone. It's not *there*! I can't believe it!' Her voice is a sort of wail. 'Somebody's dug it up by the roots.'

I close my eyes. There's a horrible silence. And then everybody's shouting. The voices are black and fierce and buzzing like angry wasps. Kenneth's stings worst of all – he's disgusted, he's outraged, and if he finds the culprit he'll . . .

I open my eyes a crack and see his face all screwed up and scary, like the Ogre in my fairy-tale book. And then Duncan starts. 'It must be vandals!' he shouts. 'Did you see anybody, Ruth?'

'No, not a soul. That's what's so extraordinary. I just can't understand it. Unless, of course' – she wheels round and grabs me by the shoulder – '*Tilly* saw someone when she went off to play on that tree? Did you, Tilly?' She makes my name sound like a swear word and her fingers are digging into my skin.

'N. . .no,' I stammer.

'Are you quite sure?'

'Yes . . . no . . .'

'And what's that supposed to mean, pray?'

'Er, yes, I did see someone.'

'Who?'

'A vandal.'

'Oh, really? And what did this *vandal* look like?'

'Big. And . . . ugly. With a scar on his face.'

Kenneth elbows Ruth aside and raises his hand for silence, like he's suddenly in charge. Then he steps towards me and bends right down, so his face is close to mine. I can see the black hairs in his nose and little blobs of sweat on his top lip. His voice isn't loud and snarly any more, but soft and sort of dangerous. 'Tilly, would you kindly open your rucksack and show us what you've got inside.'

'Kenneth!' Mum claws at his arm. 'Surely you're not accusing—?'

'I'm not accusing anybody. I'm simply conscious of the fact that Tilly's the only one who left the group and spent time on her own. As Ruth happened to notice, too.'

'I'm sorry but that's ridiculous. She just went off to explore, didn't you, love?'

I nod. I hate lying to Mum, but I feel I'm breaking into pieces.

'Fine,' Kenneth purrs, with a dreadful sickly smile. 'If she has nothing to hide, then she won't mind us seeing her rucksack, will you, Tilly?'

'No, you can't. There's . . . there's something private in it.'

'I bet there is,' Ruth mutters. Her lip is curled in a sneer.

'It's only Panda,' I blurt out. 'I know it's babyish to bring him, but Dad gave him to me, ages ago, and . . . and . . .' I'm crying. I can't stop.

Mum wipes my eyes with her hankie. 'Look, pet, no one minds about Panda. Just get him out and show them and that'll be the end of it.'

My fingers are shaking, so it's hard to get the rucksack off my back. Mum helps and then she opens it and takes Panda out and holds him up.

'Ah!' the lady in the glasses smiles. 'He's a darling, isn't he?'

I could *kiss* her, she's so nice. I wish I hadn't forgotten her name; it was something long and foreign.

'OK?' I say to Kenneth. 'Can I put him back now?'

'Just one second, young lady.' He gives me another horrible smile. 'I'd like you to take the *other* things out, if you'd be so kind.'

'Kenneth, I can't believe you're doing this! Can't you see you're upsetting her?'

'Well, let me give her a hand, then.' He snatches the rucksack and tips it up on end. Out falls the lunchbox, and he grabs it.

I stare down at the ground. I can see a tiny purple flower. I wish Miss O-L would tell me what its name is and whether it's pollinated by bees or flies or . . .

Then, before I know what's happened, there's a sort of ringing in my ears and everything goes black. I put my hand up to my face. It's burning and stinging and I feel sick. Kenneth has hit me, I think.

'You could go to prison for this!' he shouts. 'You thieving little brat!'

I'm sobbing and my nose is running and everything's wet and blurry. But I feel Mum's arms close round me and hear her shouting back at him, 'How dare you hit my daughter! *You* could go to prison – attacking an innocent child.'

'Innocent? She's a thief. *And* a bare-faced liar. She commits an act of vandalism and then swears blind she's—'

'Look at this great bruise! You might have done permanent damage.'

'And what about the damage *she's* done? Digging up a priceless specimen—'

46

'It's only a plant, for God's sake! Your trouble, Kenneth, is that you think flowers are the most important things in the world. Well, they're not. They're—'

'And your trouble, Lesley, is that you don't belong in this group. You know nothing about botany. In fact, I've come to the conclusion that you know nothing about anything.'

'If I want your opinion I'll ask for it, thank you very much! And if I'm so pig-ignorant, why did you invite me?'

'Please stop this!' Miss O-L begs. 'Let's try to behave like civilized adults. It won't help matters if we all get so worked up.'

But Kenneth takes no notice and goes on shouting at Mum. 'I certainly *wouldn't* have invited you if I'd known you'd bring your loathsome brat.'

'That's it! We're going. And I intend to report you, Kenneth Parker, for assault. And as for you stuck-up lot,' she yells at the others, 'you can *stuff* your wild flowers, you wankers!'

She seizes my hand and pulls me along, full tilt down the hill. We trip and slither on the loose stones. Trees are flying past and the path slips and slides away from us, like it's escaping too. I fall and graze my knee but she yanks me to my feet and we scramble on again. There's a roaring in my ears and I'm sure my chest is going to burst. When we reach the bottom we can hardly breathe, we're so puffed. And I've got a stitch and my cheek hurts terribly.

We sit on the grass, to recover. The sun's gone in and where everything was bright before, now it's flat and grey. And the clouds seem tired, sagging in the sky above the hill. I don't know how we'll get home. We haven't got a car. Kenneth drove us to the Centre in his Range Rover. We haven't even any money for the bus. We've left our rucksacks behind and Mum's had her purse in it. And her new wild-flower book that cost £10.99. And her lucky mascot key-ring.

Miss O-L's a liar – today *wasn't* the Eighth Wonder of the World.

'I'm sorry, Mum,' I whisper.

'That's . . . OK.'

'But what about Kenneth?'

'What about him?'

'You love him, don't you?'

She doesn't answer, just wipes her forehead with the back of her hand and looks at me for what seems ages. Then she says, 'I love *you*, Tilly.'

I don't want to start crying again, so I sit quite still and watch a tiny insect crawling up a blade of grass. The grass must seem awfully high and steep, but the bug keeps going up and up. I wonder if it's scared.

Mum unlaces her new trainers and rubs her feet. I think they must be hurting. 'I'm sorry you lost Panda,' she says.

'That's . . . OK,' I say, copying Mum's words, and the sort of slow, sad way she said them. 'It was time I gave him away. Pandas are for babies.' When Dad comes back, he'll give me something more grown up – roller skates, or a radio.

There's another long silence and I try to think of radios: what sort I'd like, what colour.

Mum's still looking at me. 'But why did you take the orchid, Tilly? I mean, what on earth were you going to do with it?'

I bite my lip. I can't explain – not yet. I've got to work things out: how to find Dad, how to make him fall in love with Mum again, even without the money.

The insect's halfway up. As I watch it, a thought jumps into my head: if it reaches the top, Dad will come back; if it doesn't, he won't.

I hate the thought – it's frightening. But inside I know it's true. Things work like that: a secret voice is telling you and that voice is always right. I've proved it loads of times.

I can hardly bear to watch as the bug moves another centimetre, then stops again, to rest. I think it's tired like Mum and me.

Get *on*! I hiss. Crawl faster. You've got more legs than us.

But it pauses, like it's lost its nerve and is just clinging on for its life. And then it lifts a feeler and I'm sure it's begging me for help.

You're nearly there, I whisper. Don't give up. You're doing well.

I keep as still as a stone so I won't put it off or scare it. I'm even trying not to breathe.

It creeps up a little bit more, but it's going slower and slower, then suddenly it falls off and lands on its back.

I touch my cheek. It's throbbing and feels hot.

'Is that hurting much?' Mum asks.

'No,' I say. If I tell her the truth she'll only be upset. She's lost Kenneth now, as well as her bag and all the other stuff.

I pick the bug up and put it back on the blade of grass. It needs a second chance. But it doesn't even try this time. It just slithers down and tumbles to the ground. I cup it in my hand and feel it tickling my palm. Dad used to tickle me sometimes when he was drying me after a bath, and then we'd have a pillow fight and he'd chase me round the room. I smile, remembering.

'What's funny?' Mum asks.

I take her hand and squeeze it and somehow manage another smile. She needs me to be brave.

Because now I know Dad *isn't* coming back.

Room Service

'In the event of a fire,' the notice on the door instructed, 'vacate your room immediately . . .'

A redundant warning, surely, Rachel thought. Did they imagine people would ignore the flames and dawdle in their rooms, finishing the newspaper? Actually, a fire might have been a welcome diversion – at least the stampede of guests would be company. For all that the hotel boasted 350 rooms, she had encountered precisely two people so far: the porter and the receptionist.

It was madness to have come – not only squandering money but risking the sack by playing truant from work. Except she couldn't work, not now; couldn't read, or think, or even summon the energy to get dressed. She was still wearing the hotel robe with its ornately embroidered crest on the pocket. No longer Rachel Williams, she was transmogrified into Linden Court.

She sat despondently on the edge of the bed – king-size, naturally. Everything was designed for couples: two cups and saucers on the hospitality tray, two sets of towels in the bathroom, two plastic-wrapped tooth mugs, two mini-bottles of shower gel and shampoo. The rooms were all doubles (so they'd said) yet the world was full of singles. Only last week she had read in the paper that more people were living alone than ever before. Which could be regarded as freedom, of course – freedom to be selfish, freedom to be lonely. Or solitary confinement. She hadn't ventured out all day for fear of crying in public; hadn't eaten a thing except half a packet of the free biscuits.

She picked up the phone and dialled Room Service. 'Yes, a steak, please, medium rare, with salad and French fries, and chocolate gâteau to follow . . .' She broke off in confusion. She was ordering Pierre's food, not hers. Was she so obsessed that she'd been subsumed by him; her own tastes supplanted by his?

Having re-ordered fish and fruit, she sat surveying the room, thinking of all the couples who had slept here: honeymooning, making love, fighting, splitting up. Or perhaps lone businessmen lying diagonally across the vast plain of the bed. Transients, like her – rootless, loveless, living out of suitcases.

She didn't even have a suitcase. Apart from the things she'd arrived in, the Linden Court towelling robe was all she had to wear.

A knock on the door made her jump. Since Pierre had gone, every knock or ring or phone-call brought with it the ridiculous hope that it might be him, returning. 'Come in,' she called eagerly.

But in walked a man in uniform – short and stout where Pierre was slim and tall. In silence he set out the plates and cutlery, transferred the dishes from the trolley to the coffee table and removed their silver covers.

'Is it still cold outside?' she asked, just to establish contact with another human being.

'Excuse?'

His English was no better than the porter's. Absurdly disappointed, she addressed him in bad French. It was the only foreign language she knew – coached by Pierre, of course.

The man smiled nervously, still uncomprehending. Despite the smile, his face was sad. Had he too been ditched, declared surplus to requirements because his partner wanted 'breathing space'? A shame they couldn't console each other, swap stories of betrayal.

'Excuse?' he said again, maybe all the English he spoke.

'Oh, never mind,' she muttered, suddenly impatient with herself and him. If she'd been less clingy and dependent, Pierre might never have left.

She gave the man a tip, which he acknowledged with a little bow before gliding away with his trolley. She willed him not to go. Come back, she howled silently, I need you! But no, the door had closed and she was alone in her prison cell again.

For God's *sake*, she told herself, don't be so pathetic. This is luxury, not Wormwood Scrubs.

Barren, though, and by virtue of its very perfection, coldly inhospitable; a colour-supplement world where a stain on the carpet or chip off the paintwork would be a heinous crime. It was *she* who was stained and chipped, a discarded item, marked down for quick disposal.

She stared miserably at the flamingoes in a picture over the bed, pink against a rosy dawn (or was it sunset?). Clearly they had been chosen not on grounds of artistic merit but to harmonize with the decor: carpet, curtains, bedspreads, wallpaper – all relentlessly pink. Pink might be perfect for healthy, glowing couples; singletons sought refuge in the shade of mourning and depression.

The food was getting cold, she realized, while she continued to sink deeper into the black bog of self-pity. The butter sauce on her fish had already formed a greasy scum, and the two salmon fillets (pink again) looked lonely on their over-sized plate, with only a sour, uncaring lemon wedge for company. She put the plate on the bedside table and climbed between the sheets. Eating in bed was a comfort, with its memories of childhood – her parents bringing soothing drinks when she was laid up with tonsillitis. But there was no palliative for losing Pierre, no aspirin to reduce the pain.

As she squeezed the lemon, a spurt of juice spurted into her eye and stung. Could you hate a lemon?

Yes, easily.

She took a mouthful of fish. Would Pierre be eating now? Unlikely at half past three. And just as unlikely he'd be on his own. She tried to picture the other woman – multilingual, no doubt, and enviably free-spirited, and attractive in a *gamine* sort of way. He'd sworn there wasn't another woman, but Pierre had always lied. Strangely, it was part of his Gallic charm. She couldn't help but admire his inventiveness, the scope of his imagination, and his obliging habit of saying what she wanted (needed) to hear.

The salmon on its own was far too rich. She should have ordered vegetables, but even a simple green salad cost £4.95. And there was only one bread roll, an insubstantial thing, more air than crumb or crust. Bread should have a doughy heart, like the dense, chewy loaves she used to make for Pierre. She imagined stacking the drawers and cupboards with them, instead of toiletries and clothes. A store of provisions might give her strength for the future, although she would need to change the recipe and add resilience and self-sufficiency to the staples of flour and yeast.

She broke the roll into pieces and mopped up the bland sauce. With

Pierre gone, food had lost its flavour. *He* had been her pepper and spice, adding pungency to everything. She remembered their first meal together, in bed, and in this hotel, but on a higher floor, room 347. She had requested 347 last night, but it was already occupied. Twice she had gone up there and stood listening outside the door, to capture an echo of Pierre. But she had heard nothing. Nothing.

Mechanically she chewed and swallowed, finishing the salmon and moving on to dessert. But no matter what she ate (grapes, banana, kiwi fruit) it continued to taste of fish. The smell had become ingrained in the very fabric of the room – the odour of rejection: putrefying, toxic. And there were grease-spots on the sheets, and crumbs and grape pips in the bed. She glanced with distaste at the flaccid banana skin. Was that how Pierre thought of her, compared with his firm peach of a new woman? Or bitter, like the lemon?

She got out of bed and emptied the sugar from every sachet on the hospitality tray into one of the cups. As a child, she had put sugar on everything; sprinkled it on sliced tomatoes, watched it melt on fried bread, made gritty sugar sandwiches, even stirred it into cold milk. Yet neither she nor the food had ever seemed sweet enough. She dropped a tea bag in the cup and switched the kettle on. Its sympathetic chunter made her feel less lonely. Perhaps in the absence of human companions, one could talk to a kettle, express concern for its predicament. It couldn't be much of a life, continually required to come panting to a boil, only to be left to go cold again. She gave it a kindly pat on the snout as it shuddered to a climax and spewed out a few bubbles at the height of its gasping passion.

Silence descended again. Strange how loud silence could be, like a barely suppressed scream. Despite the proximity of hundreds of people, there wasn't a sound to be heard. The doors were heavy, the windows triple-glazed; 'outside' no longer existed. Yet she had an uncanny sensation of being spied upon. Were there hidden cameras in the ceiling, or was some Hotel Deity sitting enthroned on the roof, His all-seeing eye scanning each room for sinners?

'Please, God,' she prayed (a rare departure from her customary atheism), 'if You're there, send Pierre back.'

Silence.

In desperation she turned on the television. Frenzied applause blared to hurting-point as the words 'BIG MONEY!' flashed across the screen. Switching channels, she was assailed by a shampoo commercial full of grotesque scarlet mouths braying out superlatives: FIRST! BEST! NEWEST! SHINIEST! If clean hair could engender such ecstasy, she would be washing hers a dozen times a day. Or stockpiling jars of Gold Blend, with its rapturous promise of coffee-flavoured romance.

As she jabbed the off-button, she realized with dismay that dusk was falling already. It got dark by four these days, and without Pierre the dark was frightening. She couldn't endure another night in this claustrophobic place. The walls seemed to be entombing her; the heavy crematorium curtains closing in around her.

She fled from the room and careered along the corridor, almost colliding with an elderly couple coming the other way. 'I . . . I'm sorry,' she stammered, conscious of her inadequate attire. 'I . . . I'm just going to the Leisure Centre.'

Leisure – an appalling word. No one seemed to have it except those who dreaded it. Why not a Grief Centre instead?

She stood back to let the couple pass, and continued at a less breakneck pace up the emergency stairs. To her surprise the door of 347 stood open, a cleaner's trolley parked outside. Hesitating only a second, she sauntered in with feigned confidence, to find a small, flustered looking woman in an overall, who quickly gathered up her cleaning cloths. 'I come back?' she asked, in a thick foreign accent.

'Yes, please.' Rachel was beginning to feel it was she and not Pierre who had gone abroad. But at least the woman hadn't questioned her right of occupancy.

Once the door had closed, she took a few dazed steps towards the bed. They were *here*, together – she and Pierre – which meant she ruled the world again. The sun rose and set for them alone, the seasons and the weather were subject to their whim, time awaited their pleasure, and every love song in history had been written in their honour.

Her eye fell on the chunky sweater draped across the chair; the pair of blue-striped pyjamas folded on the pillow. Pierre wore black silk polo-necks and went to bed in nothing but his skin. And he would never read John Grisham or eat Fox's Glacier Mints. She blinked and looked again, and the offending items metamorphosed into his well-thumbed copy of Mallarmé and a slab of Lindt *Pistache*. And the smudgy Biro jottings on the notepad rearranged themselves into his distinctive sloping script: on every sheet was written *Je t'adore.* Smiling, she opened the mini-bar: they must toast each other (and *l'amour*) in gin and Britvic orange. And on the bathroom mirror she found his rows of shaving-foam kisses. And now they were under the shower, making soapy, slippery love; then night had fallen and he was kissing her breasts in the tingling flush of a bubble bath, before luring her back to bed . . .

She turned out the lights, slipped off her robe and relaxed against the pillows. The sheets were clean and crisp – no butter stains, no smell of fish, only the seductive tang of *Eau Sauvage* and *Gitanes*. Reaching out her arms to him, she let her thighs fall languorously apart. His beard caressed her nipples, tracing mesmerizing circles, then moved down to her belly. 'I love you, Rachel,' he whispered. 'We'll be together for always.'

Pour toujours. A jamais.

The startled bed was rocking as he made her come with just his mouth: bristly chin, velvet lips. 'Yes, more!' she cried as his tongue probed and thrust. 'It's wonderful! It's wonderful!' He had peeled her like a kiwi fruit and she was all glistening-moist and sensitive as his unstinting tongue went deeper. Nothing existed in her universe save the long, slow stroke of that tongue, opening her wider and wider until the whole of him seemed to slip inside her and explore her body from the inside out. He was licking a lazy pathway from her womb to her lungs to her heart, and their bloodstreams were converging into one reckless scarlet pulse. There were no boundaries between them now: he was seeing through her eyes, swallowing with her throat, digesting with her juices. And all the Pierres that had ever been – the child Pierre, the boy Pierre, the student, poet, painter Pierre, the tender, violent, wild Pierre – were fused with her and part of her, part of her seethe and squall.

'Yes, Pierre, I'm *coming!*' she shouted, winding her fingers tighter into his hair.

Then suddenly a noise: a key turning in the lock. A harsh light snapping on, the door slamming shut, footsteps approaching the bed.

She tried to lie still. Impossible. She was almost, almost there and she could no more stop than halt a tidal wave. Even if a bomb exploded right beside the bed, she'd have to come, she'd *have* to – and would barely notice the cataclysm beneath the tumult of her own.

'Go on!' she begged. 'Go on, go on. Oh yes, oh yes, oh yes, oh yes. Oh, *Pierre* . . .'

'Actually the name's Richard,' said a voice. 'But pleased to meet you anyway.'

Life Class

'You're late.'

'Yes. Sorry.'

'Very late. My students have been waiting half an hour.'

'Sorry,' she repeated. He must have been looking for her, probably pacing up and down this draughty corridor since one minute past nine.

'It's along here,' he said tersely, striding out at such a pace she had difficulty keeping up. 'I'm Phil, by the way. The tutor.'

'Oh. Right.' She didn't like the look of him, distrusted men who dyed their hair. And wasn't it a peculiar sort of job, teaching kids to draw naked women?

'And we do expect our models to be here on the dot.'

'Yes. OK. Sorry.' Three sorrys were enough for anyone.

'So let's not waste any more time.' He opened the door to a harshly lit room with a paint-stained wooden floor. Twenty pairs of eyes turned in her direction; twenty students poised behind easels or sitting on chairs, with drawing boards. No one smiled. Just a blur of inscrutable faces. Blue jeans, baggy sweaters, the odd glint from a nose-stud.

'This is Loretta,' Phil announced.

'Lorraine,' she muttered nervously. Even her name was inadequate. Lorraine was a place-name; Loretta had style.

He drew aside the curtain to a makeshift cubicle in one corner of the room. 'Would you like to change in here, please.'

Strip, he meant. They'd laugh at her fat thighs, the scab on her knee, the little red nicks where she'd shaved her legs. Get out, she told herself – now, while there's still time.

But he had already drawn the curtain, caging her in. There wasn't even a mirror, for God's sake, just a couple of coat pegs and a plastic stacking chair.

'And please don't be too long.'

Did he have to keep labouring the point? Tetchily she removed her coat and tugged off her fur-lined boots. Minus six outside, and it was barely tepid in here. *Leave*, she repeated. You're not that desperate for cash.

She was, though. Nearly £300 in debt.

Shivering, she took off her skirt and then her tights and knickers. Her pubic hair would be on public view. She should have shaved that too. It was wild and dark and bushy, with stray hairs creeping down her inner thighs. And her toe-nails needed cutting. Slut, they'd think; not just late but lazy.

Phil coughed – a hurry-up cough. Any minute he might burst through the curtain and frogmarch her out to the class in nothing but her bra and woolly hat. She snatched the hat off, releasing her mane of tangled hair. No time to comb it. There was another impatient cough from Herr Hitler.

'OK in there?'

'Yes. Coming.' With shaking fingers she unhooked her bra. Well, at least she was stripped, as he'd instructed – a pale, plump Christmas turkey. What now? Did she emerge naked or cover herself with her coat? He would assume she knew the ropes. She'd told them she'd modelled before, airily reeling off names of other art schools. They hadn't even bothered to check. She hated lying, not because it was wrong but because people were stupid enough to believe her.

Draping the coat around her shoulders, she sauntered out. Sauntered – another lie. Stumbled, more like.

'Great!' said Phil.

What was *that* supposed to mean? She was numb with cold and fear, while he had a fatuous grin on his face. Still, better than his former scowl.

She blinked in the glare. No hiding place, no mercy; every nick and scab revealed to twenty prurient strangers.

'Right, we're ready to begin, at last. We'll start with some quick poses to get you going. You all have charcoal, I assume.'

Fuck the charcoal, she thought. What the hell do *I* do? Take up a position, presumably, in the centre of the room, where a wicker chair had been placed on a length of grubby pink fabric – another curtain, by the looks of it. But did she sit on the chair or lie on the curtain? No help was forthcoming from Phil; he was still addressing the students, running a hand through his thick, streaked, part-blond hair. 'Remember what I said earlier – life drawing is a useful tool for exploring different approaches. I want you to let yourselves go, be free and experimental. Don't worry too much about accuracy – I'm more interested in fluid action.'

She dumped her coat on the floor and walked self-consciously to the wicker chair. Hardly fluid action.

'I'd like a couple of sitting poses first, Loretta. Then a couple of standing poses. About five minutes each. OK?'

She perched on the edge of the chair and tried to cover her breasts with her arms. Could that be called a pose? She hadn't a clue, dared not even look at him.

'Wait a minute. Let's adjust these lights.'

Christ! He was walking towards her, bearing down on her; he clothed, she exposed. Cruelly he repositioned the spotlight, her every pore gaping like a crater in its stare. Even her shadow looked ungainly.

'OK, get cracking, all of you. We've wasted enough time as it is.'

She could still make a dash for it. They were unlikely to stop her if she jumped up and ran for the door – except she was being paid to keep still. Which was unbelievably difficult. Already she had developed an itch in the middle of her back that screamed out to be scratched. And she could feel a sneeze threatening, and a weird sensation all over, as if her body were out of control and trembling from top to toe. After today they would find an excuse to get rid of her. She had agreed to do every Wednesday of term, but contracts could be broken. She would have to go back to waitressing, but where, for heaven's sake, now that Big Luke's had closed down? It was all very well for students: funded by the government or subsidized by their mummies and daddies to be 'free and experimental'. Could they *see* her envy, she wondered? Perhaps they'd draw it as a black aura, or a cancerous growth distending her stomach. Her own 'Daddy' squandered his money on wifelet number four, and her Mum lived in Skanderborg with a Danish bloke who was perpetually out of work.

'Time's up,' Phil said, glancing at his watch. 'We'll try a different pose now. Could you lean back more in the chair, Loretta, and put your hands behind your head. That's better. Now we can see your face.'

Her breasts, he meant – the wanker. The nipples were erect but only from the cold. OK for him in his sweater and his thick cord trousers in that poncy shade of blue.

'Forget your preconceptions about drawing. Try to enter a karmic state and just work instinctively.'

What was he paid for all this spiel, she'd like to know. Some obscene amount like £50 an hour? She'd got less than the minimum wage at Big Luke's. They told her she would make it up in tips, but most people didn't leave tips. Once, a man had given her a fistful of French francs. A fat lot of use in Slough.

'One minute left . . . Ten seconds . . . Stop!'

Hell, time to move again. Two sitting, he'd said, then two standing. Awkwardly she got to her feet and stood in an aggressive posture, with legs apart and hand on hips, as if defying him to criticize. But he was blethering on to the class again.

'Someone asked me last term why we *do* life-drawing. It's a good question, actually, and what I'd say first is . . .'

She fought an urge to scratch her bottom. It would be criss-crossed from the wickerwork, and the students behind her might be sniggering and pointing. Just as well she couldn't see them. Or should she suddenly swing round and catch them out? Keeping still was an art in itself; a skill she didn't have. Waitressing was a doddle in comparison – on the move all day, dashing from kitchen to table and back again, and safely encased in clothes. The free food had made her fat, though; her stomach a dustbin for leftovers: stale bread, congealing meat balls, rock-hard currant buns.

'Two minutes left.'

What pose could she think of next? Her mind went blank. She had assumed modelling was a dumb job that any fool could do, even a fool like her, but in fact you had to be creative in your own way.

'OK, Loretta, this time I'd like you to imagine that you're taking something down from a shelf. Reach up high – no, higher, almost on your toes. That's it. Now put your right hand behind you and . . .'

So he was taking pity on her – the idiot who needed step-by-step instructions. His other models were professionals, no doubt: double-jointed ex-dancers, all petite size eights, who could dream up endless new poses at the merest flick of his little finger.

This position hurt her back. She'd need an osteopath tomorrow. Not that she could afford one.

'Keep the charcoal moving. Follow the lines of the model's body and be aware of her internal shapes, not just the outlines.'

Bloody cheek! Her nakedness wasn't enough; he was trying to penetrate her now. They all were. She didn't want them inside her, these alien beings with their ultra-trendy hairstyles – the guy with the pigtail, the girl with the shaven head – and stylishly shabby gear. One was wearing sunglasses, which seemed a tad pretentious for January indoors; another wore jodhpurs and knee-length riding boots. And they all possessed myriad talents, plus self-importance, confidence, purpose in their lives, and futures with a shine to them. *She'd* left school with two GCSEs.

Shit. She shouldn't be looking at them. Her head must be bobbing about all over the place, and she was in danger of overbalancing. Already she had a headache from the strain. They could probably see that too, and were drawing it, hot and throbbing. It had started as a tightness in her scalp, and now gripped her skull like forceps.

'Relax! Relax!'

She jumped. So Phil had noticed too. Then she realized he was addressing not her but the students.

'You have to be comfortable to draw, and some of you look anything but. If your posture's stiff and restricted it will affect the marks you make. Drawing is a very physical thing, so if you're sleepy, or full of drugs or caffeine, you'll draw in a different way. I suggest we take a quick break to loosen up. And if you'd like to put your sketches up on the walls, that'll clear some space.'

Instantly there was a scraping of chairs, and a shuffling of feet as they proceeded to tack up their sheets of paper.

'Loretta, is there anything you want? A drink of water? Coffee?'

Herr Hitler was relenting. She shook her head, though. A break posed new uncertainties. Did she stay as she was or put her coat back on? 'Cold,' she murmured, as an excuse to retrieve it from the floor.

'Oh, sorry. Why didn't you say?'

Why didn't you think? she bit back.

He disappeared a moment and returned with a battered fan heater, which he plugged in and switched on, directing it at the wicker chair.

Hugging the coat round her, she stood by the fire, watching the students inspect each others' drawings. She couldn't see them herself

– there were too many bodies in the way, Phil's included. He was examining the sketches, commenting, suggesting. He took a lot of trouble, treating every student's work as precious and important. Of course *they* would accept it as perfectly natural that parents and teachers should lavish all this attention on them.

She plonked herself on the chair again, wishing someone would talk to *her*. Nice to be part of a group, speak the same language, hang out in the pub together. At Big Luke's she'd been the only waitress. Big was a joke.

'It's a relief to have a young, well-proportioned model for a change,' she overheard Phil say.

She tensed. He was taking the piss – he must be. Her hips were as broad as a bus, and she'd be thirty next month, for crying out loud.

'And there's an energy about her that you've captured in your drawing, Anne.'

Energy? She'd been sitting on her arse for half of the time. Was this just more of his blarney?

'The left arm needs rethinking, though. It looks a bit tacked on.'

Lorraine got up, and approached the drawing warily, as if afraid it might bite her. She stared at it in astonishment. Anne had made her slim, not fat. Almost beautiful, for fuck's sake. Quickly she inspected the other drawings. She was slim in all of them. Thirty of her, sixty, ninety . . . Some had done multiple sketches on one sheet, others had drawn her larger. Large but slender. Elegant. A woman with a swan neck and artistic tapering fingers. In surprise, she studied her hands. She had never noticed the shape of her fingers; all she had seen was the burn on her thumb – a parting gift from Big Luke's. Were they simply flattering her? Except why the hell should they bother? She was nothing to them – a stranger, an outsider. Anyway, each seemed concerned with different aspects. One was very taken with her hair and had sketched it half a dozen times, rippling down her back; not tangled, but hanging in waves. Another had drawn her feet in touching detail. She hated her feet. ('Only policewomen wear size seven shoes,' her mother used to say. 'It's not feminine, Lorraine.') But on paper they looked fine. Elongated, yes, but delicately boned. And they had given her high cheekbones and full lips, when she'd always thought her features coarse. ('I don't know where you get that nose from, Lorraine. Not from me, that's certain.') But here was refinement in her face. And these were artists – for all she knew,

Michelangelos of the future. Surely they could see, far better than her mother, how she really looked. Wonderingly, she touched her stomach, comparing flesh to charcoal. No evidence of currant buns or decomposing meat balls, just a shapely curve. She had become another person, a Loretta.

Perhaps they'd take the drawings home and strangers would admire her: twenty sets of relatives and visitors. One day she might even be framed and find her way to a posh gallery in Bond Street. *That* would show her mother. ('You're never going to amount to much, Lorraine. Not with all your hang-ups.')

'OK, back to work. Help yourselves to more paper, if you want. Some of you still need to draw more freely. The key to good drawing is to be focused but not anxious. Loretta, we'll have a reclining pose now. And I'd like you to hold it longer – say half an hour.'

Shrugging off her coat, she stretched full-length on the curtain, lying on her side with one arm flung back provocatively. Of course she could manage half an hour.

'That's good, Loretta. Just bring your right hand forward a fraction . . . Brilliant! You've got it.'

Not quite. She rearranged her body slightly, letting her thighs fall open and making sure her breasts were squeezed together to show them off to best advantage. Then she parted her lips in a mysterious smile.

Silence fell; the only sound the scratch of charcoal on paper. *She* was the cause of this reverent hush; everyone was concentrating – on her. She too had purpose now. And power. Without her, there would be no class. Without her, the teacher couldn't teach, and the students wouldn't learn to draw. She was the most important person in the room. The lights were shining on her alone; the fire purring for her alone; every eye admiring her, including Phil's, she knew.

It was he who broke the silence, encouraging the students. 'Feel your way around the model's body. Try to have a physical response to it.'

Instantly she was aware of their response. They were, frankly, all aroused. The ones sitting just in front would be able to see her labia. She was acting out their fantasies, fulfilling their desires. Invisible lines of attraction seemed to pass from every charcoal-stick straight into her body. She was more than just Loretta; she was the goddess of the art room. And they would come here every Wednesday to worship her, pay homage.

How could she be lonely now?

Sweeties

Hilda dribbled a couple of drops of cochineal into the saucepan, and stared mesmerized at the colour. Sixty years ago, when her periods had started, she'd been terrified, disgusted. Those bright stains on her knickers meant she could make a baby. She never had, thank the Lord.

Stirring the mixture briskly, she watched the treacherous red gradually fading to an innocuous pink. A strange name, coconut ice, when it was neither cold nor shiny.

She poured the syrupy pink sludge over the white layer already in the tin, smoothed the top with a palette knife and put it beside the tray of fudge, to set. Nostalgic smells masked the usual fusty air of the flat: aniseed, hot sugar, melting chocolate, peppermint. She was the only one who took the trouble to cook. The other women just brought along shop-bought stuff, and then had the nerve to complain that Bric-à-Brac and Baby Clothes always made more than Sweets. The sitting-room was crammed with their boxes and packets, cluttering every surface. Frankly she'd be glad when Father Michael came this afternoon to take them away.

And now for a rest. Her feet were aching and she'd be on them again tomorrow all day, manning the stall and guarding her wares against the village children's pilfering. Last year the O'Reilly boys had stolen a bar of Toblerone – she was sure of it, whatever Father Michael chose to believe.

Helping herself to a peppermint cream, she was suddenly transported back to the war: her first kiss – in the blackout – hot and fierce, and tasting of peppermint.

'No, Brian,' she'd protested, trying to knee him off. Boys were dangerous. Once, she'd heard a couple kissing in the air-raid shelter; their furtive smoochings and rustlings obliterated by the crash of a bomb. A hundred and fifty dead.

Things were quieter in Devon, although she hadn't liked the country. The sky was too big, and stared at you, and she missed her mother and sisters. Brian Barton was an only child. His parents owned a sweet-shop, but she was forbidden to go in. Every evening the front door was bolted and the door from the house into the shop securely locked. One night, Brian stole the key.

'Come on,' he urged. 'They'll never know. You can have all the sweets you want.'

She eyed him with suspicion, wondering if he was telling the truth. An image of Hansel and Gretel's gingerbread house floated into her mind: walls you could eat, windows made of barley sugar. The last barley-sugar stick at home had to be divided into six.

'And comics. Anything you like – *Chips, Film Fun, The Joker.*'

She'd missed *The Joker* last week and was dying to know what had happened to Alfie the Air-Tramp. 'All right,' she said, uncertainly, 'but we'd better not be long.' She crept down the stairs behind him, looking over her shoulder. What if his parents woke up? She was bound to get the blame. They hated evacuees and had only taken her in for the money, Brian said, and for the extra ration book.

He unlocked the door and beckoned her to follow him. Little jiggles of fear and excitement wobbled through her legs as she tiptoed in, holding her breath. In the dim, ghostly light, the shop seemed not quite real and for a moment she thought she was dreaming. But as her eyes adjusted to the gloom she could make out blurry shapes. Hungrily she sniffed the air. The rooms upstairs smelt grey and sad, of damp and mothballs and homesickness, but this was a pink, happy smell, like sticking your nose into a box of Turkish Delight.

Brian flashed his torch along the shelves, where dozens of tall glass jars stood in rows, with coloured labels and identical black lids. The torchlight flickered over them, briefly bringing their contents to life: zizzy Sherbet Lemons, lumps of golden butterscotch, stripy-coated humbugs, fruit drops glowing yellow, red and green. And now the narrow beam lit up bars of chocolate, one after another – treasures she hadn't seen in months: Caramello, Whole Nut, Raspberry Creme. Then Brian shone the torch lower, on the counter, and the light was reflected on shiny metal – brass weighing scales, with a set of matching brass weights, a gleaming silver toffee-hammer and little silver shovels for scooping up the sweets. Imagine having such things in your *home*; being able to weigh out a quarter of Bull's Eyes whenever you wanted, or break up a big slab of toffee and eat it until you went pop.

'What's your favourite?' Brian asked, tapping the torch against one of the jars.

She hesitated. They were *all* her favourites, so how was she meant to choose? 'Liquorice Allsorts,' she said at last.

At once he climbed up on the counter and, with the torch tucked precariously under his chin, manoeuvred one of the jars off the shelf. He lowered it on to the counter before jumping lightly down again. Then, unscrewing the lid, he tipped the jar on its side and out tumbled not just two ounces (the most she'd ever bought in one go) but a whole glorious heap of Liquorice Allsorts.

'Go on, then – help yourself.'

Another hard choice. Round or square? Two-tiered or three-? Pink or yellow or brown? In the end she picked a white and yellow sandwich. She pulled the white square off first and ate it, fondant-sweet, then the yellow layer and finally the dark, chewy liquorice. Brian had his mouth full, too, and she noticed a tiny shred of black caught between his teeth.

'You've got a bit of liquorice stuck.'

'Where?'

'There.' She pointed with her finger, and without warning he lunged forward, closed his lips around the finger and gently bit it.

'Don't,' she said, trying to pull her hand away. His teeth grazed against her skin and gave her funny feelings.

He shrugged, and released her finger. 'Let me see your tongue.'

'Why?'

'It's all black, I bet.'

'It's not.'

'How do you know? You can't see it.'

She stuck it out at him.

'It *is* black.'

' 'Tisn't. Show me yours.'

His was pink and wriggly. He moved even nearer, and touched her face with the tip of it.

'Get off! You're foul.' She wiped the wet patch from her cheek. He was so close to her now, she could smell the stale sourness of his pyjamas. (Mrs Barton said clothes only needed washing once a month.)

She was wearing pyjamas too – a borrowed pair that were too long in the leg and felt all coarse and rough. At home she wore a nightdress.

She looked longingly at the pile of Liquorice Allsorts. 'You said I could have as many sweets as I want.'

'Go ahead. I'm not stopping you.'

This time she crammed four into her mouth. It would be lovely if she could take some home for the others, but she didn't know where home was, any more. When they were bombed out, she and her three sisters were all sent to different places. 'And can I have some Peppermint Drops as well?' They were Betty's favourites.

He clambered up for another jar, thrust his fist inside and drew out two of the chunky white discs. 'Give us a kiss first.'

'No. I don't want to make a baby.'

'Don't be daft. It's only a kiss.'

'No.' She remembered the big red spot on his chin and loathed the thought of it touching her. Even in the torchlight, she could see how swollen and angry it was.

'Please yourself.' He put one of the peppermints in his mouth and sucked it noisily, while holding the second in his hand, just out of her reach.

She snatched at it but he jerked it away. 'Changed your mind, Hil?'

'You're not to call me Hil. I've told you.'

'Hil Hil Hil,' he taunted. 'Jack and Jill went up the hill.'

'You're stupid.'

He suddenly lunged at her again and this time he put his mouth on hers and tried to force her lips apart. His tongue seemed huge and sort of furious, and made her gag. It was nearly as bad as wearing a gas mask. And his greasy black hair was brushing against her forehead. If she didn't push him off, she'd suffocate. But he was much bigger than her, and anyway his hands were locked tight around her waist. Now she'd have a baby and be sent away in disgrace, like Lilian McVeigh. (Lilian had never come back – it was almost as if she'd died.)

At last he unclamped his mouth and loosened his grip. She shook herself free, but he yanked her back and began scrabbling at the waistband of her pyjamas. The funny feelings had started again, twitching down below. Well, so what, if they sent her away? It was horrid living here. Mrs Barton gave her stale brown bread for tea, and never said goodnight at bedtime.

'What you got these on for?' He had undone the pyjama draw-string and was pulling at the elastic of her knickers.

She felt herself blushing in the dark. Sometimes she still wet the bed and she felt safer with her knickers on. Brian slipped his hand inside them. If she thought ever so hard about sweets, she wouldn't need to think about what he was doing. Best of all she would like a Gobstopper, which lasted for ages and ages, and went all different colours as you sucked it. You'd keep taking it out of your mouth to see if it had changed and it gradually got smaller and smaller until it was just a tang on your tongue.

'Lie down,' hissed Brian.

'What for?'

'Because I want you to.'

'Why should I? The floor's all dirty.'

He made a grab for the torch and switched it off. 'You can't *see* the floor now,' he taunted.

'Brian, don't! I'm scared.'

She heard him get to his knees and pat the floorboards. 'Lie here and I'll put it back on.'

'You swear?'

'Yeah. Cross my heart and hope to die. Lie *down*.'

She curled up in a ball. The wooden floor hurt her cheek and she imagined big hairy spiders crawling over her legs. The torch made jittery shadows, and at the far end of the shop there were pools of blackness where rats might live, or ghosts.

'Lie straight.' He knelt above her and uncurled her arms and legs. His voice had gone funny – high and sort of breathless.

She shut her eyes. His hands felt hot and damp. They were press-ing on her chest, right against the skin. He'd undone the top two buttons of her pyjama jacket and squeezed his fingers through the gap. And then he clambered on top of her. She lashed out with her fists, but he pinioned her arms and held them behind her head. He was such an awful weight he was squashing the breath from her body.

'Listen, Hil' – his voice was still gaspy and odd – 'if you do what I want, you can have a whole jar of toffees.'

She shook her head. Sweets were dangerous. They rotted your teeth and gave you spots. The spot on Brian's chin seemed to swell to bursting-point as his face loomed over hers.

And then, with a terrific noise, the door was flung open and crashed back against the wall. 'Brian! Hilda! What the devil's going on?' Thunderous footsteps made the floor quake, and a fierce beam of light flashed right into her eyes. Brian rolled off her, and she lay, transfixed by the light, like a stunned and blinded rabbit. And there was a loud ringing sound in her ears that only increased her terror.

On and on it jangled and finally she realized it was the phone. She pounced on it and, almost choking through the peppermint cream, whimpered in a shred of voice, 'It was *Brian*, Mr Barton. He made me come down here, I didn't want to, honest, but – *Who?* . . . Oh . . . Oh . . . I'm sorry, Father Michael. I didn't recognize your . . . Yes, of course. The sweets are ready. They just need a bit longer to cool . . . Yes, half past four will be fine.'

She put the phone down, crimson with embarrassment. Whatever must the priest have thought? How could she look him in the eye this afternoon? Or face him at church on Sunday? She caught sight of herself in the mirror – her apron was dusted with icing sugar and straggles of hair were escaping from her bun. She jabbed the slipping hairpins more tightly into her scalp and removed the offending apron. She must tidy herself – and the flat – before he arrived.

Yet she felt strangely sick and dizzy as she limped into the sitting-room. She clutched at the wall for support, before sinking into a chair. Was she twelve, or seventy-four? Alone, or at the Bartons'? Sweets were everywhere – boxes of Black Magic, tins of humbugs and barley sugars, Maltesers, Turkish Delight . . .

She closed her eyes and saw the tall glass jars again, glowing and ghostly on the shelves. Brian had promised her toffees, but she had never got to taste them. She had been packed off in disgrace, back to London and the Blitz.

All at once there was a muffled *crrr. . .rrrr. . .ump* as a bomb exploded further along the street. Shock waves juddered through the air-raid shelter, and brick-dust rained down from the roof. Shouts and screams outside cut across the frantic squawk of the ambulance bells. Fear made her wet her knickers; the hot, shameful trickle soon turning squelchy-cold.

'Brian!' she cried. 'Please help!'

And suddenly there he was – a different Brian, decent and respectful. He didn't live in Devon but in Southwark, right next door. He knew that she was frightened, so he held her hand and softly stroked her hair. No need to push him off – she could trust this special new

Brian. He would never be rough or bullying, and would only do what she agreed he could. And in return he would give her loads of sweets.

'What are your favourite toffees?' he whispered, edging up beside her on the grimy wooden bench.

'Banana Splits.' Little toffee sandwiches with a creamy yellow filling. There weren't any real bananas any more.

He unwrapped a Banana Split and popped it into her mouth. His hands were nothing like the other Brian's, but smooth and kind, with clean nails. And his eyes were a lovely light blue, not burnt-toast black.

She sat, contentedly sucking, his arm around her shoulder. The all-clear had just sounded but she didn't go back home. She felt safer staying here, in the air-raid shelter sweet-shop. It no longer smelled of smoke and dust but of candyfloss and Pear Drops and Dairy Butter Mints. And even if the shop should be bombed, its pink, happy smell would never disappear, but would linger in the air, wafting hope and sweetness over the craters and the rubble.

'Would you like some Sherbet Lemons, Hilda?'

She smiled. Of course she would. As she crunched one in her teeth its glassy shell burst open and released a tingling fizz. Her mouth was full of sweet and sour: banana, sherbet, toffee, lemon. Still sucking the last sharp lemon splinter, she started on the Dolly Mixtures – everything in miniature: tiny sugary jellies, weeny pastel-coloured cubes and discs.

Tenderly Brian kissed her cheek, then moved his hand towards her chest. 'If you let me touch you – *there*, Hilda – I'll give you a Walnut Whip.'

She nestled closer. The funny feelings were coming back, but much nicer than before. And his fingers were so gentle she wasn't scared at all. And anyway Walnut Whips cost tuppence-ha'penny each, so she'd only ever had one tiny lick of Betty's.

'Let me show you how to eat it,' he said, cupping it in his palm. 'First you bite the walnut off – like this.'

She watched his teeth close round the nut, which he passed from his mouth to hers, softly brushing her lips. The nut was oily and slightly bitter, an exciting, grown-up taste that made the quivery feelings creep like tickly mouse's paws down into her knickers.

'That leaves a little hole – see? Just enough to poke your tongue inside.' He narrowed his tongue until it was pointy at the end and used it like a spoon to scoop out the cream filling.

Dreamily she stretched beside him. She was no longer made of blood and bones but of luscious soft white creamy stuff, and his tongue was deep inside her, lapping at it, sucking . . .

'And last of all the chocolate shell. You can either lick it till it melts . . .'

'Mm,' she murmured, as his tongue caressed her melting shell and she felt herself dissolving into smooth velvety chocolate squish.

And now he was giving her a baby – not a nasty real one that screamed and wet its nappy, but a tiny yellow Jelly Baby. She bit its head off, chewed its little body, then nibbled its red twin. No one sent her packing like Lilian McVeigh. And no one punished Brian. *He* had stopped the bombs, ended the eerie blackout, brought bananas back, and eggs, refilled the hungry chocolate machines. And although the war was over, he would stay with her day and night, constantly offering new Bounty: the hard creaminess of a Milky Bar, Aero full of bubbles, the honey crunch of Maltesers, Winter Warmers, Love Hearts . . .

She sat up on one elbow. Somewhere, far away, she thought she heard a doorbell. Yes, there it was again, louder and more insistent. *Brian*, come back to find her, to ask her hand in marriage. She scrambled to her feet and dashed out to the hall.

All her life she had been waiting for the ring.

Mantra

'Could you lie face-down for me, please?'

Nervously she climbed up on the couch. At least face-down her breasts would be concealed. Being naked in front of a stranger – and a man at that – was rather an unsettling experience. When Janet had offered her the present of a massage she'd assumed it would be performed by a white-coated beautician, not a swarthy chap in frayed jeans.

'Relax,' he urged. 'You're very tense.'

Wasn't it counter-productive, telling a tense person to relax? It just seemed to make her muscles more knotted than ever.

'Try to let yourself go, Emma, and surrender to the process.'

As his hands made contact with her back he let out a great sigh. Was he tired before he'd started or, worse, bored? Another deep sigh followed – almost a groan of pain.

'Is something wrong?' she mumbled into the couch.

'No, everything's just fine. I'm simply releasing my own stuff before I start the treatment. This is your time, Emma, so I need to focus on *you*. I intend to work on your chakras, to balance the different systems of the body, and then go beyond the body and fine-tune the spirit too. I guess Janet's told you that I'm really more of a healer than a masseur.'

'Yes, she did say something about—'

'I've trained in many traditions and techniques: shiatsu, iridology, crystal healing, ayurvedic medicine . . .'

OK, he was well qualified, but she rather wished he'd shut up. She'd had her fill of babbling Americans for one day. The couple beside her on the plane ('We're from Idaho and we just loved your beautiful country!') had given her an exhaustive account of their travels across the length and breadth of England, followed by alarmingly intimate details of their forty-two-year marriage. And she had missed most of the film (billed as a bitter-sweet romance) while they regaled her with the talents of their teeming brood of children and grandchildren.

'And I was lucky enough to study with Gurinder Singh at his ashram in the Punjab. I've also travelled with nomads in Mongolia . . .'

He was evidently more adventurous than she was. A Heathrow–LA flight was not exactly on a par with a trek across Mongolia.

'And my treatments last ninety minutes, minimum. A shorter time would be unfair to both of us. I'm not into superficial. I go deep, in every sense.'

'Going deep' sounded ominously like a warning of pain to come. Already he was prodding the bones along her spine with vigorous (vicious) fingers. This was not at all the evening she'd envisaged: relaxing on the sofa with Janet and a glass of wine, catching up on old times. Still, the massage was intended as a treat, so she ought to try to enjoy it.

'Your muscles are absolutely rigid, Emma, which of course doesn't surprise me after such a long flight. And I hear they lost your baggage . . .'

'Yes, it was put on the wrong plane.' She pictured her smart blue case exiled in some foreign land – part of *her*, displaced. Any loss was difficult just now.

'Did they say when you'd get it back?'

'Tomorrow, hopefully . . .' The man at the lost luggage desk had been offhand to the point of rudeness, but how could he know that, deprived of her clothes and personal belongings, she'd felt her identity crumble to dust.

'You have very bad adhesions in this area. They need breaking down, or you'll suffer permanent damage. Your whole back's in spasm, Emma.'

'Well, could you use a bit less pressure, please? It's hurting.' Rather an understatement: this was more like assault and battery than massage.

'Mm. There's psychological pain, as well. I'm tuning in to a deep malaise. You've been through some sort of trauma – that's what my hands are telling me.'

How on earth did he know? Janet had promised not to say a word, and Janet would never break a promise.

'Have you suffered a recent bereavement?'

It *had* been like a death: shattering and sudden. He must be psychic in some way, reading her like a book. But she wouldn't bore him by raking it all up. It was unfair, if not ill-mannered, to unload your problems on to other people. 'Look, would you mind awfully if we don't talk?'

'Sure. You're tired – I'm aware of that. I picked up the exhaustion as soon as I touched your body. Let me put on some music to help you relax. It's a compilation tape I made of Buddhist prayers, Sanskrit texts, Mongolian overtone chanting and various other things from my travels. You'll find it uplifts you spiritually and physically.'

This prompted an image of her levitating gently to the ceiling – well, it would be a lot more comfortable than having her nose squashed into a couch. Turning her neck with difficulty, she watched him wipe the oil from his hands and slot a cassette into the player. Freed, if only briefly, from his pummelling, she considered her chances of escape – not just from him but from the States. She should never have come in the first place. LA was stifling and noisy, and Janet had changed. (The Janet she'd known in England would-n't dream of consulting gurus and healers, even if any had been available.)

There was a low moaning sound from the tape, which rose gradu-ally in volume and intensity until it filled the room. It seemed to reflect her own feelings – more so when Xavier returned to the couch and resumed his punishing onslaught. His hands, travelling the length of her spine, had the weight and rigidity of a flat-iron, ruthlessly level-ling out every bump and furrow in its path.

And then an odd thing happened. He laughed – not a quiet reflec-tive chuckle but a great bellow of a laugh. Followed by another. What the hell was so funny? He could at least share the joke: it was a long time since anything had even made her smile.

'Yes, yes, yes, yes, yes!' he exclaimed, assailing her neck with such ferocity she feared her head might snap off. 'Do you realize, Emma, this was *meant*. Your being here today is no accident. You were sent to me, I'm convinced of it. And I'm laughing because I'm so happy – just knowing what I can do for you and what changes I can make in your life.'

The only change she wanted was to have her job restored. Which was beyond his powers, or anyone's. Dumped at forty-two – it still seemed unbelievable. And that brutal instruction to clear her desk within the hour, as if she were a leper who might taint the other staff.

'I'll give your back a rest now, and work on your legs and feet. Feet hold a lot of tension, so you should feel a great release.'

After fifteen years, for God's sake. It was worse than a divorce. Gibbs & Shaw had been her home, her family, her *raison d'être*, her future – or so she had stupidly thought.

Her friends said airily that of course she'd find another job, but the few interviews she'd had so far gave little cause for hope. Without work, life was purposeless and shapeless. At Gibbs & Shaw twelve-hour days were the norm, so she had never needed hobbies.

'Oh, just listen to this prayer, Emma! It brings back blissful memories. I recorded it in a Hindu temple my last day in the Punjab.'

She had taken it all for granted: the camaraderie, the in-jokes, the gossip, the shared goals. And in her mind she was still at her desk, fighting to meet deadlines, initiating ideas. Even if she were *sixty*-two, she wouldn't succumb to golf or gardening. Time was too precious to be frittered away in a bunker or a potting-shed.

'What he's saying is, "Bear all and do nothing; hear all and say nothing; give all and take nothing; save all and be nothing." Doesn't that just freak you out?'

'Mm.' Her colleagues had promised to keep in touch, but she knew they'd soon forget her. She was an outsider already, a has-been.

'I learned so much wisdom in the East. For instance, "Speak with Love and it becomes Truth." That's beautiful, don't you think?'

Her alarm clock still went off at six and she would leap out of bed, only to remember that there was nothing to get up for. She might never need an alarm clock again in her life. *Or* a smart suit. Or—

'Come on, lovely leg – reee-laaax!'

God, he was talking to her limbs now, while massaging the inside of her thigh. His hand was going right up to her groin, yet the process left her cold. Had she lost her libido along with all the rest? Surely she should feel *some*thing when a man touched her naked body? He wasn't unattractive, although rather an enigma, with his Spanish name and American accent, his dark foreign-looking skin and grey-green eyes.

'Ah! – now we've moved from India to Tibet. This song's very special. You know, every time I hear it, it reduces me to tears.' The mournful chanting in the background had given place to a throbbing plaint, interspersed with drumbeats. 'Did I tell you about my pilgrimage to Lhasa and—?'

'No.'

'It was the high point of my life, Emma. I visited all these monasteries and temples, and achieved my own nirvana on the bank of the Yarlong Tsangpo River, in sight of Mount Everest.'

He was working on the soles of her feet, and seemed to be tickling them deliberately. She held her breath in an effort not to giggle or cry out.

'Of course the persecution's terrible, but you have to go beyond that and learn from the Tibetans themselves. There they are, occupied by a foreign power and living in dire poverty in a harsh environment, yet you get the feeling that they're richer and more blessed than we are in the West. Those I met were so content, so full of human courage. One afternoon, in Gyantse, I watched this group of men building a house in the broiling sun. It was real back-breaking labour – they didn't have machines, only picks and shovels. Yet, all the while, they were singing with such joy you'd never think it was work. Shit! This music really gets to me. I'll be sobbing all over the couch soon. The gist of what he's saying is "You are what you are looking for." Deep, huh?'

She made a strangulated noise, still tortured by the tickling.

'You sound a bit blocked up, Emma. Shall we turn you over? You'll be more comfortable that way.' He repositioned the towels to preserve her modesty as she wriggled up and over, momentarily dazzled by the glare. Her body clock was still set to English time, so by rights it should be dark by now, but the brash California sun was flooding through the window. At least she had things to look at now that she was lying on her back, although Janet's bedroom struck her as faintly absurd: thick pile carpet the colour of clotted cream, gold-weave linen wallpaper, cream lace bedspread elaborately ruched and frilled. The bed itself (king-size) was piled with fluffy toys and heart-shaped velvet cushions. Yes, Janet had changed. She remembered the austere flat they'd shared as students – Blondie posters on the walls and the two narrow, lumpy beds littered with clothes and books.

'Even now, the Tibetans aren't that used to seeing Westerners. I was in the market place one day and an old peasant woman came up and pinched my arm. Apparently she was amazed by how hairy it was and wanted to check I was real!'

A surreptitious glance at his arms confirmed that they were unusually hairy. And a tangle of coarse hairs sprouted above the neckline of his T-shirt. 'Ouch!' She winced as his hands moved to her stomach.

'Yes, that's tender, isn't it? There's a blockage in the colon. Are you constipated?'

'A bit,' she mumbled, blushing.

'We'll sort that out, don't worry. We need to get some movement here.' He began kneading her flesh energetically, as if he were making bread.

'Er, how long were you in Tibet?' she asked, as a diversion from the topic of her bowels.

'I can't answer that, Emma. You don't measure these things in weeks or months. Time stands still in Tibet.'

In LA too, apparently – surely the ninety minutes was up?

'I remember once I was travelling to Shigatse on the Friendship Highway. The bus was packed with Tibetans, and although I didn't speak the language they included me in their group. One offered me a piece of his dried yak meat; another pointed at the monasteries we were passing – all destroyed, of course. Just pathetic piles of bricks and shale clinging to the mountaintops. And then we came to a monastery that was being reconstructed, rising from the rubble like a shining symbol of hope. And it wasn't until that moment, Emma, that I really understood the concept of the Wheel of Life – things rise and fall, then rise again and fall again, and—'

'Xavier, I . . . I'm going to close my eyes and have a bit of a doze. I hope you don't object.'

'No, go ahead, that's great! Janet asked me to stop by today because she could see you were strung up. And if I've succeeded in relaxing you, I can go home a happy man. This session has been incredibly therapeutic. In fact, dare I use the P word?'

Pretentious? Phoney? Pseudo? Painful, certainly. He was still mauling her protesting colon.

'Pro-*found*,' he intoned. 'I'm just blown away by the transformation I see in you. The reward I get from my work is restoring clients' hearts and minds. I don't expect material rewards . . .'

Oh, no? She guessed he charged hundreds of dollars per session. Janet was nothing if not generous.

'. . . just the knowledge that I've worked a little miracle.'

'You have,' she lied. 'And I'm grateful. But you know, Xavier, I think I've had enough now. You've made me so relaxed I feel I could sleep for hours.'

'I'm thrilled to hear that, Emma, but we haven't finished yet. I still need to work on your face and upper body. And your head, of course. All the busy thought-traffic needs to be slowed way down, and the brainwaves switched to alpha-mode.'

'Perhaps some other time?'

'Well, there's one thing I insist on, and that's giving you your personal mantra. I devise one for each of my clients, something specific to their individual needs. I call it the icing on the massage-cake.'

'Could you give it to me now?'

He frowned. 'We still have another twenty minutes. I don't like to cut things short.'

She forced a smile. 'Well, let's pretend we're in Tibet. Time does-n't matter there.'

'Emma' – he leaned over her supine body and gently kissed her forehead – 'you're so wise, my child.'

Child, indeed! She caught a whiff of sweat, and recoiled from the pungent garlic on his breath. Perhaps when you had achieved nirvana by some obscure Tibetan river, in sight of Mount Everest, you didn't bother with petty things like soap and toothpaste.

'I do hope I'll see you again? How about another session next week?'

'I'm, er, not sure what Janet's planned.'

'Well, just let me know. I can drive down any time. And now for your mantra. I'm going to say it in Sanskrit, because Sanskrit's a sacred language and this is a sacred moment.'

'Could you translate it then, or it'll be double Dutch to me.'

'There's no need for translations. Sanskrit works on us like music – we understand it on an instinctive, intuitive level. Even though the words might seem strange, their effect is amazingly powerful. Just listening to the sounds and rhythms can nourish our spirit, enhance communication, reconnect us with primal harmony, transform us inwardly . . .'

She was sorry now she'd asked. Would he ever stop?

'And what's so extraordinary is that it's survived for twenty-five centuries, more or less unchanged. And it's full of paradox. It's an ancient language, but also the language of the Eternal Now. And the language of enlightenment, which at the same time connects us to our child-self. And it's called a difficult language, yet I've known some people who've never heard a word of Sanskrit suddenly produce these spontaneous outpourings, as if they know it in their inner soul. But most important for *you*, Emma, is that it can free us from the bondage of past illusions, and bring deep peace and happiness.'

'I can't wait.'

'The word mantra itself comes from Sanskrit, but I guess you knew that already.'

'No.'

'It means literally "to free from the mind". I don't want to bombard you with all the stuff, but there are fifty letters in the Sanskrit alphabet and fifty corresponding spots along the chakras, which we translate from Sanskrit as "petals". So if you recite a mantra containing certain seed-sounds, the petals on the chakras vibrate in specific ways and you'll get a surge of spiritual energy, like a whale ingesting plankton.'

Petals, seeds, whales, plankton – this was turning into a biology lesson.

'The ultimate goal of a Sanskrit mantra is spiritual growth, spiritual evolution and finally spiritual freedom. And along the way many wonderful things can happen.'

And now, arms outstretched, eyes closed and face contorted in a grimace, he began reciting with great solemnity. To her it was just gibberish and he looked so utterly ridiculous, she felt a bubble of laughter welling up inside. Embarrassingly, she couldn't contain it and erupted into giggles.

Yet far from being offended, he gazed at her with a beatific smile. 'Emma, this is awesome! I've lifted your sadness at last. I never thought I'd hear you laugh.'

And *I* never thought I'd hear such a load of rubbish, she muttered, struggling up from the couch. Her back hurt, her neck throbbed, and every muscle ached, but still she couldn't control the giggles. 'Thank you, Xavier,' she spluttered, eyes streaming with helpless laughter, 'for a . . . well, *unique* massage.'

Resplendent in pink shorts and designer sunglasses, Janet stood at the worktop, juicing oranges. 'It's such a glorious morning I've laid breakfast on the balcony. How did you sleep?'

'Never better. I went out like a light.'

'That's Xavier. He has the same effect on me.'

Emma said nothing. It was more likely good old-fashioned exhaustion.

'I thought we'd have a proper American breakfast – waffles with bacon and maple syrup. Or there's blueberry muffins if you like.'

'I'll try the waffles, although it sounds a peculiar mixture!'

'No worse than pork and apple sauce. And by the way I've booked lunch at Smokey Joe's. I've planned a few treats for us today, in honour of your visit. But first we ought to give Doug a call. He's got fingers in so many pies in London and LA I'm sure he'll be able to find you a job.'

'I don't want a job.'

'*What?*'

Emma sank into a chair. The statement had shocked her, too. Didn't she want a job more than anything in the world? 'I . . . I need more time to myself.'

'But you've had *weeks* to yourself. And you've been saying how empty your life is, and how you're desperate to get back to work.'

'I was wrong,' she said. Or rather somebody else said, someone speaking through her. 'Gibbs & Shaw was a kind of . . . slavery. I worked those appalling long hours, and never had a minute free to think.'

'Emma, this is nonsense! You loved it there. Your letters were always full of the place.'

'I was just kidding myself, accepting other people's values. I didn't even like my colleagues. Oh, I thought I did, but all they really cared about was money and promotion.'

'Emma, you hypocrite! Those things are important to you.'

'They *were*. I told you – I fell into the trap of wanting what you're meant to want. And I was always so frantically busy, there wasn't time to work out what matters in life. I ignored my whole spiritual side.'

Janet shot her a look of alarm and irritation. 'I'm sorry, I'm flummoxed.'

Me too, thought Emma. And yet her words had seemed utterly right, as if the truth had been revealed to her at last.

'How will you survive, though? You can't live on air.'

'I've got my severance pay.'

'That won't last long. Besides, you're a workaholic. Even at university you put us all to shame. You can't change your basic nature.'

'It's not my basic nature,' she said, quietly but insistently. 'Being a workaholic was a way of avoiding reality. I don't need to do that now.'

'Emma, what's got into you? I just don't understand.'

'Nor do I.' She shook her head in mixed wonder and confusion. 'I suppose you could call it . . . a little miracle.'

Janet snorted. 'Miracle my eye! Jet lag, more like. This simply isn't you.'

'It *is*, Janet. The real me.'

'But you're young, for heaven's sake. You've got to do something with your life. You can't just potter about in carpet-slippers for the next thirty years.'

'I don't intend to. I have plans.'

'What sort of plans?'

'Well, I'm going to learn Sanskrit for a start.'

'*Sanskrit*?' Janet stared at her, open-mouthed.

'Yes. Some people think that, given time, it could become the universal language.' How ever had she known that? She didn't remember Xavier saying it.

'Emma, I'm worried about you, seriously.'

'It's OK. I'm on top of the world. Everything's simple and easy. I feel like a child again.'

'Second childhood, you mean,' Janet grunted.

'Well, yes, exactly. We lose so much by growing up. We become judgemental and closed off and full of fears and anxieties. We need to be children again to possess a state of natural wisdom.'

'OK' – Janet scooped up the squeezed orange skins and flung them into the bin – 'so you're fluent in Sanskrit and playing with your dolls again, then what?'

'I'll travel.'

'Well, at least that means I'll see more of you.'

Emma walked slowly to the window. Outside, the slim trunk of a date-palm pointed like a finger to the sun – a beneficent sun showering its largesse on every lustrous leaf and twig, every radiant blade of grass. In the distance she could just make out the craggy mountain peaks, snowed with clouds and blurring into mist. It was still early, still daybreak; time still young and stretching to infinity. 'I'm going East,' she smiled, 'not West. In fact, I'm going to Tibet.'

Heron

Stupid pond, thought Paula, banging down her coffee cup.
Pretentious waterfall. Absurd tribe of plastic frogs. The frogs were
Maureen's choice, no doubt, while Eric toiled Sunday after Sunday,
building his mini Niagara. Between them they had ruined the whole
garden, and now they were talking dahlias. *Dahlias*, for heaven's sake
– horrid garish things, about as subtle as Maureen's taste in clothes.

Yet Eric treated her like royalty, scurrying up with drinks for her
when she was reclining on the sun lounger, even picking up her
magazine if she dropped it. Maureen read *OK!* and *Real* – neither
aptly named.

Paula unfolded *The Independent*. An article on torture in Peru,
which once would have stirred her to righteous anger, now had little
impact. She'd become uncaring – not to mention bitter, petty, snob-
bish and bone idle, spending her days staring out of the window.
Next thing, she'd be counting the daisies on the lawn – except there
weren't any since Eric and Maureen had taken over. Every anarchic
weed had been rooted out, every patch of moss ruthlessly extermi-
nated in the pursuit of perfection.

After a perfunctory look at the book reviews, she turned to
Appointments. As usual it was full of managerial positions – nothing
remotely suitable for someone whose only skill was in drawing and
painting. International Business Adviser, Director of Human
Resources, Head of Supply Management . . . Nobody wanted artists.
There was always voluntary work, of course. Perhaps she should train

as a Samaritan. 'Yes, go ahead and kill yourself. It's much the best solution.'

Enviously she studied the items on next door's washing-line. Eleven nappies, three Babygros, four pairs of Y-fronts, six pillow-cases . . . Joyce was a model of diligence, probably at this moment ironing dusters or wallpapering the garage. Everyone was busy – Eric and Maureen notching up more sales at work, the woman opposite running her crèche, a couple of magpies in the garden collecting twigs for their nest, and a hyperactive squirrel leaping from branch to branch in the copper beech. Even Joyce's washing looked sprightly, billowing in the breeze.

Billow, pillow . . . Words were peculiar things. Divorce – seven letters destroying seven years. A home divided into two flats, one up, one down. Losing Matthew meant losing the house and garden too; losing her point in life.

Perhaps she'd make another coffee. It helped to fill the time, provided a tiny ritual: boiling water, heating milk, even choosing a pretty cup. As she rose from her chair she noticed a movement over the rooftops – a large grey bird, which she recognized as a heron, flapping languidly down to the garden and alighting on the fence. It perched there, motionless, its eyes fixed on the pond, home to Eric's Koi carp. He wouldn't be exactly overjoyed to lose them to a predator.

Go on, *take* one, she urged. But the bird remained absolutely still, a stone sentinel alert to its prey. She had never seen a heron at such close quarters. She could make out the dark tips of its wing feathers and the black crest on its head, the spindly legs and stiletto-sharp yellow bill.

And suddenly, after eighteen months of lethargy, she felt an urge to draw again. With Matthew gone, she hadn't so much as picked up a crayon or pencil; she had simply crammed her painting paraphernalia into the landing cupboard and tried to forget it was there.

Nervously she stood in front of the cupboard, willing herself to open the door. Her fingers closed round the handle and turned. Inside was her *life* – her former life – paints, palettes, brushes, paper: the tools of her trade. The brushes had gone hard, the bundles of paper were creased, and her precious portfolios were lightly filmed with dust. She took out one of the portfolios and placed it on the table. The pages were weighted with memories: the bluebell wood she had sketched on honeymoon, the ancient sagging yew that Matthew had christened Methuselah, the pouting lips of the orchids he had given her on their second anniversary.

She shut the book impatiently. This was no time for nostalgia – she must get back to the heron before it flew away. Returning to the window with a sketch book and a charcoal pencil she was relieved to find the bird still there, positioned now right beside the pond. However, she was unable to take advantage of her model's obliging stillness and proximity. Her hand seemed to have forgotten how to hold the pencil, as if paralysed by a muscle-wasting illness. Yet the desire to draw was surely something positive, like regaining the feeling in a long insentient limb.

She glanced from bird to pad and back again and, roused at last to action, decided to start with the head. Her initial strokes were tentative, even clumsy, but she tore out the page and started on a clean one, determined to persevere. The heron must be her exemplar. Its attention never wavered, as if it existed solely to catch fish – as *she* existed to draw.

And slowly, hearteningly, the lines began to flow with greater ease. She had caught the shape of the head, in essence, and the dagger-like thrust of the beak, although the neck posed more of a challenge, with its pronounced S-curve and subtle gradations in colour.

Then all at once the heron stirred – disturbed by Joyce next door, emerging with another basket of laundry. With a squawk of complaint and a disgruntled shake of its wings it launched itself into the air and disappeared over the copper beech.

Paula continued drawing, from memory. If she stopped now she might never restart. With luck, the heron would return, enabling her to do a sequence of studies, first black and white, then colour. There was even a chance of exhibiting again. Normally she made excuses if the gallery phoned to ask about new work, but perhaps her artistic stagnation was over at long last.

The adjustment on the binoculars was stiff from lack of use, but eventually the heron sprang into focus and she spent several minutes studying the texture of its plumage: the downy softness of the chest in contrast with the silken wing. And similarly the tension in the neck muscles as the bird stood poised to strike. This was its fourth visit to the pond, although it hadn't yet taken a fish. Maybe they were camouflaged by the aquatic plants or lurking at the bottom, out of reach. At least its lengthy vigil gave her time to draw – already she had progressed to a second sketch book. The bird's continued presence seemed to have released her from the stupor of grief. Like her, it was always alone. She knew that herons were supposed to live in heronries, but she couldn't imagine this one a member of some noisy, squabbling colony. It was a solitary, a philosopher.

She was rethinking the proportions of the body to the legs when she almost dropped her charcoal in surprise: with startling speed the kinked neck straightened and the snake-like head stabbed down into the water, reappearing with a flash of gold and scarlet in the beak. The pinioned Koi squirmed frantically, spraying showers of silver droplets in its struggle to escape. But the heron's grip was tenacious and she watched in mingled alarm and fascination as it began to swallow its prey in a series of undulating gulps – a procedure not without hazard, given the size of the fish. Quickly she resumed her drawing, trying to capture the gradually descending bulge in the heron's throat, and the way it threw its head up to facilitate the process, and then, mission accomplished, the impressive wingspan as it flapped ponderously away, long legs stretched out behind.

She was so absorbed, she didn't hear Eric and Maureen return. As a couple, they were more or less inseparable, and had made togetherness an art form not only at home but at work. Employed by the same company, they even shared an office and a boss. And every day, as soon as they got back, they would sally out to the garden, still in their formal business suits, to feed their beloved Koi. She could see them now from the window, scattering fish-food on the water. But their fond expressions soon darkened as they realized one of their precious babies was missing – precious in all senses: those exotic creatures had cost over £100 apiece.

Instinctively, she drew back out of sight. She had no wish to risk another interrogation, like the time Eric mislaid his briefcase. She knew they thought her weird, having neither job nor husband, and being so tearful when they'd moved in downstairs. Anyway, whatever questions they might ask, she would say nothing about the heron. After its successful catch today, it would surely come back for more tomorrow, and she would be there to observe it.

She surveyed the room with satisfaction. The heron had long since outgrown her sketchbooks and now surrounded her on every side. She had pinned up sheets of cartridge paper wherever there was space and used the walls as drawing boards, depicting the bird in flight, or standing fishing with its head sunk into its shoulders, or walking with its stiff robotic gait. In the last two weeks she had learned more about the species, bringing home books from the library to research its breeding habits, its calls and songs, its migratory patterns and even the myths in which it figured. The heron, she'd discovered, was sacred to Freyja, Norse goddess of love and fertility. When Freyja's husband disappeared, permanent winter descended on the land. But after many barren years, spring burst out again to celebrate their reunion, the animals of farm and forest mated, and flowers bloomed in swathes of scent and riotous colour. A positive message, surely. Divorce or no, she was still Matthew's wife – in spirit, in intent – and she refused to give up hope of his return. She needed patience, that's all, and she was learning it from the heron, learning stillness and calmness, the ability to wait. She had done a lot of waiting in her time. Matthew's job as a reporter meant frequent trips abroad, so she had often sat vigilantly by the phone, expecting calls from Berlin or Bucharest, Marseille or Madagascar. And now it was the heron she awaited, watching for its arrival as she had once listened for the sound of Matthew's car. The bird was more than just a companion – it had become a sort of tutelary god, to inspire her and protect her. Its presence structured her days, provided a sense of purpose. Not only was she drawing again, her work was better than ever before.

'Oh, hello, Paula! We haven't seen you for ages.'

She put her bags down, cursing under her breath. Just her luck to arrive back from the shops at the very moment Eric and Maureen were getting out of the car. She hated these enforced neighbourly chats, usually about the weather. If you no longer had a garden, what did it matter if the rain held off or you'd been spared an overnight frost?

'We've just been down to Squire's,' Eric told her.

'Oh?' She wondered what grotesque new garden feature they were planning next – a rose arbour complete with plastic Venus and a string of fairy lights? A dinky little wishing-well?

'Yes, we wanted some advice about the pond. I'm afraid we've had a major tragedy. Over the last fortnight nearly half our fish have gone.'

'Oh dear . . .'

'We thought a cat must have got them, but the chap at Squire's said it was more likely to be a heron, and advised us to buy a decoy. Apparently herons hate competition and if they see one by a pond, they'll go elsewhere to feed. So' – he manoeuvred a bulky package from the boot of the car – 'meet Henry!' He stripped off the protective wrapping to reveal a hideous dummy heron in dull grey plastic, with a leering red eye and a pole instead of legs. 'You stick this pole in a flower pot filled with earth and, hey presto! – he keeps all rivals at bay.'

'We've bought some netting, too,' Maureen added, 'to put over the pond. We can't afford to lose any more. I don't know whether we told you, Paula, but the Ochiba Chigura – one of the fish that was taken – was worth over two hundred pounds.'

'Really,' Paula murmured, blushing as if she personally had stolen it. Which in a sense she had. In the interests of art, she had to experience the swallowing process exactly as the bird did; feel her throat distended by the fish, the muscles stretching and straining to an almost unbearable degree, and then the convulsion in her gullet as the slimy threshing body finally shuddered down. And despite the physical distress, there'd also been a surge of elation with each new fish devoured. She and the heron were allies in the battle against Eric and Maureen, working silently together to reduce their influence, their power.

Eric slammed the boot shut. 'And if the netting doesn't work,' he said, with a conspiratorial grin at his wife, 'or Henry doesn't do his stuff, we're going to buy a bloody gun!'

Paula flinched. 'I . . . I'd better be getting in,' she said, edging past them to her own entrance.

She dragged herself upstairs, feeling a rising tide of panic, as on the day that Matthew left. Eric and Maureen, far from waning, seemed to swell and fill the garden. Their shrill triumphant voices shattered the Sunday peace, and the lurid tropical flowers on their matching Hawaiian shirts blazed against the green ache of the lawn. Eric was carrying Henry, while Maureen tottered behind in her slingbacks, the roll of plastic netting under her arm. Having secured Henry in his flower pot, they placed him by the pond on the exact spot where her heron had stood, and gave him an affectionate pat on the neck. How could they imagine he resembled a real heron? He was no more than a caricature, a fitting companion for the plastic frogs, the fishing gnome and the fake-marble Buttercup Fairy. The fairy was unspeakably coy, with her flowerhead hat and fluted frock, her perky wings, simpering smile and long, cascading ringlets. Paula shut her eyes, remembering the garden that she and Matthew had nurtured: the purple haze of buddleia planted to attract butterflies, the herb bed pungent with rosemary and sage, the grass unmown as a haven for wild flowers. And if they had ever decided to build a pond, it would have been for the benefit of dragonflies and (real) frogs, not pampered, status-symbol fish.

She turned away from the window and walked wretchedly into her bedroom, which looked out on to the street. The woman at number nine was just saying goodbye to her grandsons – towheaded twins, each clutching a balloon. Matthew had never wanted children. 'I'm going to keep you all to myself,' he'd laughed, and she'd felt secretly flattered to be needed so exclusively. Now he and Diane had a baby daughter.

She drew the curtains on the family, and stretched full length on the bed. It was still daylight outside but midnight in her head. She closed her eyes and prayed for sleep.

Sitting listlessly at the window, she jotted down a few colour notes for her final composition. Legs – greenish yellow. Chest – pearl grey with black markings. But what was the point? Eric's loathsome decoy had ruined everything, keeping away not only her heron but her inspiration, her will to create. She ripped the sheet of paper off the pad and screwed it into a ball, tempted to do likewise with the sketches on the walls. The bird's pervasive presence in the room only emphasized its absence outside. The heron had deserted her, like Matthew; a double divorce, a double betrayal.

She glanced at Matthew's photo on the bureau. His dark eyes gazed directly into hers; his sensuous mouth was half open in a smile. Should she destroy the photo, destroy the heron sketches, stop fooling herself with images when the reality had gone? But just at that moment her eye was caught by a movement in the sky – a glimpse of grey that grew steadily larger. Tense with anticipation, she followed its approach above the rooftops. Could it be. . . ?

She hardly dared to watch as it took shape. But the long trailing legs were unmistakable, and the sinuous neck hunched tight against the body. Such was her relief she seemed to take wing herself, soaring with the heron over the trees and gardens, then gliding lazily down – lower, lower, towards the pond. But would it alight with Henry standing guard? Seemingly oblivious, it swooped down beside the dummy bird and adopted its familiar pose, its gimlet gaze registering every ripple on the water as it waited in stealthy ambush.

Elated, she seized her pencil. She was *not* abandoned, *not* rejected, and that meant she could draw again. Indeed her hand seemed almost inspired, moving with such confidence she had soon covered several pages.

Glancing back at her model to check a detail of the pick-axe bill, she was just in time to see the neck shoot out and plunge into the water. Oh God! she thought, it'll get entangled in the netting and do itself an injury. She held her breath in fear, but within seconds the head bobbed up again, unscathed, and on this occasion its catch was not a fish but a frog. With the frog's hind legs dangling from each side of its beak, the heron began its usual attempts at swallowing, with great choking, heaving gulps. But the frog was having none of it. Although smaller than a Koi, it seemed just as determined to escape, and writhed in vigorous protest. It was such a comical sight, she couldn't help but laugh. The sound was nearly as startling as seeing the bird return. She hadn't laughed since Matthew left. It was something other people did – normal happy people, with partners, children, jobs.

But she *had* a job: a new picture to plan. She darted to the landing cupboard and got out the old Clark's shoebox that housed her tubes of acrylic paint. Should she depict her model small against the backdrop of the garden, or in close-up, to fill the page? And what should the weather be? Grey and overcast, as now, with the heron's plumage reflecting the sombre tone of the sky? Or a bright day with strong shadows?

She pulled her easel from the cupboard, dusted it off and set it up by the window, then took her dry, caked brushes and ran them under the kitchen tap. Brushes were easily softened – all it took was soap and warm water.

Returning to the window, she peered down at the pond. The heron was still devouring the frog – devouring Eric and Maureen, devouring the past, her bitterness, her despair. She could start again, alone and self-sufficient. Her Protector had shown her the way. He had ignored the decoy and the netting, cocked a snook at Eric's attempts at deterrence, come back because he had no choice: fishing was his *raison d'être*. She must learn from his example, rise above the difficulties, ignore the loneliness, and focus on what gave meaning to her life.

She laid the tubes of paint beside the easel, with a jar of water, the clean brushes and a rag. Even if the heron didn't appear again, would it really matter? He was here, in essence, in her sketches. Critically she scrutinized each drawing on the walls. Yes, her careful observation had paid off. Every detail was correct: the soft white bushy breast-plate; the thin, gnarled legs with their feathered ruff at the top; the four long-clawed toes, three pointing forward, one back.

As she moved from sketch to sketch, she seemed to hear the thrum of wingbeats and the harsh *krornk-krornking* cry. She had brought the bird to life in her sitting-room, and nothing could obliterate him now.

She was wrong only in one particular. If anatomy must be correct, then so must terminology: this was no longer a sitting-room – it was an artist's studio.

Heart to Heart

'Sensitive but lonely gentleman seeks special lady to share life's deepest moments, and for tender, lasting, loving, caring relationship.'

She re-read the adjectives – tender, lasting, loving, caring. Exactly what she was looking for. And so different from the more earthy requirements that cropped up with such depressing regularity: fun-loving, tactile, adventurous, uninhibited . . . And how refreshing that he called himself a gentleman rather than the usual 'male' – a sensitive gentleman, what's more, who valued life's deepest moments.

Of course, she was bound to be disappointed as soon as she heard his voice. The other recordings she'd listened to had all been uninspiring: the first boasted he was 'fanciable', the second dropped his aitches, the third sounded overbearing, and the fourth wanted a compatible star sign – Pisces, Cancer or Libra (she was Virgo).

Nervously she picked up the phone and dialled the number once more, to be greeted by the breezy female voice. 'Welcome to Heart to Heart! Please enter the four-digit code of the advertisement you've chosen.'

She dialled 2109, noticing it was the date of her birthday. Could that be significant?

'Hello! I'm Christopher . . .'

An attractive voice, at least – rich and dark like *Sachertorte*. And she was glad he didn't shorten his name, unlike Chris, the office joker, whose idea of a deep moment was a discussion of Arsenal's chances in the Champions League.

'I . . . I'm afraid I'm not very good at talking about myself, so this is just a short message . . .'

She liked his self-deprecation – a rare trait in the few men she'd known, and entirely lacking in the other advertisers, who, it seemed, ranked among the most handsome, articulate charmers in the land, not one more lowly than a company director.

'. . . but I do believe that someone out there will listen to these few simple words and know intuitively that we should meet. That's how these things happen, don't you think? It's in the lap of the gods . . .'

There was a nerve-rackingly long pause. 'Yes, go on, go *on*,' she prompted.

'. . . So if you feel, as I do, that nothing is more important in life than real, honest, tender love, and commitment to another until death, please do leave me your name and number.'

Real, honest, tender love – she couldn't have put it better herself. And the Biblical ring of commitment until death suggested genuine seriousness of purpose – as did his reference to the lap of the gods. This man, whoever he was, had a spiritual dimension to him that she found immensely appealing. Maybe Fate was on her side, for once.

'If you wish to reply,' the cheery girl was saying, 'please leave your message after the tone.'

She cleared her throat. 'My name's Gemma,' she began, only to dry up. Lord! – he'd think she'd changed her mind and rung off. 'Like you,' she continued desperately, 'I'm not much good at talking about myself, but I'm, er, thirty-eight, and I work for an insurance company.' How boring she must seem, but then he had stipulated honesty. 'I . . . I'm five foot three, with grey eyes and mid-brown hair. I wouldn't say I'm pretty – on the other hand I don't think I'm ugly either. Oh, and I'm single, of course, but . . . but I've got a lot of love to give.' She felt herself blushing. She wasn't used to talking about love, especially to a disembodied stranger. '. . . And I feel, as you do, that there's more to life than just having fun. I'm interested in the big questions – where we've come from, where we're going . . .' It sounded awfully pretentious – safer to stick to practicalities. '. . . So perhaps we could meet – for a coffee, or a drink.' Why on earth had she mentioned drink when she never touched it? – now he'd get the wrong impression. 'I mean,' she added hastily, 'just an orange juice or something.' Which only made it worse, as if she were too stingy to spend money. Best to shut up before she made a complete hash of things. She blurted out her phone number and banged down the receiver.

He wouldn't ring back anyway. He was seeking a 'special lady' and, judging by the competition, there was nothing particularly special about *her*. Most of the Females Seeking Males claimed to be charismatic superwomen, cultured and curvaceous, dynamic and outgoing, even 'absolutely adorable' in one case. *She* was absolutely ordinary. Angrily she bundled up the newspapers and shoved them in the bin. She'd survived on her own for twenty years, so she might as well resign herself to another twenty.

The café was in an unfamiliar street and sited (inauspiciously) between a launderette and a betting shop. She dithered outside, not wanting to look over-eager. They had arranged to meet at six and it was not yet twenty to. Perhaps he was there already, though – terrified, like her, of being late. But a surreptitious glance inside revealed only two men sitting on their own, and neither seemed to have a copy of *Hard Times*.

She had warmed to that small detail – a fellow Dickens fan. And might his choice of title hint at secret suffering? He had described himself as lonely in his ad, and loneliness could be a scourge, as she had every reason to know. He was courageous, in her opinion, to have admitted to it at all, when the very word had connotations of failure. Although of course you could be highly successful yet still lonely – a writer, for example, who worked in isolation, or an academic researcher who spent his days in the hushed cell of a library, surrounded by voiceless tomes. He had told her very little on the phone, but she imagined him a poet or professor, or someone with an interest in philosophy. Well, she'd find out soon enough. And in the meantime she'd walk to the corner and back, to give him time to turn up.

At five past six she peered through the café window again. Still only the same two men, but she was going in, regardless. It had just begun to rain, and she didn't want her hair reduced to rats' tails when she had taken such pains to make it look presentable.

Choosing a seat in the corner, she took out her own copy of *Hard Times* and placed it four-square on the table. No one approached, however, except a rather haggard waitress.

'Yes, love, what can I get you?'

'Er, it's OK, thanks. I'm . . . waiting for someone.' (Suppose he didn't come. The humiliation would be unbearable. She would never, ever reply to a personal ad again.)

She tried to distract herself by studying the menu. Cheese and commitment omelette. Chicken Christopher . . . It was silly to over-react. There might have been a hold-up on the tube, or he'd tripped and sprained his ankle – anything could have happened. Real, honest, tender rump steak with loving, caring chips. If he was an absent-minded professor, he might have got the date wrong.

Or *she* might. But no – the evening paper abandoned on the next table confirmed that it was indeed Friday the fifteenth.

Just at that moment a shambling bear of a man with unkempt ginger hair appeared from the direction of the toilets. Spotting her *Hard Times*, he stopped in his tracks and flushed a deep brick red. 'G. . .Gemma?' he stammered.

For a second she simply gaped at him, before she managed to recover herself, hoping he hadn't noticed her first shock of disappointment. The poet-professor of her dreams had been slender and distinguished-look-ing, and, of course, well-groomed. Christopher was frankly a mess. His trousers were badly creased and his unflattering green shirt failed to disguise a sizeable paunch. Worse, he had glasses on a cord round his neck and a bum-bag strapped to his waist, and surely few things were less conducive to romance than bum-bags and glasses on cords.

She had made an effort, and not only with her hair, but now her best black skirt and lacy blouse looked absurdly formal.

'I'm Christopher,' he said (needlessly), giving a shy smile. 'May I join you?'

No, go *away*, was her immediate reaction, but she hadn't the guts to say it. Could she invent an emergency: her tortoise had escaped; her widowed mother was being held at gunpoint. . . ? 'Er, yes,' she murmured. 'Do sit down.'

Close to, she was aware of his smell – nothing as crude as sweat, more a faintly musty tang, as if he'd lain forgotten in a dank cupboard since last year.

'I'm sorry, I forgot the book.' He gestured to her Dickens. 'I was frightfully nervous at the thought of our meeting and everything else went out of my head.'

He looked so vulnerable she softened. It was unfair to judge by appearances. After all, Mozart was short, Shakespeare bald, and for all she knew Einstein might have worn his glasses on a cord. 'I'm nervous, too,' she said. 'I've never done this sort of thing before.'

'Nor me.'

Silence.

Fortunately the waitress came over again, pad and pencil poised. Gemma passed Christopher the menu, aware of a gnawing chasm in her stomach. As they had arranged to meet for an early supper, she had decided to skip lunch, and breakfast had been a single slice of toast.

'Oh, I couldn't eat,' he said, lowering his voice to a whisper. 'I . . . I'm afraid I've got the runs. It's stress again, I'm sure. I've been here since quarter past five and I've had to . . . go three times already. But please do order something yourself.'

'No, I'm not hungry either.' A sudden vision of the contents of the toilet bowl had killed her appetite stone dead. 'I'll just have a cup of tea.'

'And for you?' The waitress looked pityingly at Christopher.

'Water, please.'

'Still or sparkling?'

'Tap.'

The woman departed with a disgruntled sniff. Gemma, though, felt duty-bound to give the poor fellow a chance – it would be cruel to write him off when they had barely exchanged a word. A deep philosophical discussion was probably out of the question, given the condition of his bowels, but she ought at least to show some interest in him. 'What sort of work do you do?' she asked, pressing her hand hard against her stomach to disguise its audible rumblings.

'Well, nothing at the moment.'

His Adam's apple was pulsing, she noticed, like a tiny, frightened creature trapped in the cage of his throat. 'Oh?' she said, encouragingly. Perhaps he was an academic, preparing to write a thesis, or—

'I . . . haven't been well.'

'Oh, dear. Nothing serious I hope?'

'Well, yes . . . no . . . It wasn't exactly an illness, more a sort of . . . breakdown.'

'Oh, dear,' she said again, beginning to feel out of her depth.

'You see, my mother killed herself.'

She stared at him, aghast. 'Goodness – that's . . . that's terrible. I'm so sorry.' (How strange, though, that in the aftermath of such tragedy he should be attempting to meet women.) 'Did it happen recently?'

'Oh, no. When I was three.' All at once tears filled his pale blue eyes. 'But even now I'm overwhelmed by the feeling that no one's . . . there for me. I sit alone in my flat at night and I try to imagine how it felt when my mother held me as a baby.'

This was worse and worse. What on earth was she meant to *say*? 'But . . . but, who looked after you? I mean . . . after she'd. . . ?'

Dumbly he shook his head.

'Wasn't your father around?' she prompted.

'Don't mention him!' Christopher snapped. 'Not ever. *Ever*. Do you understand?'

She flinched at his harsh tone. This wasn't going to work – he was obviously in no condition to start a new relationship. Was there any means of escape? A back exit from the toilet, maybe? From where they were sitting now, the main door was all too visible.

She was relieved to see the waitress arrive. Even a tiny diversion was welcome. But she could hardly sit drinking tea when Christopher was so distraught. 'Here's your water,' she said gently. 'Have a sip. It might help.'

'Don't patronize me, Gemma.'

Stung by his unwarranted hostility, she shrugged and turned away. The couple at the next table, she noted enviously, were not only tucking in to steak and chips but were engaged in lively conversation.

Christopher blew his nose – a trumpet-blast – on a none-too-clean checked handkerchief: a ploy to regain her attention, no doubt.

'Oh, I know you don't want to listen, Gemma. Other people's tragedies are such a bore, aren't they? But my mother's death has blighted my whole life.'

'Yes, I see that.'

'I felt if she didn't value me enough to stay alive for my sake, I couldn't be worth loving.'

'But it might have had nothing to do with you. I mean, if she'd been suffering from depression or something it could have made her act irrationally.'

His eyes narrowed. 'So you're siding with her, are you?'

'No. I'm just trying to understand.'

'No one can understand.' He took a noisy gulp of water, then unexpectedly his whole face brightened, like a little boy recovering from a tantrum. 'I'm sorry,' he said. 'It's been an appalling day. You see, I . . . I convinced myself that you wouldn't turn up, and that brought back awful memories of being let down and left alone and . . .'

'Well, I did turn up, didn't I?'

'Yes.' He managed a smile. His teeth were large and uneven. 'And I'm so grateful. Honestly.'

'That's OK.' Perhaps she could take a sip of tea now, without being accused of callousness.

'You know something?'

'What?' She put the cup down.

'In your message you told me you weren't pretty. But you are. In fact you're beautiful. The most beautiful girl I've ever met.'

She blushed. 'No, really, I . . .'

'You didn't mention your long hair. My mother had long hair. I've seen it in her photographs. And you look like her in other ways as well. You've both got delicate features and lovely big grey eyes.'

'What a strange coincidence.'

'No, Gemma, it's not a coincidence.' Solemnly he raised his hand in an almost priestly gesture. 'This whole thing was fated to happen – your responding to my ad, and then turning out to be so like my mother. It's as if she's come back to me at last.'

She gazed at him in horror. She had no wish to be a mother, and certainly not to a child of fifty-odd.

'Oh, God!' He clutched his stomach suddenly and lurched up from his chair. 'I need to . . . go again,' he groaned. 'But don't leave, Gemma, will you?'

'Well, I . . . I mustn't be too long. I . . . I'm expecting an important call.'

'Promise me you'll stay,' he begged. 'Oh, *please* . . .' Another spasm of pain creased his fleshy face.

This was little short of blackmail. Any more delay and he might have an accident, right here on the floor, and she'd die of shame and embarrassment. The adjacent couple were already casting curious glances in their direction. 'OK,' she muttered. 'I promise.'

Disconsolately she watched his departing back. She couldn't walk out on him anyway, when he was in such a precarious state. She must try to help this once – if only to offer a listening ear – but then somehow make him understand that they couldn't meet again. There was no need to hurt his feelings; she could fabricate an excuse: a trip abroad, or—

'Anything else you need, love?' The waitress was passing with a tray of plates.

Yes, she thought – a kind way of telling this unfortunate man that it's over before it's begun.

'What a gorgeous flat!' he said, peering at the picture above the mantelpiece, having finally managed to disentangle the twisted cord of his glasses. (At least he hadn't brought the bum-bag today.)

'Well, it's only very modest . . .'

He lowered himself into a chair, stretching out his legs in their rain-bespattered corduroys. 'I feel I ought to take my shoes off. I wouldn't want to spoil this lovely white carpet.'

Yes, a good idea. His shoes were sodden, and the carpet was brand new. He seemed too big for the flat altogether, his outsize body dwarfing the dainty chair, and his ginger hair clashing wildly with the subtle rose-pink velour.

'The thing is, I have a problem with oughts and shoulds. You see, after my mother's death I was surrounded by people telling me I *should* be a good boy and I *ought* to be doing this, that or the other. And my stepmother especially kept should-ing me and ought-ing me, so now whenever I hear the words I want to open my mouth and scream.'

She made a mental note to avoid them, along with the other words and phrases on his blacklist: father, positive thinking, job centre, feminist. She already had a headache and if he started screaming it might develop into a migraine. 'Can I get you a drink?'

'Just water, please. It's funny – whenever I see you my insides turn to mush and I can't eat or drink a thing. All I can think of is my mother: she loves me, she's come back.'

'I'll, er, get the water.' In the kitchen, she poured herself a vodka. After a lifetime's self-imposed abstinence, she had started drinking alcohol only this last week, and although still unused to its effects, she found it helped her survive the time she spent with

Christopher. She turned the oven off; no point wasting electricity if he couldn't bring himself to eat. A pity, though, after she'd gone to so much trouble mincing beef and braising onions for a meat loaf – his favourite, he had said, as long as it was made to his mother's recipe.

She put his glass of water on the coffee table, then sat in the chair furthest from his, bracing herself for more piteous revelations about his childhood.

'Oh, Gemma, it's so marvellous to be here! You make me feel . . . well, safe, and I've never felt that with anyone else before. Even at school I had no friends. The other boys tended to avoid me just because my mother was dead.'

She gave a sympathetic murmur.

'It's as if, ever since I was little, I've been surrounded by a high brick wall. I can't get out and no one can get in. But now you're dismantling the wall, brick by brick by brick.'

'Good,' she said, eyeing the bowls of nibbles. Would it seem uncaring if she helped herself to a Twiglet?

'And another thing – I'm growing up. I'd been stuck at three emotionally all my adult life. But in the short time we've known each other, I've advanced by several years.'

Where was he now, then – six, seven, or even eight? And how long before he reached his chronological age and she could return to blessed solitude?

He took a sip of water and sat looking at her intently. 'You know, you're like my mother in temperament as well. My uncle used to tell me how unassuming she was, and gentle.'

'Well, I'm not sure I—'

'As far as I'm concerned, any lady worth the name is submissive and sweet-natured. And a mother supremely so. I find the bra-burning brigade utterly repellent. They're self-centred, misguided and a danger to their children . . .'

While he continued his habitual rant, she reached out for a crisp. These days she felt permanently hollow, having lost half a stone in a fortnight. She tried to chew quietly – any crunching noise might interrupt his flow – but he suddenly broke off in mid-sentence and lumbered to his feet. 'Gemma,' he whispered, in a sort of gasping croak, 'there's something I have to ask you. Something desperately important.'

Alarmed, she too stood up and backed towards the door. 'Wh. . .what is it?'

'I want you to hold me, very tight. Just like my mother would. I'm a tiny, tiny boy and you're pressing me against you, with your arms clasped round my back so that I feel completely safe.'

'Well, no, I don't think—'

'Oh, *please*, Gemma. I've imagined it so often – my mother actually holding me in the flesh.'

'Look, I'm not your mother, Christopher.'

'Oh, but you are. A manifestation of her – an embodiment, an incarnation.'

She was beginning to feel light-headed, and not only from the vodka. The words he used made her doubt her own reality. Even the flat seemed alien with him standing here in the middle of the room. Normally she didn't ask people back, but he had talked her round, as usual.

'I promise, Gemma, on all that's sacred, not to take advantage of you – if that's what you're concerned about.'

'No, it isn't that. It's—'

'I just have to know what it feels like to be cuddled by my mother.'

'And suppose it upsets you?'

'Of course it won't upset me. In fact it's the only way I'll ever heal the pain.' And with that he lunged towards her, kneeling on the carpet so that his head was level with her chest. Pressing his face against her breasts, he let out a moan of pleasure. 'Put your arms round me, Mummy.'

Stiffly, she obeyed, staring down at his shock of coarse red hair. His nose was stabbing into her chest and his hands gripped her waist like fetters. Soon she had cramp in her left leg, but she dared not move a muscle. He was keeping so still himself, it was like a sort of sacrament. A car droned past in the street, merging with the lament of the rain. The world outside seemed increasingly dim and shadowy, as if nothing else existed beyond their two yoked bodies. Yet in spite of their physical closeness – hearing each other's intimate sounds (tummy-gurglings, heartbeat), inhaling each other's smells, feeling each other's clammy warmth, breathing the same thimbleful of air – never had she felt so separate from another human being, so locked into the prison of her self.

And then his shoulders began to shake and she realized he was crying. 'Oh, Mummy!' he sobbed. 'This is a miracle, a miracle! I don't think I can bear it.'

He was trembling so violently she could hardly hold him now. Revulsion urged her to push him away, but it was comfort he was seeking, words of reassurance.

Briefly unclasping his hands, he drew his head back to look into her face. His hair was dishevelled, his eyes red-rimmed. 'Say "I love you, little Christopher",' he pleaded.

She said nothing. Her white silk blouse, she noticed, was streaked with tears and snot.

'*Say* it!' he demanded.

A familiar pattern: when he didn't get his way he switched from entreaty to petulance. Shutting her eyes in resignation, she allowed him to press close once more while she stood listening to the weeping of the rain. 'I love you, little Christopher,' she said.

'Gemma, did you hear me?'

'Yes . . . No.' She was worried about the dreadful state of the flat. Christopher's stuff was everywhere: his sleeping-bag in the sitting-room, his Complan in the kitchen, his shoes and shirts and trousers in her wardrobe, his bulk supply of Imodium supplanting her codeine in the bathroom cabinet. Even his smell hung in the air – no longer musty cupboards but a faint odour of hot pennies and damp string. 'I'm sorry, what were you saying? I . . . I didn't quite catch . . .'

'About my mother. She had a blouse exactly like yours – white with a lacy front.'

'Oh, really?' She tried to stifle a yawn. She hadn't slept for the last six nights. Christopher cried out in his sleep and she could hear him through the wall.

'Yes, I've seen it in the photos. There's even one of her in her night-gown. I think it must have been taken when she was ill.'

'Ill?'

'Yes. She suffered a lot from migraine and according to Uncle Henry often had to retreat to her bed.'

Gemma ran a hand across her forehead. Her own migraines had become more frequent of late – ominously so. There was little chance of retreating to bed, however, until well into the early hours, when Christopher finally fell asleep.

'And she had a serious bout of pneumonia when she was only eighteen. Apparently she wasn't expected to live.'

Gemma drew in her breath. She too had had pneumonia, also at eighteen, and had pulled through only after high doses of antibiotics. 'How did she actually . . . die?' (She hadn't dared to broach the question before, but it seemed increasingly relevant.)

'Jumped.'

'What?'

'Eighteen storeys. From a tower block in Southwark. Smashed herself to pieces.'

Gemma shuddered. Who had picked up the pieces? Identified the body?

He gave a sudden throaty laugh. 'But she isn't dead. She's here. And she's going to feed her precious little lamb.' With a triumphant smile he produced something from behind his back and held it out towards her – a baby's bottle, complete with rubber teat. She stared in disbelief.

'Oh, you'd rather breast-feed, would you? I do agree – it's much better for the baby.'

She sank into a chair, feeling suddenly nauseous. It was bad enough giving him his Complan – just looking at the white, curdled liquid often made her gag. 'You . . . you told me your mother couldn't breast-feed. She developed an abscess, you said.'

'Yes. Poor Mummy.'

'Well, how could she feed you with an abscess?'

'That's why I bought the bottle – to spare her pain. There's some powdered milk in the kitchen. You mix it with boiled water, but be sure to let the water cool. And don't forget to sterilize the bottle. Babies are so susceptible to germs.'

She hid her head in her hands. Her temples were throbbing and her throat felt blocked, as if she was choking on a lump of granite.

'*I* can't do it. I'm only a tiny scrap of a thing. You wouldn't want me to starve, would you? Your own flesh and blood?'

She forced the granite down, grimacing at the bitter after-taste. 'No, of course not,' she murmured, dreading the thought of another outburst. Two days ago he had broken half her china.

'So you will do it?'

Wearily she nodded.

'And you'll let me sit on your lap, and hold me like a proper baby?'

'Mm.'

'Right – here's the bottle. Go and make it up while I get into my cot.'

Waiting for the water to boil, she glanced listlessly at the stack of unopened post. With a baby in the house she couldn't seem to get to grips with anything. The papers, too, were piling up unread. News was just strings of syllables; arts and sport mere squiggles on the page. Besides, she might stumble across those loathsome Heart to Heart columns with their deceitful promises: 'real, honest, tender, love . . .' As for work – it was out of the question. After taking a week's sick leave, she had handed in her notice.

There was a bellow from the sitting-room, a summons from her child.

'Mummy's coming,' she called, picking her way to his sleeping-bag-cot through a tide of discarded clothes. He had wrapped himself in a blanket ('shawl') and was lying curled in the foetal position. 'Time for your bottle, Christopher.'

She heaved him up from the floor and pulled him with difficulty towards her nursing chair. The shawl kept slipping, revealing odious glimpses of the naked, freckled flesh beneath. She tried to settle him on her lap but his body was so cumbersome she felt as if her bones were being crushed. There was no part of her that didn't hurt – her breasts crushed by his shoulder, her neck cricked at an awkward angle, her thighs pinioned by his massive rump, her back aching from his weight.

Supporting his head with her arm, she inserted the rubber teat between his lips. At once he began greedily sucking, making loud slurping noises. She focused instead on the rhythm of the rain, lashing at the windows, streaming down the panes in angry rivulets. It had been raining continuously since the day they met.

His face was so close she could see the scurf of stubble on his jaw and the enlarged, blackened pores around his bulbous nose. Milk dribbled down his chin on to her blouse. It was ruined anyway – like her best blue dress (stolen from her wardrobe as a memento of his mother, and returned covered in blotchy tear-stains). *He* was happy enough, though, gulping his feed and gazing adoringly into her eyes, and the milk was almost finished, thank God. Tilting the bottle, she let him drain the last few drops. 'That's it, Christopher – all gone now. Time for your nap.'

'No,' he spluttered, releasing the teat. 'First you have to wind me.'

'What?'

'Put me over your shoulder and pat my back, to bring up the air I've swallowed.'

She hadn't the energy to argue. Instead, she pushed at his bottom to turf him off her lap and tried to haul him to his feet. He resisted with all his might, dislodging the shawl in the process. His bare body was grotesque – hairless, mottled and veiny, with a great roll of doughy flesh around his middle that all but hid his genitals. She quickly thrust the blanket across his lower parts to conceal the offensive sight.

'Treat me gently!' he whimpered. 'I'm your darling little baby boy. You mustn't pull me about.'

He was now half crouching on her lap but with his upper body twisted, so that he was facing over her shoulder. 'Rub my back!' he commanded. 'No, not so hard. Just massage it in little circles. That's better. Oh, that's beautiful. You're such a lovely Mummy.'

All at once he gave a monstrous belch and she felt a spurt of warmish milk trickle down her back. 'Finished?' she asked.

'No. I need my nappy changing before you put me back in my cot.'

Pain was blurring her vision, hammering through her head. 'I . . . I haven't any nappies.'

'Use a big white towel. And I've seen safety pins in your bedroom. Go and fetch them, would you?'

'But I can't move with you on my knee.'

Grudgingly he stood up. 'And don't be long – you mustn't leave a baby on its own.'

She returned with the pins and a bath towel, to find him lying naked on her antique Persian rug.

'It's my changing mat,' he told her.

'OK,' she said with a shrug. The sooner she put on his nappy the sooner she would be spared the sight of his puckered, lumpy testicles, his shrivelled penis and sparse gingery pubic hair. With difficulty she squatted down beside him, trying to ignore her protesting muscles. Somehow she would have to lift his bottom up, to slip the towel underneath. He made no attempt to help, so she pulled feebly at his leg until at last he raised his buttocks. Having got the nappy in place, she secured the fiddly pins, jabbing her finger and making it bleed.

'Oh, Mummy, I'm in heaven!' he crowed.

'Well, be a good boy then and help Mummy settle you down for your nap.'

Enchanted by her compliance, he crawled on his hands and knees towards his cot, the bulky towel sagging beneath his groin. 'Kiss bubba goodnight.'

She kissed his stubbly cheek.

'No, a proper kiss. On the lips.'

As she bent over him again, another rapier-blade of pain stabbed through her head.

'And now I want you to sing me a lullaby and sit beside my cot till I fall asleep.'

Drawing her chair up to the sleeping-bag, she began to sing in a soft, mournful tone,

'Hush a bye baby,
On the tree top . . .'

His eyelids were growing heavy. It had been a long day for them both.

'. . . When the wind blows
The cradle will rock . . .'

When she heard his breathing deepen she tiptoed from the room and, putting on her raincoat, slipped out of the front door. She trudged along the dark, empty street, battered by the rain but still singing to herself,

'. . . When the bough breaks
The cradle will fall,
And down will come . . .'

The lift was out of order so she had to climb the emergency stairs. Eighteen floors was much further than she'd realized. She toiled up and up the dimly lit, discoloured steps, forced to stop at intervals as her legs grew gradually tireder. Every stop afforded a new perspective. A few floors up, she was level with the tree-tops, then the roofs of houses, gleaming wetly in the rain, then higher than a church spire, casting its long shadow across the shimmering Thames. And by the eleventh floor, she could almost touch the moon and stars, or push away the brooding clouds that threatened to engulf them. Yet still she laboured upwards – above the clouds, above the stars – until she reached the topmost landing. Peering through the glass, she was gripped by a wave of vertigo and had to flatten herself against the wall.

Once the dizziness subsided, she ventured out on to the open roof, catching her breath at the sight of the bleak stretch of concrete surrounded by a parapet. Somehow it seemed familiar. Clinging to the railings, she steeled herself to look down, and again the view stirred memories: the lights of Southwark glittering below, and beyond, the whole of London spread out in a ghostly sheen of black and silver, rain and river, ripple and reflection.

Calmer now, she inhaled the cool night air, exulting in her freedom – freedom from the burden of motherhood, freedom from the world. Nobody could reach her here; nobody come close. She felt weightless and ethereal, released at last from pain. Indeed, at this majestic height she could almost be a goddess surveying her creation. Far, far below, the cars crawled along like glow-worms between strings of fairy lights, past shops and houses as small as children's toys. And she stood supreme above it all, blissfully alone.

Smiling, she unbuttoned her coat and left it folded on the balcony. Then, squeezing through a gap in the railings, she balanced on the very edge of the parapet, looking up into the sky. The soft rain caressed her cheek, the wind ruffled her long hair, and, as she watched, the moon slipped through its dark cage of clouds and lit her final path.

'Goodbye, baby Christopher,' she whispered and, smiling still, she jumped.

Mr Hush

Dark.

Disappointing.

If it was still dark, it couldn't be six. It was light at six – just – and she hated getting up before the sun. It made the day too long, pulled it out of shape.

She groped for the clock. She kept it face-down at night because the fluorescent hands could affect your pineal gland – or so she'd read in the *Daily Telegraph*. She wasn't sure what a pineal gland was but, as life had taught her, better to be safe than sorry.

She peered at the impassive green hands: five to four. Too late to go back to sleep and too early to get up. She would relieve herself, then lie down again and feign sleep.

She struggled out of bed and fumbled underneath for the chamber pot. It was a long trek to the bathroom and she couldn't risk an accident. With every year things became less reliable: bladders, eyes, the buses.

It was difficult to squat. Her muscles protested and a bone in her leg creaked alarmingly. When at last she reached a sitting position, she felt not relief but tedium. She had done this too many times; done everything too many times – made beds, washed stockings, laid breakfast for one. Three hundred and sixty-five breakfasts every year. If she lived another decade, it would be thousands more, all on her own, of course. She might live even longer – a hundred was nothing nowadays. There was an island in Japan where centenarians still planted beans, tended sheep and goats. Nice to have a goat. Someone to talk to, someone to look after.

She picked up the heavy chamber pot and set it carefully on the bedside table. Safer there than on the floor. Once, she had kicked it over; once, she had dropped a pill inside. She always emptied it in the morning and four o'clock wasn't morning. Four o'clock was prison time.

Ten past six. She squeezed a strip of toothpaste onto the brush. Sainsbury's own, 30p cheaper than Macleans. The brush was blue: her father had wanted a boy. He hadn't been much in evidence. Fathers didn't hang around for girls. She couldn't remember his face, only his smell: Brylcreem and Woodbines and Fox's Glacier Mints on his breath. His voice was a shout that made the house shake.

She rinsed her mouth with water. How many times had she cleaned her teeth? It must be close to a million by now. Did other people get bored with the same routine – her neighbours, for example? But they would have more variety: children to dress, husbands to feed, briefcases to pack. And they probably wouldn't be up yet, but still lying in their double beds, belonging and entwined. She had never shared a bed.

She dressed and went downstairs. Her cup and plate were waiting on the table. She always laid breakfast the evening before, as her mother had done for her father, even when he wasn't there. She picked up the crested jam spoon, remembering her mother polishing the silver, the acrid tang of silver polish mingling with the smell of mutton stew. Her mother had left her the contents of the house – loved, familiar things that were fast becoming fossils: tallboys, horsehair mattresses, three-tier cake-stands, a proud iron beast of a mangle. And the ivory-handled fish knives and forks, wrapped in tissue, like babies in shawls, and kept in the top bureau drawer. When she passed on, those shawls would become shrouds. No one used fish knives any more. Fish were different, too, these days. They no longer had bones or heads and tails, but were anonymously breadcrumbed into oblongs and squares. And tea was made in the cup with a teabag. No, not even a cup – a mug.

She took the blue-flowered teapot down from its shelf. Another fossil, along with its knitted blue tea cosy. She ought to knit herself a person-cosy, with the holes for arms, instead of handle and spout. She could pull it right down past her knees, to keep her warm and snug. How many times had she made the tea, measuring out her life in PG Tips?

She put in two heaped spoonfuls, one for her and one for the pot.

Today it didn't seem enough. She added two more for her parents, then another three for the siblings she had never had. She continued to spoon in tea, feeling stronger with each spoonful. Four for the next-door neighbours, six for the people opposite, eight for the sheep and goats. The packet was almost empty.

Abruptly, she switched off the kettle and went out to the hall. She put on her coat, locked up back and front, and set off briskly down the road. There wouldn't be many buses at this hour of the morning, but at least the bus stop had a seat. And she had time.

'A table for one, madam?'

'No, two, please.'

'Certainly, madam. This way.'

She was aware of her unfashionable clothes. The hotel had changed since she had last been here, long, long, long ago. Then it had been plump waitresses in baggy skirts and blouses; now tall, supercilious waiters in black coats. And the red gingham tablecloths had given place to starched white damask, with matching napkins as big as towels. The place was surprisingly full. And the sun was not only up, but washed, dressed and poking golden fingers through the window. Her journey had taken an age. There hadn't been a bus for half an hour, and then she'd got on the wrong one by mistake and landed up in Sydenham.

She glanced around the dining-room. Mostly men. Men in twos, in suits.

The waiter handed her a menu, which was covered with the same stiff maroon leatherette as the hymn books in St Andrew's. But twice the size. English breakfast cost £16.95. A fifth of her pension. No matter – she could always sell the fish knives.

'Will you be having the full breakfast, madam?'

'Oh, yes, please. For both of us.'

Her companion would be a gentle man. A gentleman. He wouldn't smoke. Or shout. His name was most important. No Christian name (too familiar), just a safe, unobtrusive surname. Mr Hush, perhaps. Yes, perfect. He would be nicely mannered, beautifully turned out. She fixed her eyes on his crisp white shirt and classic navy tie. His shoes were so highly polished she could see her face in them. 'He won't be long,' she told the waiter.

'Can I get you some tea or coffee while you wait, madam?'

115

'No, thank you.' It would be rude to start without him. He was a busy man: perhaps a doctor or a surgeon – someone who might be summoned, meals or meetings notwithstanding, at any hour of the day or night.

However delayed he might be, she had plenty to admire: the gilt-framed pictures of racehorses, the tiny vase on each table containing a rosebud and a sprig of fern, the ruched pink curtains tied back with gold cords. And the enormous menu, of course. At home it would be tea and toast. Here she was spoilt for choice – Loch Fyne kippers (proper fish, with eyes), bacon, sausage, mushrooms and tomatoes, and eggs in such variety they took up four whole lines: boiled, poached, scrambled, coddled, fried. Coddled, she decided. Lovely to be coddled, especially by your father, told you were pretty, petted and indulged. And what would Mr Hush have? Kippers, she hoped: strong, distinctive, and with just a hint of danger from the bones.

The waiter brought a basket of bread rolls, some delicately white and sprinkled with pale seeds, others dark and crusty, a couple coiled like shells.

She wouldn't touch them, of course, until Mr Hush arrived. He might have been called to a cardiac arrest and be engaged in delicate heart surgery. It was already getting on for nine o'clock. Everybody was eating except her, and no one else was sitting on their own. The noise level rose as people laughed and chatted, clattered knives and forks. She watched a man at the next table cut off a knob of sausage and chew appreciatively. She could taste it in her mouth: porky, sweetish, and with a slight after-glow of spice. She hadn't eaten since high tea yesterday. And teas got lower every week. Never mind – Mr Hush would come, just give him time.

'I'm sorry, madam, but we finish serving breakfast at ten. If your friend isn't here within the next few minutes, I'm afraid . . .'

'No, he will be. He's on his way.'

'Are you sure I can't get you something?'

'I prefer to wait, thank you.'

'Or you could help yourself from the buffet table to cereals and fruits . . .'

'No, thank you.' She had never liked the idea of help-yourself. And nor, she knew, would Mr Hush. He would be used to proper service.

'I'll wait,' she repeated. 'He'll be coming any moment.'

Nearly everyone had gone by now – the men in suits, the two middle-aged couples, the pair of giggly young girls. *They* had all helped themselves, returning from the buffet table with bowls of prunes or grapefruit, cereals and yoghurt, before being served with cooked breakfast on vast white dinner-plates. Mr Hush would eat in moderation. In fact, she realized, this wasn't quite the place for him. After performing an operation he would probably need to rest, and would prefer a meal much later, in quiet, unpretentious surroundings. Her home would be ideal. Chestnut Close had very little traffic and the neighbours were mostly out all day. Once he had washed and changed, they could sit down to high tea together, and this time it must be high. Perhaps a nice piece of smoked haddock, served with thin-sliced bread and butter, and a little salad to add a dash of colour – nothing indigestible, just a leaf or two of lettuce and some diced beetroot and tomato. And home-made seed cake to follow, sitting in state atop the cake-stand, with almond fingers below and macaroons on the bottom tier. They would use the fish knives, of course – use all her mother's things: the sugar tongs and cut-glass jam pot, the butter knife and napkin rings.

He might agree to stay the night. Mr Hush wouldn't balk at a horsehair mattress, or a marble-topped washstand with a flower-sprigged bowl and ewer. She would make up the bed in the spare room, air the sheets, put a lavender sachet under the pillow. And she would bring him tea in the morning: three spoonfuls in the pot and her best embroidered tray cloth. How did he like his toast – thick or thin, pale or dark? They could even use the toasting-fork, although it would need a good polish first.

After breakfast, they could go for a walk, up to the park and back. If he wanted to talk about his patients, she'd provide a sympathetic ear. She was very good at listening. She never interrupted . . .

'I'm sorry, madam, but it *is* now five past ten. We have to close the dining-room to prepare the tables for lunch. If you'd like to order for yourself, I can bring you anything you want, but I'm afraid I shan't be able to serve your friend.'

She rose to her feet, with difficulty. She had been sitting too long and her legs had stiffened. 'It's all right,' she said, 'I have to be getting back.'

There was a lot to do: the house to clean, the fish knives to polish, the tablecloth to wash and starch. Mr Hush was used to things done properly.

The waiter drew back her chair. 'I'm sorry, madam, you've had a long wait for nothing.'

She smiled. For nothing? How wrong he was.

Leaning over, she plucked the rosebud from the tiny vase and pushed it through the buttonhole of her blouse.

A red rose.

For love.

Jezebel

'You're not going out *again*, are you?'

'What do you mean, again?'

'You were out last night.'

'So?'

Her father banged on the floor with his stick. 'Don't take that tone with me, Jane!'

'Look, Dad, I'm only going into town to get your bloody pills. That's not a crime, is it?'

'Watch your language, child. Your mother never swore.'

'I'm not a child.'

'Well, you behave like one.'

She grabbed her bag, slammed the door and ran down the street full pelt, as if she expected him to come trundling after her in his wheelchair.

There'd be more trouble tomorrow. She wouldn't be back till late – very late. Ryan couldn't get away before nine.

She stopped to catch her breath, sucking the name like a sweet. Ryan Steffano: half Irish, half Italian – an irresistible combination. He had picked her up so brazenly, putting his hand on her thigh and fixing her with that blue hypnotic stare. 'Darlin',' he'd announced, not caring if the entire pub overheard, 'I've waited all me life to find you.'

No other man had been so forward – not that she had the chance to meet many. There'd been John last year, of course, who was intense but rather dull, plying her with dreary questions like what job she did ('Nursemaid to my father') and where she lived ('A bloody cage'). Perhaps it wasn't surprising that things had fizzled out between them. But Ryan was a different proposition. He'd quoted poetry, romantic stuff, whole chunks of it by heart. And he'd taken her hand and kissed the fingers one by one, lingeringly and tenderly, like a Hollywood film star in the forties. And then he'd said, 'Will I be seeing you tomorrow, darlin'?'

But tomorrow was Friday – her father's night at the Social Club. She had to wheel him there and stay all evening, making stupid conversation with the other daft old cackers.

'Well, Saturday, then. Saturday's me birthday. And if you're not there for me birthday, I'll die of a broken heart. No, don't laugh, I'm serious. We're made for each other, darlin'. I knew it the minute I saw you.'

Could this be her chance to escape? She and Ryan in Dublin, or better still in Italy. Yes, she was standing on the terrace of his luxurious Tuscan villa, surrounded by vines and olive groves, and gazing up at a sky of deepest blue. His handsome brothers (all with the same slim build and thrill-black hair) were treading grapes with their naked feet, and his gentle, loving father (sound in mind and body) was holding out his arms to embrace her as a daughter.

The automatic doors slid open. How had she reached Boots? Only seconds before, Ryan had slipped the ring on her finger in the quaint Italian church. The villagers had turned out in their Sunday best, and were weeping with emotion at the sight of the radiant bride from England. She glanced at her left hand, amazed that the ring finger was bare.

Brushing confetti from her shoulders, she queued at the pharmacy for her father's Hexopal. He also needed Sennakot and denture cleaner. No part of his anatomy seemed to function any more – his bowels were stubborn, his legs as weak as drinking straws, and his mind lucid only in bursts.

On the way to Dental Care she passed the beauty counters. It was years since she'd bothered with make-up. Why glam yourself up for an irritable old sod who didn't notice anything except the ladder in your tights? But Ryan had told her she had a gorgeous mouth. She'd never even thought about her mouth, but as they were leaving the pub he'd suddenly seized hold of her and whispered, 'Luscious lips!', all soft and breathy right into her ear. Then he pressed his long, lean body against hers and gave her a tingling love-bite on the neck. She'd almost died with excitement. Perhaps she'd buy a new lipstick in his honour.

She was examining the scores of different ranges when the woman at the Lancôme counter caught her eye and smiled. 'Can I help you, madam?'

'Er, yes . . .' She felt intimidated by the awesome mask of foundation and blusher; the eyebrows plucked to a fine interrogative arch. 'I was wondering about a . . . lipstick.'

'We've just brought out a new line,' the woman enthused, unsheathing a slender gold case. 'It's kissproof and long-lasting – guaranteed to stay on eight hours.'

Ryan's lips met hers and their kiss lasted eight hours easily. And, yes, the lipstick stayed on – on and on and on, as day dwindled into night, spring turned to summer, summer to winter, and then to another spring. And still the colour didn't fade as they grew old together, but not a whit less passionate.

'What you do is apply it first – I'd recommend two coats – then blot your lips thoroughly, and use this little brush to put on the fixative . . .'

Ryan had captured her tongue with his and the sensations were exquisite. She wanted to concentrate on each subtle smooch and rasp, but the wretched woman's voice would keep intruding.

'I'll, er, think about it,' she mumbled, moving to the display racks, where she could try out the testers in peace. The colour must be exactly right – too pale and she'd look anaemic; too blatant and Ryan would think she was a tart.

Max Factor had a 'Rose' range: Tea Rose, Rose Dawn, Rose of Cyprus. Rose was her mother's name and therefore best avoided. Anyway, flower names were too demure. Why be a Sweet Pea when she could be a Tornado or an *Agent Provocateur*?

Honolulu Honey – now that sounded promising: no longer mousy little Jane who spent half her day helping her father on and off the toilet, but a sophisticated Caribbean island-hopper. Some hope. If she hightailed it to Honolulu, her Dad would be on the phone at once, whining for her to come back and cut his toenails. Besides, the colour was too orangey and vivid, as if a thousand tropical sunsets were condensed into the tiny stick.

She picked up another tester, a puce pink called Miss Fizz. Miss Fizz shimmied up to the counter, auburn curls aglow – a babe, a goer, a girl who lived for pleasure and would feel no guilt at dishing up a shop-bought Cornish pastie for her Dad instead of cooking meat and two veg. But the colour was still not right. The trouble was, she didn't know Ryan's taste. He liked poetry, yes, and whisky chasers, but when it came to women, would he prefer a Rebel or a Tiffany?

'Discover a New Look!' invited a notice above a mirrored unit crammed with beauty samples. All the product names seemed to reflect her feelings for Ryan: Addiction, Obsession, Reckless, Freedom, Frenzy. She applied Freedom to her lips and studied herself in the mirror, less struck by her mouth than the pallor of her cheeks. She needed the Italian sun – and Ryan – to give her a glow without and within.

Turning her back on the ill-natured mirror, she plunged deeper into unknown territory, discovering ranges with peculiar names like Trash and Urban Decay. And the individual lipstick-names were equally distasteful, downright menacing, in fact: Burn-Out, Scream, Asphyxia, Crime and Punishment. Last time she'd shopped for cosmetics there'd been nothing remotely like this. Had the world changed so much in her absence? 'Bruise,' she murmured, flinching with ecstatic pain as Ryan lashed her naked breasts. 'Scandal. Outrage. Scarlet Gash.' He was standing astride her as she cowered, chained and handcuffed, on the dungeon floor. 'Chaos,' she moaned, thrilling to the swish-swish of his whip. 'Fire Down Below. Just Deserts.'

'Excuse me!' A middle-aged woman elbowed her aside and took a lipstick from the display rack, seemingly at random. She didn't bother to read its name or try it on her wrist, just dropped it in her wire basket as she might a packet of crisps. But then she was wearing a wedding ring, and choosing the right lipstick wouldn't be so critical if you had already snared a husband.

Still, it was no use standing dithering here all day. Why not trust to Fate, just reach out and touch a lipstick without looking, and let that be the one.

Fate was on her side. The colour was perfect: an attractive coral red, neither too pale nor too deep. And its name? – she did look now – Jezebel.

Bloody hell! Wasn't Jezebel some harlot in the Bible? And it was a term her father used to describe Mrs Hughes next door – presumably because she was on husband number five and wore black fishnet tights.

Well, why not? Ryan would adore black fishnet tights. Indeed, she could feel him running his hand up her leg, higher and higher, almost to her groin. She would need new knickers, lacy-black and crotchless, and a new tight slinky skirt. And a low-cut glittery top, and long sparkly earrings that jangled as she laughed. Jezebel would laugh a lot, and drink a lot, match Ryan glass for glass.

She would just have to change in the pub – get there early and slip into the toilet, stuff her old clothes in the bin. She wouldn't need them any more. Jezebel and Ryan were about to embark on a new life.

She walked home in triumph, jauntily swinging the carrier bags from Top Shop and Miss Selfridge – the skirt was dynamite and she'd even managed to get it half-price. Better still, people had treated her with unaccustomed respect. Janes were patronized and put-upon, whereas Jezebels, she'd come to see, were assertive, self-assured. Even the weather had changed; the earlier sullen drizzle giving place to fitful sun. And Jezebel had used her power to accelerate the spring. The cherry trees near home, still blackly bare a couple of hours ago, were now foaming with pink blossom, and the tight fists of the horse chestnut buds were unfurling into lush green candelabra. 'All lovers love the spring,' she hummed, crossing the road to the local parade of shops. Jane's singing voice was thin, but Jezebel's rich contralto carried over the sea to Italy, where the Steffano brothers had paused in their work to listen dewy-eyed.

'Special Offer. Jus-Rol Pastry – two for the price of one.'

The placard in Mr Patel's window brought her up with a jolt. She had clean forgotten her father's tea, and it was the Social Club this evening so they would need to eat earlier than usual. Instead of fobbing him off with a sandwich, she could buy the two packets of Jus-Rol and make him a steak and kidney pie. And an apple pie to follow. She owed him that much, surely. After all, she was planning to walk out and leave him – a poor defenceless invalid. Just as her mother had. But her mother had left a child as well as a husband; abandoned her only daughter without a backward glance.

She couldn't be that brutal. She would contact the Social Services and make arrangements for his care. And she'd come home for the occasional visit, although always with Ryan, of course. And today she'd cook his favourite things to accompany the pie: mashed potatoes, buttered carrots, parsnips roasted with honey. This evening she'd be conscientious Jane, but tomorrow night with Ryan she'd become outrageous, reckless Jezebel again.

'You've been gone for *hours*.'

'Sorry, Dad.' Once, she used to keep a count of all the Sorrys, but had given up when it topped the hundred-a-day mark.

'Where on earth have you been?'

'I . . . I had to wait ages for your prescription. Then I went to Patel's and got a load of stuff for tea. I thought I'd make a steak and kidney pie.'

'What's that in aid of?'

'Well, you like it, don't you?'

'Like it? I'll say! But I've almost forgotten what it tastes like.'

'And apple pie for pudding.'

He stared at her, confused. 'Is . . . is it my birthday?'

'No, Dad.' He had difficulty with dates. It was *Ryan's* birthday and she'd bought him a pair of cufflinks in the shape of little silver hearts and a Pisces birthday card. It said in *Star Signs for Lovers* that Pisces men were romantic, dreamy, impulsive, sensuous . . . 'I just decided to cook, that's all. So you sit and watch the News while I get on in the kitchen.'

Cooking was hard work, but she did it happily. She was cooking for Ryan – braising meat, peeling potatoes, chopping and coring apples. He kept stealing up behind her to run his fingers through her hair, or kiss the back of her neck.

In the end, she jettisoned the rolling-pin and flung away her apron. Love was more important than food, and if he wanted to take her there and then, ravish her on the kitchen floor, she would willingly submit . . .

'OK, Dad, let's eat.' She wheeled him up to the table and began the arduous process of transferring him to the dining-chair. He had to lean on his stick with one arm and lean on her with the other, before lowering himself stiffly on to the waiting air-cushion. She put a second cushion behind his back, moved his chair in a little and tied a napkin round his neck.

The dishes were ready and waiting on the table. She had used the best white china, found a pretty flower-sprigged cloth and even remembered to warm the plates. She cut into the pie, giving him a generous piece with a pastry rose on top, then piled his plate with vegetables.

He took a mouthful. 'Mm, it's good,'

She nearly dropped the serving spoon in shock: he hadn't paid her a compliment in years. Perhaps she ought to cook for him more often. Except it was too late now. In Tuscany, she and Ryan would live on grapes – and love.

'Very good,' he repeated, chewing vigorously.

Maybe just once in a while she would invite him to the villa, to give him a taste of Italian life and food. She bit into a parsnip, imagining the wedding feast the Steffanos would provide: a boar's head in pride of place, surrounded by steaming platters of risotto, cannelloni, scalloppine, calamari . . . She swallowed the piece of parsnip, tasting garlic, exotic spices.

Her father mashed a carrot in a pool of Bisto gravy, then paused with his fork halfway to his mouth. 'Someone phoned,' he said.

'Who?' No one ever phoned.

'Some Irish chap. Can't remember his name.'

She gripped the edge of the table. 'What did he say?'

'I didn't like the sound of him.' Her father stuffed the carrot into his mouth.

'Dad, *please* try to remember. It's important.'

'Who is he, then? The doctor?'

'No.' She felt faint, weak, hot and cold at once. 'Er, yes – an Irish doctor. I . . . phoned him about your dizzy spells and he said to come and see him tomorrow – you know, to talk it over.'

Her father looked at her suspiciously. 'You didn't tell me.'

'No. I . . . I thought I'd wait until—'

'Dublin, that was it. He had to go to Dublin.'

'*Dublin*? Why? When?'

'Tomorrow. He's going tomorrow.'

'Tomorrow?' She could only repeat his words like a moron, numb with incredulity.

Her father put down his knife and fork, frowning in an effort to concentrate. Remembering wasn't easy for him – it involved an elaborate ritual of screwing up his eyes, tapping his forehead, biting his lip.

He screwed, he tapped, he bit.

'Yes, Dad?'

All at once his face brightened. 'I've got it – yes, a sudden change of plan, he said. That was it. A sudden change of plan.'

'But did he leave a phone number? Somewhere I can contact him?'

There was a long, almost unbearable silence while her father tapped his forehead again, bit his lip and screwed up his eyes so tightly he looked grotesque. 'No,' he said, at last. 'He said you weren't to ring him. He'll be gone, he said.'

'Gone?'

Her father nodded. 'Gone,' he repeated. 'Gone. Gone. Gone. Gone.'

Slowly she stood up and walked to the door.

'Where are you off to now, Jane?'

'To get . . . a glass of water.'

'There's water on the table.'

Ignoring him, she went up to her bedroom. The leopard-skin skirt and low-cut glittery top hung side by side in the wardrobe. She took them out, folded them with care and laid them on the bed. Then she opened her underwear drawer, where she'd put the fishnet tights and lacy knickers. Before adding them to the pile, she held them against her face for a moment to feel the whisper-soft scratch of the lace, the warp and weft of the net. Next she got out the cufflinks and the Pisces birthday card. The cufflinks nestled on a satin cushion in their elegant black box, and the two shimmering fishes on the card were passionately entwined.

The last item was the lipstick. She caressed its tooled gold case, exploring every tiny protuberance and groove, then slipped it into her pocket and carried all the other things downstairs. Taking a box of matches from the kitchen, she stepped out of the back door.

The light was dying; a blue haze blurred the colours, but she could still see the signs of spring: pink whorls of confetti-blossom on the trees and the daffodils' brave bugles tooting to the moon.

She prised the lid off the incinerator and pressed down the garden rubbish to make room for the clothes. There was a smell of rankness, deadness – rotting cabbage, last winter's leaves. She struck a match and tossed it in, and stood listening to the crackle of the flames. Burn-out. Chaos. Fire Down Below.

She threw the cufflinks on to the pyre, followed by the card, and watched them char to cinders in a trice. Scream. Outrage. Crime and Punishment.

Again, last to go was the lipstick. She took it from her pocket and twisted the base to its full extent until the red rod reared up stiff, tumescent. Smiling, she consigned it to the fire. Bruise. Scarlet Gash. Asphyxia.

Inside, the apple pie was cooling on the worktop. She carried it to the sink, turned on the waste-disposal unit and fed it in piece by piece, poking the lumps down with a fork. The custard went the same way. Trash. Scandal. Just Deserts.

Then she took a tray into the dining-room and placed the dishes on it – pie, potatoes, parsnips, carrots – carried them out to the kitchen and patiently and methodically disposed of each in turn. The whirring, grinding noise was soothing, and drowned her father's bewildered cries. Poor old man – he deserved better from his daughter.

Yet his plate, too, must go.

'I haven't finished,' he whimpered, trying to cling to it.

'Don't worry, Dad.' Gently she kissed the top of his head. 'We'll have a nice little snack at the Social Club before your game of dominoes.'

Madame Martinez

'Madame Martinez of New Malden – never fails to reunite the separated.'

The advertisement seemed to leap right off the page. Carla hardly ever read the local paper, and certainly not the classifieds. Could her eye have been guided here by Keith?

Madame Martinez's credentials took up several lines: *First Lady of clairvoyance, psychic, healer, the answer to your prayers . . .*

Carla wasn't in the habit of praying. Even at the funeral, rage had prevented her from joining in the responses.

'My cosmic gifts are awesome. I predicted the death of Princess Diana, and Brazil winning the World Cup . . .'

It struck her as rather peculiar to link two such disparate events. Yet psychic powers couldn't be dismissed out of hand. That thing on Channel 4, for instance, about the man who'd won the Lottery six times in succession, using the teachings of the Universal Kabbala . . . The programme had convinced her that, explicable or not, there must be more to it than blind chance.

'A £9.99 administration fee secures you an hour-long consultation worth £50, in which I guarantee you contact with your loved ones . . .'

£9.99 was peanuts. The funeral had cost two thousand, and she would pay double that just to hear Keith's voice again. Her friends would think her stupid for even entertaining the possibility, but there was no need for them to know. (Just as they knew nothing of her continuing visits to the hospital, sneaking along to Churchill Ward to soak up Keith's last traces). She hesitated only a moment longer before dialling the New Malden number.

A man with a thick accent answered. 'Yes? Hello.'

'I, er, wanted to speak to Madame Martinez.'

'She not here.'

'Could I arrange an appointment with her?'

'Wait. I get her book.'

Carla waited, listening to the music in the background. It didn't sound very spiritual, more like Kiss FM.

'You want come tomorrow?'

Tomorrow? She'd assumed Madame Martinez would be booked up weeks ahead. 'Yes, possibly . . . What time?'

'Ten o'clock?'

It would mean taking the morning off work, and she was already in danger of being sacked. Since the funeral, she couldn't seem to concentrate on sales figures. Her mind kept returning to the question of Keith's ashes: would scattering them mean losing him for ever? 'OK. And the address?'

'Number three Fletcher Road. You turn right out of New Malden station and . . .'

She jotted down the instructions and rang off. Her heart was beating at an alarming rate – as Keith's had done, that hideous day . . .

But number three was lucky. Wasn't it?

Turning the corner, she surveyed the row of mock-Tudor semis – smug-looking houses with net curtains and neat gardens. Somehow she had imagined Madame Martinez living in a watchtower, wild ocean waves crashing round its base. Ridiculous. Surrey wasn't On-Sea.

The door chime was a tinny version of 'The Ride of the Valkyries'. She wondered about its significance – or might this be the wrong house? No one seemed to be in, and she certainly wasn't late. In fact, she had arrived at the station forty minutes early and had killed time in the Oxfam shop. The day after the funeral she'd taken all Keith's clothes to the British Heart Foundation shop, then regretted it the instant she got home. The clothes were hardly likely to turn up in the New Malden branch of Oxfam, but she had found it strangely comforting hunting through rails of shirts and trousers and recognizing lookalikes. She'd bought a blue-striped tie, identical to Keith's.

'No, I don't want a bag,' she'd told the assistant, tenderly rolling the tie and putting it in her coat pocket. She'd been stroking it ever since, and gave it an extra squeeze, for luck, as she rang the bell a second time.

She was about to give up in despair when the door was opened by a dumpy middle-aged woman, still buttoning her jacket as if she hadn't finished dressing. Her eyes were an undistinguished blue, with heavy crêpey lids. The Crimplene two-piece strained across her hips, and her greying hair was scraped into a bun.

'Hello! Hello! So sorry to keep you. I don't usually see people before twelve.'

'But the, er, gentleman said . . .'

'Oh, Ivor' – she gave a disparaging shrug – 'what would he know? But do come in.'

Carla stepped into the poky hall. There was a smell she couldn't place. Incense? Joss sticks? Herbal cigarettes?

'Would you like a cup of tea?'

Tersely she declined. She wasn't here for tea and small talk.

'It's no trouble, dear. I've got the kettle on.'

'Well, all right. Thank you.' She mustn't seem ungracious. 'You are Madame Martinez?' she added quickly, before the woman could disappear. She had pictured the First Lady of clairvoyance dressed in something floaty or dramatic, not puddle-coloured Crimplene. And those dreadful canvas shoes with Velcro fastenings, the sort advertised for people with bunions. Still, as Keith was fond of saying, you shouldn't judge by appearances.

'But of course I am. And you're Carla.'

The simple statement hit her like a thunderbolt. She was sure she hadn't given her name on the phone, prompted by some instinct to remain anonymous. On the other hand, grief played havoc with one's memory, so could she be mistaken? 'H. . .how did you know?' she asked.

Madame Martinez gave an inscrutable smile. 'I know a lot of things, dear. Now you sit here in the warm and I'll go and fetch the tea.'

Warm was an understatement. The room was stifling, indeed claustrophobic, with the curtains closed and the gas fire turned up high. Carla perched on the edge of a chair, listening to the ponderous ticking of the old-fashioned clock on the mantelpiece. The poor thing sounded bronchitic, and showed the time as twenty-five to four.

She opened her purse and took out a £10 note. What was the procedure? Did she pay up front, or only after the consultation? And was £9.99 enough? Judging by the threadbare carpet and battered thirties' sideboard, Madame Martinez wasn't exactly loaded.

She left the note conspicuously on the coffee table, to indicate her willingness to pay. Keith, she begged, I need to know that you're all right. If there's the slightest chance you can co-operate—

'I hope you don't mind soya milk? I'm allergic to dairy products.' Madame Martinez had reappeared, carrying a tray with two cups of curdled-looking tea and a bowl of damp brown sugar. 'The sugar's for me. You don't take it, do you?'

'Well, no . . .' She mustn't over-react. There was a fifty-fifty chance of someone not taking sugar. It was hardly proof of awesome cosmic powers.

'And if I'd brought biscuits, you wouldn't have eaten them.'

Correct. Since Keith had gone, she'd felt constantly sick and faint, and had been living on nothing but Complan, which reminded her of baby-food. She and Keith were planning a baby, now that he was less pressured at work.

Had been, she meant. She kept using the wrong tense. For Keith there wasn't any 'now'.

Madame Martinez sugared her tea, took a noisy sip, then settled back in her chair. 'Well, what can I do for you?'

She sounded like an assistant in a dress shop rather than a clairvoyant. Shouldn't she *know*, for goodness' sake? After all, she'd just claimed to know 'a lot of things'. 'It's my, er, husband,' Carla murmured.

'He's on the Other Side.'

'I beg your pardon?'

'Hush!' Imperiously holding up her hand, Madame Martinez closed her eyes and inclined her head, as if listening to a disembodied voice. After a protracted pause, she spoke again, in a softer, more mysterious tone. 'Does the name Michael mean anything?'

Carla shook her head, dumb with disappointment. If the woman had picked up *her* name from the aether, then why not Keith's?

'No, wait. I'm coming up with John.'

John must be the most common name in England. And Michael not far behind. 'He's called Keith,' she said, to forestall further guesses. Madame Martinez herself was probably plain Mrs Smith.

'Ah, Keith. Yes.'

Another awkward silence fell. The clock's rasping tick seemed infinitely sad, as if it too had suffered a bereavement.

'I see a tall, broad-shouldered man, with floppy hair combed back.'

'Keith isn't tall,' she snapped. 'He's short and slender. And his hair's close-cropped, not floppy.'

'You're right, my dear. It's not Keith, it's his father. They're together on the Other Side, chatting about old times.'

'I'm sorry, I find that hard to swallow. Keith's father walked out when he was only six and they never saw each other again. So they certainly wouldn't be chatting.'

'I can understand your surprise. But you see, on the Other Side all earthly animosities are healed.'

'But it doesn't make sense. Keith's only forty-one and his father died at eighty. How could you possibly confuse them?'

'Wait . . .' Again the hand was held aloft. 'It's coming clearer. I see a short, slim man, with thick black hair . . .'

'Well, of course you do – that's what I've just told you. Except his hair isn't black, it's fair.'

'Could it be his brother?'

'Keith's an only child. We both are.' Which was why they wanted a big family – two boys and two girls, ideally. But they'd left it too late.

'Ah! I'm getting a stronger sense of him now. And you'll be relieved to hear he's looking very happy. He's obviously at peace.'

'But you *would* say that, wouldn't you? – just to make me feel better. Why the hell should he look happy when he was cut off in his prime? God! That bloody ambulance . . . If they'd only got there sooner, he might still be alive.'

'Death is not the end, Carla. It's a new beginning. And Keith's passage to the Other Side is a chance for you to see things in a completely different way, and to be aware of a whole aspect of life closed to you before. I know Keith himself would want that for you.'

'You don't know anything about him.' Angrily Carla clutched the chair-arm, accidentally dislodging its cover, to reveal stained and fraying fabric underneath. No wonder the woman lived in penury when she was so obviously a con.

'Oh, but I do. I know he loves you very deeply, Carla, and he's worried that you're distressed.'

'That's pure conjecture. And it could apply to anyone. Come on, if you're so damned clever, give me something specific.'

The crêpey eyelids closed once more and the sallow face contorted in a spasm. Carla waited, involuntarily glancing at the clock, which still said 4.35. How weird, she thought, that although its hands hadn't moved, the lugubrious ticking continued. Could that itself be proof of some strange power? She began counting the ticks, trying to calm her breathing: five, ten, fifteen, twenty-five . . . There was still not a sound from Madame Martinez. Had she fallen asleep?

But just then her eyes flickered open, and the lips parted in another utterance. 'Keith loved sailing, didn't he?'

Finally losing patience, Carla sprang to her feet. 'No! Absolutely not. We had a trip on a Thames pleasure boat once and he began throwing up the minute we left dry land.'

'Ah, but I could be tuning in to something symbolical. Sailing on the sea of life, perhaps.'

'I've never heard such crap! And your ad's an utter fraud. So much for never failing – you *have* failed this time, haven't you?'

'But, my dear, we've hardly started. It's quite normal for things to be a little . . . fuzzy before I get into my stride.'

'I'm sorry, I can't waste any more time. I should be in the office.' Angrily she eyed the £10 note – she'd need money when she got the sack. 'My boss is already doing his nut about all the time I've had off.' She seized her bag, to leave, then stood awkwardly by the door. 'Can I use your toilet, please?' Another after-effect of the death: a bladder as over-sensitive as she was.

Madame Martinez seemed put out. 'Oh, dear. We haven't a downstairs toilet. And it's awfully cold upstairs.'

'That's OK, I'm boiling. Just point me in the direction.'

Madame Martinez rose stiffly from her chair and hauled herself up the stairs, Carla following impatiently.

'It's that door there. I'll wait for you on the landing.'

So she wasn't to be trusted – she might creep into the bedroom and make off with the family jewels. Although judging by the brooch on Madame Martinez's lapel (a cat, with glittery green eyes all too clearly made of paste, not emeralds), there wouldn't be much jewellery worth stealing.

'The Smallest Room' said the plaque on the toilet door. Dead right. It was so cramped that sitting on the seat, her knees were about three inches from the door.

And it was agony to pee! She seemed to have cystitis now, on top of everything else. She couldn't even drum up the energy to go downstairs again, but remained hunched on the pink plastic seat, fighting back the tears. Life was hard when there was nobody to share it with.

She shivered in the arctic chill. Presumably Madame Martinez couldn't afford to heat the upstairs. And to make matters worse, an icy draught was knifing in from overhead. Craning her neck to find the source of it, she let out an astonished cry.

Keith! He was *there*. In person. Smiling at her through the skylight. He must have climbed up on to the roof and crawled across the slates to this particular window, knowing he would see her.

Rubbish. Keith was dead. Gone. Reduced to ashes. She didn't even believe in the Other Side. In any case, if he was meant to have 'passed over', what was he doing on the rooftops of New Malden?

Deliberately she averted her eyes from the skylight and stared instead at the chipped pink floor-tiles – a different pink from the seat. When she looked up again, the mirage would be gone.

But it wasn't gone. And it wasn't a mirage. It was Keith, in the flesh – a living, breathing, calmly smiling Keith. 'He's obviously very happy,' Madame Martinez had said.

'Darling, are . . . are you happy?'

He put his finger to his lips, but the smile remained – a genuine and, yes, joyous smile.

She pinched the skin on the inside of her wrist, hard. And then again. She was hallucinating – she must be. But why now, for heaven's sake? Even in the darkest days, before and after the funeral, she hadn't conjured up ghosts or spectres. Desolate she might have been, but not delusional.

It was a trick of the light, surely? She blinked a few times before daring to glance up again. Keith was still there, and in no way ghostly or spectral. In fact, he was dressed in a cheerful red sweater and had a Band-Aid on his thumb. Ghosts didn't wear Band-Aids.

'Keith,' she implored. '*Is* it you? Are you . . . are you real?'

He nodded, grinning, as if amazed that she should doubt it.

'Speak to me. Oh, please, darling! Just say a few words – something to help me carry on. It's so terrible without you. I can't sleep; the bed's too big. And I don't cook any more. There's no point – no point in anything.'

'There *is* a point,' Keith said, speaking softly and ethereally. 'And that's our baby. It's vital that you look after the child. And yourself.'

'*Baby*? *Child*? What on earth do you mean? Keith, wait . . . don't go. You must explain . . .'

Too late. He'd vanished and she could see nothing but a pane of clouded glass.

Stumbling to her feet, she stood leaning against the wall. She hadn't had a period for weeks. She'd hardly registered the fact till now – grief obliterated all else. And she'd put her recurring nausea down to stress. But it could be morning sickness. And the cystitis too could be another sign. Pregnant women often suffered with their bladders. Pregnant . . . The very word was a beacon of hope. To be carrying Keith's child, part of him living on in her, redeeming him, giving her a reason to survive. But why had he appeared here, in Madame Martinez's house, rather than at home?

Warily she unlocked the door and peered out. There was no one on the landing, so she ran downstairs and burst into the sitting-room. Madame Martinez was ensconced on the sofa, calmly drinking her tea.

'Did you *know*?' demanded Carla. 'And if so, why in God's name didn't you say?' She broke off, ashamed of the aggression in her voice. And earlier she had been downright rude. 'I'm sorry,' she muttered. 'I was just so disappointed. I mean, you didn't seem to be coming up with anything. But now . . .'

Madame Martinez gave her an affectionate pat on the arm. 'I told you, my dear, sometimes these things take time, especially if there's cosmic interference. I'm delighted for you, believe me, but I suggest you go home and rest – you do look a little peaky. Remember,' she added, and suddenly, uncannily, the whole timbre of her voice changed – deepening, as if she were speaking through Keith: 'it's vital that you look after the child. And yourself.'

One Million Rosaries

Lilian stooped to pick up the letter from the mat. No doubt it would be a circular or one of those rubbishy mail-order catalogues. But no – she peered in surprise: a large vellum envelope emblazoned with a cross and a white dove. She carried it into the kitchen and carefully slit it open with a paper-knife. Out fell a glossy calendar with a picture of the Blessed Virgin Mary on the front, and a letter addressed to her by name.

Dear Miss Thompson, Friend in Christ and Faithful Defender of Life . . .

She smiled. The description was pleasing.

Every year in the UK alone 190,000 babies are murdered through abortion . . .

She put a hand to her throat. She had been in the middle of breakfast and the thought of abortion quite put her off her poached egg. But the statistic was horrendous. She imagined the pathetic little corpses laid out in a line, stretching from Land's End to John O'Groats. Not that she was particularly fond of babies – noisy, smelly creatures – it was the principle that mattered, though. Murder was a heinous sin.

By the age of 44, a third of all women in Britain will have killed the child in their womb . . .

Yes, Mrs Wainwright, for one. Nobody had admitted it in so many words, but the whole episode was deeply suspicious. Spending a day in hospital when there was patently nothing wrong with her, and blushing to the roots of her hair when questioned about the matter. *And* she'd stopped going to Mass.

We need your help to counter the Culture of Death . . .

Gladly. She'd never liked Mrs Wainwright anyway, and her five children were arrant hooligans – although at least she hadn't aborted those.

Immoral practices are rife: cohabitation, contraception, adultery, fornication . . .

No need to spell it out. She'd seen it with her own eyes. Even in a quiet, leafy road like this there were all sorts of goings-on. Mr Baines, for instance, was known to spend most evenings at number twenty-five, where that hussy of a girl lived – a so-called single parent. Single! She must have had dozens of 'lodgers' over the years, all male, of course. And Ken and Suzanne at number twelve weren't married. They'd moved in together as bold as brass and proceeded to procreate without a by-your-leave. What had become of the Sacrament of marriage?

She bit sharply into her slice of toast. In her view the priests were to blame, certainly modern ones like Father Collingwood – 'Jim', as he liked to style himself. If 'Father' wasn't good enough for him, what business had he training for the priesthood? No seminary worth its salt should have accepted him in the first place. Now, at forty-five, he spent more time than was healthy at the youth club, playing that ridiculous guitar, or running classes in motorcycle maintenance. He'd be better occupied teaching the children their Catechism and preparing them for the Sacraments.

Children as young as nine are familiar with condoms . . .

Yes, there it was in black and white – the shame of it. She had never seen a condom, nor wanted to. The very thought was repellent. Even rubber gloves she avoided – they had a sinister feel about them that she was sure could only be sinful.

86% of all teenage girls are sexually promiscuous . . .

She had never been a teenager. Neither the word nor the concept had existed in her day (and nor had that brazen word 'partner', except of course in the business sense). No wonder the church was half empty on Sunday if all the youngsters were cavorting in bed with each other. And their parents at it, too, no doubt, like that wicked film on Channel 4 last week. She'd had to turn the sound down in the end, so intense was the moaning and gasping. The next morning she'd penned an extremely strong letter to the television authorities, registering her disgust. But like as not, she'd receive the usual lame reply: that the programme had value in reflecting social reality.

Threatened as we are by a tidal wave of pornography, a raging epidemic of sexually transmitted diseases . . .

Mr Baines was bound to have a sexual disease. Once, meeting her in the street, his hand had brushed the sleeve of her coat and although she was on her way to the shops, she had gone straight home again and washed in disinfectant.

We must engage in a cosmic struggle against the Powers of Darkness and the Forces of Satan. May we enlist you as a Warrior?

Yes. A resounding yes. What could be more important in life than to fight the Powers of Darkness? Already she felt stronger; perhaps invigorated by those capital letters. Her life had mostly been lived in lower case, but joining the Crusade would mean that her every action henceforth would be imbued with Point and Purpose.

The chief weapon in our struggle is the most Holy Rosary – described by Pope Adrian VI as the Scourge of the Devil. As a Warrior for Christ, we beg you to join our One Million Rosary Campaign. We have purposely set our target very high because only by such heroic spiritual endeavour shall we overcome the modern assault on Life. Every Rosary you say is another Victory for Faith and for the Family. Please return this pledge today.

The pledge was a printed form with a little box to tick and space at the bottom for a signature. *Yes,* she read, *I pledge to pray the Rosary for the year 2002, to hasten the Defeat of the Evil in our midst.*

Without hesitation she ticked the box and signed her name. If someone didn't take a stand, people would be fornicating openly in the streets.

Only by praying the Rosary can we encourage the young to lead lives of holy chastity.

Chastity – a lovely word, and as rare a commodity these days as self-discipline and old-fashioned good manners. And it was one of the Twelve Fruits of the Holy Ghost. She remembered learning them at school, coached by Sister Scholastica. Some of them were difficult to spell (benignity, longaninity) but she'd finally mastered all twelve, along with the Seven Spiritual Works of Mercy, the Eight Beatitudes, the Six Sins Against the Holy Ghost, the Four Sins Crying to Heaven for Vengeance, and of course the Ten Commandments and Twelve Articles of the Creed. The various numbers had been a source of comfort – the fact that everything was meticulously counted and spelt out. God would be a man like her father, who did double-entry book-keeping and divided his busy day into hours and minutes, each with its allotted task. One needed Order in the world, the reassurance that the Divine Accountant's figures added up.

In 1988, Pope John Paul II asked Catholics to say the Rosary for the conversion of Soviet Russia. Just one year later, the Berlin Wall came crashing down, along with Communism itself – a victory inconceivable without the power of the Holy Rosary . . .

Amazing. She, Miss Lilian Thompson, could actually influence world politics, destroy corrupt regimes and fifteen-foot-high walls. She pushed away her plate. It would be unseemly to sit eating toast and marmalade when she had just signed a solemn Pledge.

If you would like to buy a Rosary, please send a cheque or postal order for £6.99.

No need for that. She had rosaries for every day of the week. The oldest and most precious was the mother of pearl one she had been given for her First Communion. She tended not to use it now, for fear of wearing away the already fragile beads. The black one was more practical, and more powerful too, as it had been blessed by the Holy Father only last year. Could it have been he who had given them her name? (How else would they have contacted her?) Certainly she felt a special bond with the Pope. Not only were they both engaged in God's work, but she, too, had taken a vow of chastity – at the age of thirteen, in fact, when her menstrual periods started. Hateful, defiling blood, month after month, for close on forty years. The menopause had come as a great relief. Hot flushes and night sweats were a small price to pay for being freed from the curse of Eve. The hysterectomy, too, had left her feeling considerably cleaner and lighter. In truth, she would gladly be rid of other parts of her body – her liver and kidneys, perhaps, or her gall bladder and spleen. Flesh was a constant burden.

Please accept this calendar with our compliments. Circle every day you say the Rosary and at the end of each month, add up your total, enter the figure on the tear-off slip and return it to us at VICTORY FOR LIFE. *In January next year, the person with the highest number will present the Rosary Bouquet to Our Blessed Lady at her shrine at Walsingham.*

She clasped her hands in delight. *She* would be that person. What an honour and a privilege. The Bishop would be there, of course, and priests from the length and breadth of England. Possibly a cardinal or two, or even the Holy Father himself. But during the ceremony all eyes would be on *her* as she walked slowly up to the statue of the

Blessed Virgin and presented the bouquet. They might allow her to say a few words, describe her lifelong battle against immorality. Imagine addressing Pope John Paul! The perfect climax to her life.

She studied the calendar closely. It wouldn't really be adequate. The months were divided into their constituent days, but by no means would she restrict herself to a single Rosary a day. She would have to make her own version, listing every hour of every day in the year, and aim to circle each one – the daylight hours, at least. Obviously some time must be set aside for housework and shopping, and for personal chores such as bathing and dressing, and bandaging her leg, but otherwise she could devote the whole day to the Rosary. They would be astounded to see the figures on her tear-off strips: the highest scores ever achieved for VICTORY FOR LIFE.

'Hail Mary, Full of grace, The Lord is . . .'

Her second name was Mary – Lilian Mary Cecilia: three times pure. Cecilia was a virgin betrothed against her will, who was martyred when she refused to consummate the marriage. And, faced with a philanderer like Ken or that heathen Mr Baines, she would have done the same. Mr Baines probably compounded his sin of fornication by using contraceptives. An image of his erect and rubbered organ suddenly sprang into her mind. 'Lord save me, or I perish,' she muttered, hastily making the sign of the Cross. She was dreadfully tired and the Devil was known to take advantage of lowered states such as hunger or fatigue. Already today she had clocked up forty Rosaries, scarcely pausing to eat or drink. Before continuing into the night, she ought to make a cup of tea or see if she could find a tin of soup among the dwindling supplies in the cupboard. Yet such was her exhaustion she could only rise stiffly from her knees and collapse into the nearest chair.

There was a film of dust on the table and the narcissi in the vase were dying. Normally she took pride in her home, but in wartime different standards must prevail. You couldn't be fussing about with a duster whilst Satan's arrows fell thick and fast on the world. Besides, there was ample recompense for the neglected house, the unmade bed, the weariness and pain. All she had to do was read the Fifteen Promises of Our Blessed Mother to Those Who Recite the Rosary, which were printed on the calendar in Our Lady's colour, blue. She'd read them so often she knew them off by heart.

Whoever shall recite the Rosary devoutly shall never be conquered by misfortune nor shall perish by an unprovided death . . .

Death had been a worry, certainly. Could she trust 'Jim' to administer the Last Sacraments? Or would he arrive in his bovver boots and leathers and play her 'Kumbaya'?

The advocates of the Rosary shall have for intercessors the entire celestial court at the hour of death . . .

What a consolation! In the presence of the entire celestial court, she could safely ignore 'Jim' and his guitar.

The faithful children of the Rosary shall merit a high degree of glory in Heaven . . .

Her favourite Promise of all. She could already see herself seated at God's right hand, along with His Blessed Mother, Saint Peter and Saint John. Mr Baines, of course, would be in Hell. 'Jim' had announced to the congregation last Sunday that there was no such place as Hell. The minute she got home, she had written to the Bishop to complain. It was yet another example of this new-fangled modern theology – everything was watered down, even sin. If 'Jim' chose to believe that God's love and mercy overruled His justice, he was courting disaster for himself and his flock. She was extremely fortunate in that she had been properly instructed in the tenets of the Faith, at home as well as school. Those women at the convent up the road (she refused to call them nuns – they wore jeans and lipstick, and for all she knew, smoked cigarettes, or worse) couldn't hold a candle to the pious souls like Sister Scholastica and Sister Aloysius who had taught her at *Le Sacré Cœur*. No wonder the Holy Father looked so ill and frail; he was grieving for the modern world.

Proudly she surveyed the extra page she had inserted into the calendar, listing every hour in January. Forty circles today, thirty-seven yesterday, thirty-three the day before and thirty each on Saturday and Sunday: a hundred and forty already. By January next year the total would be tens of thousands. Time no longer dragged – in fact she had never been so busy. None the less, it was often hard to concentrate. When you were saying the Hail Mary over and over and over again, the words began to lose their meaning. And even the usually bracing 'Glory Be' seemed less powerful now. Sometimes the mere ticking of the clock could put her off her stroke, or the toot of a car outside, and she would forget where she was up to and have to start the decade again. This morning she was almost sure she'd left out

a 'Hail Holy Queen', so she'd recited it twice at the end of the next
Rosary, and then a third time, as penance.

And later in the day, while meditating on the Sorrowful Mysteries,
she'd had a most disturbing experience. Her attention had been
devoutly fixed on Christ and Saint Veronica when all at once they
turned into Ken and Suzanne. Horrified, she'd said an Act of
Contrition, but still she couldn't get the image out of her mind: their
bodies sprawled naked on the bed, yet the details remaining blurred.
It had set her wondering what they actually *did* together, which was
even more unsettling. Could it be the Sin of Sodom? The Sin wasn't
explained in the Catechism, except as one of the Four Crying to
Heaven for Vengeance, so she had no idea what it was. There were
nine separate ways you could share the guilt of another's sin, and one
of them was Silence, so it was really her Christian duty to report the
dissolute pair. She had reported Mr Baines already. Not that it made
a jot of difference – she had spotted him last night again, slinking
across the road to Melanie's with that lascivious look on his face. And
what sort of name was Melanie, she'd like to know? The value of
having a saint's name was that you received their protection all your
life. Saint Cecilia was like her devoted elder sister, and Mary, as well
as being Mother to the Universe, was her specific mother, prepared
night and day to succour her.

Succour. Another beautiful word, with its connotations of 'suckle'.
Sometimes she imagined herself suckling from one of Mary's breasts,
while Jesus fed at the other. Nice to have been born a twin. Twins
were never lonely.

'Blessed art thou amongst women,' she murmured, reaching for her
Rosary once more. Surely God would understand if she said the next
few Rosaries from the comfort of her chair instead of kneeling on the
floor? Her knees were swollen and rubbed raw, but she couldn't waste
precious time going to the doctor. Every minute of her day must be
dedicated to the Defeat of Evil.

The shriek of the alarm clock jolted her from sleep. She awoke to
pain: her knees throbbed and a tight band gripped her head. No
matter. She'd simply increase her dose of pills; they had worked well
enough yesterday, despite the unfortunate side effects of taking them
on an empty stomach. She groped for the light switch and peered at
the clock – half past two. Three hours' sleep was quite sufficient when

you were Fighting for a Cause.

Struggling out of bed, she smoothed her crumpled skirt. It had become a spiritual challenge to cut extraneous activities out of her life: undressing at night, for instance, or washing herself or her clothes. Frankly it appalled her to think of the hours she had frittered away poaching eggs or grating cheese for Welsh rarebit, listening to the News or idling to the shops – all lost opportunities. But now they were into February she was achieving a minimum of seventy Rosaries a day. Sometimes, it had to be said, she was assailed by temptations of the flesh: to sleep in a little longer, or cook herself a meal or – shameless indulgence – soak in a hot bath. But she had only to remind herself of the lovely piece printed on the back of the calendar about 'dryness of soul and interior discouragement' to be restored to the path of virtue.

Never give up, it urged. *However arduous you find your prayers, remember Christ's Agony in the Garden. 'Being in agony, He prayed the longer.' Just follow His example.*

That had ·proved a great help. What were her petty ailments, compared to Christ's Agony? Her knees might be burning and her fingers sore from the pressure of the beads, but at least she wasn't nailed to a Cross nor crowned with thorns. Although actually it did feel as if a hundred long spikes had been rammed into her head, and the dizzy spells were becoming much more frequent. Yesterday she had fallen and been unable to get up for half an hour. But she had simply lain there on the floor and meditated on Our Blessed Saviour falling three times while carrying His Cross. Which meant that in a way she was continuing the Rosary, even though she was too weak to say the prayers.

And today she would recite the Sorrowful Mysteries again. The Joyful and the Glorious Mysteries held much less attraction. Even as a child she had preferred the Sorrowful. Sister Aloysius had taught them in Form One that life was a Vale of Tears, a punishment for sin (like menstrual periods) and that to expect happiness in this world rather than the next was presumptuous, if not heretical. Indeed as true children of Christ they should actively seek to crucify themselves. Above her bed there'd been a Crucifix, faithfully depicting the nail-holes in His hands and feet, and the scarlet gash in His side. Every night she had poked her finger deep into those holes, and felt a peculiar thrill, a glow of warmth suffusing her whole body.

No chance of any glow just now. It was bitterly cold in the house. The central heating seemed to have gone wrong, but she had more important things to do than call out the Electricity Board. She put on an extra cardigan and got creakily down on her knees. 'Our Father,' she began, 'Who art in Heaven . . .'

She longed to join Him there. In Heaven you were freed from your physical infirmities and had the entire Heavenly Host as company, whereas here on earth conversation was restricted to the few odd words exchanged each week with the girl on Sainsbury's check-out, and 'Jim's' inane chatter after Mass.

'Give us this day our daily bread . . .'

No, she dare not think of bread or she might succumb in the morning and go out and buy a loaf. Or even a cake. Her mouth began to water as she pictured the delicious little almond slices in Marshall's Bakery. And their Victoria sponges, oozing jam and cream. And the trays of sugared buns . . .

'Lead us not into temptation . . .'

The worst temptation wasn't cakes but Ken. He would keep intruding, unannounced and naked, into the sanctuary of her mind. The only naked male body she had ever seen was Christ's, and *His* private parts were always covered with a loincloth.

'Get thee behind me, Satan,' she commanded, taking comfort from the fact that the Devil had tempted the greatest of the saints, and Our Lord Himself, of course. In fact, the closer you were to God, the more His wily Adversary would try to wrest you away.

'. . . but deliver us from evil. Amen.'

'Amen,' she repeated desperately. 'Amen.'

He was there. In the room. The Archfiend. And lesser demons sneered and writhed on every side. It was impossible to pray, or even kneel, so stiff had her legs become. Bands of promiscuous teenagers were fornicating on the floor, the chairs, the sofa. Adulterers and cohabitors were upstairs in her bedroom – she could hear their gasps and moans. Babies were swelling in a hundred and ninety thousand wombs, waiting to be murdered by their hundred and ninety thousand mothers. And 'Jim' was doing unspeakable things with a dozen boys from the youth club, gleefully stripping off his clothes and theirs.

'Go away!' she whimpered. 'I'm falling behind with my Rosary. I haven't circled a single hour today.'

147

But now there came a new terror: the jangling of a bell. It rang on and on, getting louder, louder, louder. She clutched the sideboard in mortal fear. It must be the Last Knell.

'Help me!' she cried, but her voice was lost in a thunderous knocking. *'Behold I stand at the gate and knock . . .'* Could it be Christ? Come to save her? To take her up directly into Heaven as He had His blessed Mother?

Gathering her last shred of strength, she dragged herself to the front door, nearly losing her balance as she struggled with the bolt.

Two black uniforms towered before her; two accusing faces leered down into hers. And beyond them, in the street, a sleek white creature crouched: a slavering beast of prey, about to spring forward and snatch her in its jaws. Panic-stricken, she shrank back into the hall. They had come to lock her up. For adultery, fornication. She had sinned in mind and heart, which was as iniquitous as committing the act itself. She had fornicated shamelessly with Ken and Mr Baines, with Mr Wainwright and 'Jim', with the priests and bishops of Holy Mother Church – even, God forgive her, with the Pope. But there was no forgiveness for such heinous sins, Sins that Cried to Heaven for Vengeance. Already the world was going black and she was staggering and floundering – falling down, down, down, down, down to Hell.

'Now, Miss Thompson, what we'd like to do is admit you for a couple of days. That leg of yours needs attention, and you're badly dehydrated, so we're going to put up a drip and give you some fluids. I understand you haven't been eating . . .'

'You don't understand anything,' she said, her voice a feeble croak. 'I'm not staying in a hospital.' Hospitals were Places of Death. It said so in the letter: abortion, sterilization, vasectomy, euthanasia – all such horrors took place in hospital. Doctors were Abortion Merchants, 'the deluded human allies of the Powers of Darkness'. Every year worldwide they murdered fifty million babies in the womb. And they practised IVF, destroying embryos by the billion, or subjecting them to cruel, inhuman experiments. And they gave women the Pill, handed out condoms as freely as sweets to innocent children, killed old ladies in their hospital beds . . .

'You were lucky, Miss Thompson, that your neighbour noticed the milk bottles on the step. If he hadn't alerted the police . . .'

Lucky? Certainly not. This whole unfortunate episode had inter-fered with her Crusade.

'But now you're here, we can start building up your strength.'

'I'm not staying,' she repeated. 'I have work to do at home.'

They'd bandaged her leg and given her a cup of tea and two diges-tive biscuits. Thus fortified, she could continue with her Rosaries. Of course it would take its toll; of course she wouldn't have time to eat, or wash, or shop, or clean the house. But in the ambulance, when she realized she was saved – that God in His infinite mercy had spared her from Eternal Damnation, despite the rankness of her sins – she was struck by a brilliant idea. *She*, alone and unaided, would say the One Million Rosaries required by VICTORY FOR LIFE. Why leave it to other Catholics, who might have demanding jobs and families, or who lacked her own commitment and endurance? It would mean making a new calendar, something on a mammoth scale, but that would be simple enough. And she would have to restrict her sleep to an hour per night, but as it was only for a year it would do no lasting damage.

Walsingham was all that mattered and her momentous role at the shrine. She would be the first person in the history of the Church to recite one million Rosaries in the space of a single year. So even if she had to crawl there on her hands and knees or be carried on a stretcher, nothing and no one – whether nurse, policeman, doctor or priest – would stop her presenting the Rosary bouquet.

No Room at the Inn

'It's no good – I've got to have a breather. These damn things are cutting my hands to ribbons.' Geoff put down the bulging carrier bags, which collapsed around his feet. 'I told you we should have brought the car.'

'We'd never have parked. It's bad enough at normal times.'

'Couldn't you have got all this stuff before? I don't know why you always leave it to the last minute.'

Ingrid felt a scream rising in her throat. She had gone shopping practically every evening this week, as well as a couple of lunch hours. 'I have got most things,' she said, through gritted teeth. Over the years she had suppressed so many screams, their silent skeletons must be silting up her insides. 'But then you invited Tom and Rosie. That's another six for lunch.'

'Five. The baby doesn't eat.'

'No, six. They're bringing the au pair.'

'God, not that dreadful Polish girl.'

They'd met Gizela only once, and Ingrid had found her instantly likeable, if rather domineering. Gizela would be a natural screamer, her complaints emerging loud and fully-formed. And she would have packed Geoff off to do all the shopping on his own. 'I can't see anything wrong with her.'

'Her English is appalling.'

'Better than your Polish, I should think! Come on – I must get home. There's still masses to be done.' She picked up her shopping bags, and some of his, and began battling through the crowds again.

A tinny rendition of 'Jingle Bells' was being relayed from a loud-speaker in the square, competing with the shouts of the market traders. And outside the church a group of parish worthies, muffled in coats and scarves, were singing carols to a flute accompaniment.

'O come all ye faithful, joyful and triumphant . . .'

In fact, joy and triumph were conspicuous by their absence. Frustration and fatigue seemed more in evidence as grim-faced shoppers trudged from stall to stall, pausing only to snap at their children or glower at passers-by.

'O come ye, o come ye to Be-e-e-thle-hem . . .'

Ingrid thought of the gruesome footage on last night's news, showing the dead and wounded in the latest Bethlehem riot. No joy or triumph either for the grieving Jews and Arabs.

'Bloody hell!' Geoff muttered, ducking out of the way of a jauntily bouncing balloon attached to a child's buggy. 'Let's walk back along the river. You can't move in this crush.'

They crossed the square into Thames Street, cut along an alleyway and descended the steps to the riverside walk. Dank swirls of mist hung above the water and the lamp-posts cast long, distorted shadows on the path. Ingrid shivered. Away from the shops the air was colder, as if the gaudy reds and greens of the Christmas decorations could impart warmth as well as colour. The sun hadn't shown its face all day, and early in the afternoon the sky had taken on an eerie purplish-yellow tinge, like a bruise, subsiding prematurely into twilight. And now that it was truly dark, the clouds parted only fitfully to reveal a pale rag of moon.

There was a sudden rush of wings and a raucous honking – a skein of Canada geese flying overhead. Ingrid watched them pass. In her mind she was soaring with them, no longer earthbound and solitary but buoyed up within the safety of a flock.

'Damn birds!' Geoff muttered. 'Shitting all over the place.' He inspected the sole of his shoe in disgust. 'They don't belong here anyway – bloody foreign creatures.'

She, too, was foreign, but she stifled her retort, as usual, and sought distraction in reading the names of the boats moored along the bank: *Sea Myth, Aphrodite, Norma Jean* . . . 'Oh, lord,' she exclaimed, 'I've just had an awful thought. Isn't Norma vegetarian?'

'No idea. I can't keep up with all her damn-fool diets. I seem to remember last year she wouldn't eat wheat or dairy.'

'Why didn't you *remind* me? I'll have to cook her something separate and I might not have the right things.'

'Come off it – the house is groaning with food already, quite apart from the fifty-odd quid we've just spent.'

'Yes, but she's—'

Ingrid broke off as a figure emerged through the gloom, a tall, lean, youngish man walking purposefully towards them. Despite the temperature he was wearing only a shirt and jeans – no coat, not even a sweater.

'Excuse me' – his voice was surprisingly refined – 'I'm sorry to trouble you, but I wonder if you might happen to know of a bed-and-breakfast place in the area?'

'Mm, let me think . . .' she said, reassured by his courteous tone. 'There's the YMCA in Derwent Road. They do accommodation, don't they, Geoff?'

The only response was a non-committal grunt.

'They're fully booked,' the stranger said. 'I've just come from there.'

'Oh . . . well, how about the King's Arms? It's quite reasonable, as far as I know.'

'They're full, too.'

'Oh, dear. I'm sorry, I can't think of anywhere else . . . Well, except the Carlton Court Hotel, but that's rather pricey – about a hundred pounds a night, I believe.'

The man smiled politely. 'Out of the question, I'm afraid. I'm looking for somewhere fairly basic. You see, I'm homeless at the moment, and out of work. I've nowhere to go for Christmas.'

Ingrid bit her lip. 'That's terrible. I . . . don't know what to suggest.' She turned to her husband and whispered, 'Can't *we* do something?'

He shook his head vigorously. 'You know my opinion of scroungers,' he said, making no attempt to lower his voice.

She flushed in embarrassment. She could slip the man some money – or might he be offended? He didn't look anything like a down-and-out: his clothes were clean, if inadequate, his hair was neatly trimmed, and there was a sensitive cast to his features, suggesting intelligence and breeding.

'Come *on*.' Geoff seized her arm almost roughly.

'It's not easy being homeless at this time of year,' the stranger continued, and his voice faltered, betraying emotion for the first time.

'Yes, it must be dreadful. I just wish we could help . . .'

Geoff pulled her away and marched her along the path. 'Don't believe a word of it. It's a sob story, a con – that's all. He's probably got a perfectly good home.'

'But he didn't even have a coat, poor thing.'

'Well, of course not. Another ploy to gain sympathy from suckers like you.'

'Oh, Geoff, don't be so callous. No one would choose to be out in shirtsleeves in this weather. It's bitter.' A wind had sprung up, cantankerous like her husband, raising angry little flurries on the water, and harassing the trees. 'Let's go back and give him something. If not money, then some of this food.'

'For heaven's sake – you said a minute ago we hadn't got enough.'

'But darling, he's got nothing.'

'Rubbish! He's evidently got the wherewithal to pay for bed and breakfast, and those places don't come cheap.'

She skirted a puddle, gleaming blackly in the lamplight. 'Yes, but it's no good if they're all full.'

'There must be shelters for the homeless – Salvation Army hostels or some such.'

'Where, though? Anyway he wouldn't fit in. He seems a cultured sort of man.'

'Oh, sure – William bloody Shakespeare. We know nothing whatever about him. He could be a maniac, or a rapist, or God knows what kind of criminal . . .'

Seeing a light in one of the houseboats, she stooped to peep through the window. The cabin looked cosy and Christmassy, hung with garlands of tinsel, and a young couple were sitting side by side deep in conversation. The man was laughing – actually laughing!

'I think we should invite him home. For Christmas Day, at least.'

'Are you out of your mind? With all the family there? What do you think they'd say?'

'They'll probably complain, as usual,' she murmured, more to herself than him, 'so it won't make any difference.'

'And what's *that* supposed to mean? If you object so much to having them, why—?'

'I don't object. It's just that . . . well, I suppose it would be nice,

one year, to do something different. You know, go away somewhere –
to a hotel, or on a cruise, or—'

'You must be joking! Cruises cost a fortune at the best of times, and
most hotels charge double at Christmas. Anyway everywhere's
booked solid months ahead.'

'We've never tried it, though, so we can't be sure . . .'

'Besides, it wouldn't be fair on Mum and Dad. You know how they
hate change.'

'OK, OK, we'll keep Christmas the same as always. But I don't see
why we shouldn't include that poor man.'

'Because I don't want us to be burgled or murdered in our beds.'

She lifted the tray of mince pies from the oven and transferred them
to racks to cool. She really ought to make another batch: with fifteen
for lunch tomorrow this lot wouldn't go far. And there was still the
problem of Norma. If she couldn't eat wheat or dairy products, none
of the puddings would do. It might be best to phone her and check,
but that would involve an hour-long exposition on the vagaries of her
bowels. The simplest solution would be to make a fruit salad, and a
vegetarian main course, just in case.

Wearily she sat at the kitchen table, riffling through recipe books.
It was already ten, and there were still the sprouts to prepare. Easier
to do it tonight when there weren't children underfoot.

The wind, stronger now, was soughing round the house, rattling
the loose pane in the cloakroom window – no night to be out. Had
that man found a place to stay? How pitiful it seemed that he had no
family or friends to take him in. Could he be a sort of Christ figure,
come again, and hoping this time there might be room in the inn? It
was years since she'd been to church, but odd phrases from the Bible
drifted into her mind. 'He came unto His own, but His own received
Him not . . .'

She could easily make up a bed on the sofa, lay another place at the
table tomorrow. It would be interesting to talk to him and learn something of his life. Even with a houseful of relatives, Christmas could be
lonely. Geoff always drank too much and fell asleep after lunch, the
children invariably squabbled, and there'd never yet been a year that
Bill and Patrick hadn't had a mammoth slanging match. Without relatives or children of her own, she often felt she didn't quite belong. In-
laws weren't the same; you didn't share blood or genes with them, or

habits. All you shared was the person you'd married, and Geoff was no longer the person she'd married. After twenty years he'd . . .

'You're not still at it, are you?'

'Mm.'

'Can't you call it a day for now and start again in the morning?'

'I'd rather not. I'm making a nut loaf for Norma and I need to shell a load of nuts.'

'Well, I'm going to bed.'

'OK.'

'Don't be long.'

'No.'

'And don't wake me up.'

She imagined a rather different exchange: 'Would you like some help, darling?' Or: 'I'll stay and keep you company, my love.' Or: 'Goodnight' at the very least. If she had asked the stranger to stay, they might be sitting here talking, like the couple in the houseboat. How she would enjoy that conversation, even if it touched on painful subjects Geoff refused to discuss: childlessness, for instance, and still feeling an alien in your adopted country after twenty years – indeed, the problems of marriage generally. Was the man married, she wondered? And homeless because his wife had thrown him out? It seemed unlikely somehow. There was an unusual sort of detachment about him, even an otherworldliness. It hadn't been a chance encounter – she was becoming convinced of that – but a deliberate test of her compassion. A test she had failed, through her meek acceptance of Geoff's hard-hearted stand. But she had long ago settled for submission, cultivating smiles and patience, like flowers sown in a minefield. Hypocritical, perhaps, but better (and safer) than provoking Geoff's foul temper.

The noise from outside drew her to the window. The wind was working itself into a frenzy, battering plants and shrubs in the front garden, littering the path with snapped-off twigs, even wrenching over a dustbin. She couldn't just continue with her cooking while that man was out there somewhere, in desperate need of shelter from the storm. The least she could do was take him a coat and a blanket, and a supply of food to last him over Christmas.

She found a sturdy basket and filled it with provisions: a loaf, a slab of cheese, the pâté intended for Boxing Day, half-a-dozen mince pies, and a Thermos of coffee. The coat was more difficult. She didn't dare take one of Geoff's or go upstairs for a blanket, so she removed the throw from the sofa and stuffed it into a big carrier bag with the old gardening jacket that hung in the hall cupboard. Then, pulling on her sheepskin, she let herself out of the house.

Instantly the wind assailed her, tearing at her clothes and trying to drag the bags from her hands. It had already vented its wrath on the street – whole branches ripped from trees and a For Sale board lying crippled on the pavement. She stepped over it, pressed on. The years with Geoff had taught her that anger was something you couldn't control. It raged; you simply waited for the lull.

Eddies of rubbish from the overturned dustbin were trapped against the wheels of the Johnsons' car, and its windscreen was spattered with wet leaves. She had never learned to drive. In the early days there wasn't the money for lessons, and Geoff refused to teach her in 'his' precious Allegro. And now that they had the money, her nerve had been destroyed by his (frequently expressed) conviction that she would be a liability behind the wheel. Yet searching the area on foot was a near-impossible task. The man might be anywhere by now, even safe in a hotel. Somehow, though, she knew in her bones that he was still in the vicinity, actually waiting to be found.

She crossed Luxmore Gardens and turned towards the embankment. Her eyes were streaming in the wind, but her hands weren't free to wipe them. She hadn't cried in years. It took confidence to cry, the same as to rant and rage – both involved the belief that you had rights or grievances.

Finally reaching the river, she found more devastation. The boats were straining at their moorings, bobbing like flotsam at the mercy of the wind, their pitiful creakings and flappings lost in its manic howl. Buffeted by a violent gust, she sought shelter in the lee of a wooden stand containing a lifebuoy. 'In emergency, release catch . . .' A lifebuoy would have proved a more useful wedding present than bed-linen or china. But she was forgetting her mission: it was the man who mattered, not her – homeless, friendless and freezing cold, yet perhaps a redeemer and a deliverer.

She had hoped to see him huddled on one of the benches along the embankment, but they all stood pathetically empty, many with broken slats and scrawled with graffiti. There was not a sign of life; no bird on the water, no car on the road beyond; even the cosy houseboat now dark and uninhabited. The world had become a wilderness, stripped bare by the psychotic wind.

But then, a little further ahead, she made out a hump on the ground. Approaching warily, she saw it was a human shape, shrouded in something that looked like sacking. The wind tugged at the sacking but whoever was inside lay absolutely motionless. Was this the man she was seeking, already dead from cold or hunger? Had she arrived too late?

Frantically she scrabbled at one end of the sacking and managed to pull it back. A lined, stubbly face stared up at her, ingrained with dirt and fringed with matted hair. The bloodshot eyes narrowed in rage. 'What the fuck. . . ?'

No cultured voice, but a furious drunken bellow. Geoff's words of warning jangled in her head: maniac, rapist, murderer . . . Any second he'd attack her.

'Can't a man get some sleep, for fuck's sake?'

As he struggled up to a sitting position, she could smell the booze on his breath. He might have an empty bottle, smash it into her face . . .

'What the hell are you playing at?'

'I . . . I'm sorry,' she stammered, pushing the food and the bag at him.

'What's this?' he demanded.

'Er, just a few things for . . . for Christmas. And . . . and a coat and . . .'

Frowning in suspicion, he thrust a filthy hand into the basket, pulling out a package wrapped in greaseproof. Clumsily he clawed at the paper, but the wind pounced on it and whipped it away, tumbling the mince pies into his lap. He peered at them, then bit into one greedily. It was demolished in a couple of bites, and he started on the next.

'There's . . . cheese as well, and some bread . . .'

'Who the fuck are you, then – Lady fucking Bountiful?'

She blushed. 'Just, er, well – nobody, really.'

'*Nobody*? Well, fuck off, nobody, and leave me alone.'

She didn't wait to be told a second time but fled back along the path, stumbling and tripping in her haste, and not stopping for breath until she was level with the houseboat. Nervously she looked over her shoulder. He wasn't blundering in pursuit, thank God, or yelling more abuse. Yet she still felt sick and shaky, and despite the cold she was sweating.

She took several slow, deep breaths to calm her thudding heart, concentrating on the reflections in the river: inverted boats, trembling trees, the blurred bulk of a landing-stage. But the water itself was no longer ruffled and choppy, and she realized with surprise that unaccountably the wind had dropped. And towards the east the sky was lightening, the clouds rolling back to reveal a glimmer of stars. Only now did she fully savour the relief of her escape. She could have been left for dead or hideously scarred; instead all she had lost was an old jacket and a basket.

Then all at once came a sound of bells – church bells from St Mary's on the other side of the river. It must be nearly twelve and the bells were summoning the faithful to Midnight Mass. How exuberant they sounded, joyful and triumphant, like the carol. And full of hope as the carillon rang out above the town, announcing the birth of Christ in an ass's stall because there was no room at the inn. And, as she watched, a much brighter star appeared above the river, gilding the oil-black water. She kept her eyes fixed on it, suddenly knowing in her heart that, whatever Geoff might say, next Christmas would be different. In fact she wouldn't even be with him, but somewhere far away, possibly back in her own country, living a new life. It was a flash of revelation – mysterious, inexplicable, but beyond any shadow of doubt.

She continued gazing up at the star, as the cascade of bells rejoiced and exulted around her. It was the man who had brought this to pass; *he* who had ordered the wind to be still, and lit her way with a star. And tomorrow he would be there, keeping up her courage amid the quarrels and complaints – the courage to take flight.

'Thank you,' she whispered. Then she opened her mouth and screamed – not in anger or frustration but in freedom and release, the sound surging up to heaven with the sweet clamour of the bells.

Pay-Back

'Hello, Tina. This is Peggy Wright. You still haven't rung me back. And it's very inconvenient. What I need to know is, are you coming this Sunday or is it Sunday week?'

'Neither,' Judith snapped. Hadn't the wretched woman realized by now that she was ringing the wrong number? Whoever Tina was, she didn't live here, thank God. (It had taken only one disastrous flat-sharing experience to put her off the idea for life.)

Having deleted Peggy Wright, she listened to the other half-dozen messages. Would she phone Susanna, tonight if possible? Was she coming to the Conservation Society dinner next month? Would she mind helping with the Famine Relief collection. . . ?

Yes, actually she would mind. Work was so pressured at the moment, she couldn't fit in a social life, let alone take on more commitments. And the dreadful noise outside the office was like a form of torture. The screech of the electric drills never seemed to stop. Surely it didn't take four weeks to repair a gas pipe?

Here at home it was mercifully quiet, but there was still a backlog of unanswered post and e-mails, piles of unread newspapers cluttering the flat, the laundry basket overflowing . . .

'Relax, Jude!' Tom had warned this afternoon, as the resources meeting disbanded. 'You're heading for a burn-out.' And then he'd saddled her with yet another project, even though he knew she'd been in since seven.

Her cup of cold breakfast coffee stood untouched on the draining-board. She tipped it down the sink, washed up last night's supper things, then opened a tin of tuna and ate it, standing up, from the can. Supper thus dispensed with, she unpacked her briefcase and turned on the computer, to amend the report for tomorrow's presentation

161

(putting the answerphone on mute to forestall interruptions).

After half an hour she had managed only a couple of sentences. Strangely, her lack of concentration seemed to stem from Peggy Wright, whose whiny petulance and martyred tone so resembled her mother's. And thoughts of her mother were totally unconducive to work, provoking the usual churning backwash of rage, resentment and guilt.

In frustration she decided to stop and have a coffee, but on her way to the kitchen she noticed the answerphone was flashing again. Another message from Susanna, no doubt. She turned the sound back on.

'Hello, Tina. This is Peggy, still trying to get in touch. I phoned you twice yesterday and again this morning. Usually you ring straight back. I hope you haven't gone on holiday. You know I like you to tell me if you're going to be away . . .'

I'm not bloody Tina and I'm not on bloody holiday, Judith muttered through clenched teeth.

'Can you ring me the minute you get this, and tell me when to expect you. You see, Ray's promised to bring some plants over so that you can put them in for me, and if it's not this Sunday he'll . . .'

She already knew about the plants. Ray and his dratted begonias had featured in yesterday's messages, as had Peggy's worsening asthma. Uncanny, the similarity to her mother – the repetitive demands, the self-pitying sighs of exhaustion, as if she were on the verge of nervous collapse.

'Ray's bought these lovely begonias. And some marigolds and lobelia. And pansies, he said – mixed colours. And three dozen dwarf zinnias. But if you don't intend to come, Tina, they'll all shrivel up and die. Ray can't put them in. His leg's playing up again. So the least you can do is pick up the phone and . . .'

She wrenched the receiver from its cradle and dialled 1471. Peggy Wright could go to hell – or find herself a jobbing gardener.

'We do not have the caller's number to return the call.'

With a curse she resumed work on her report, although she couldn't seem to concentrate any better than before. Did other people hate their mothers, even after they were dead? Or was she a vile, unnatural daughter who deserved to be punished for such sentiments? At various times during childhood and adolescence, she had conjured up alternative mothers: a sweet, easy-going mother, who praised rather

162

than criticized (and never, ever sighed); a strong, self-sufficient mother, for whom a daughter was more than a book-end to prevent her falling flat; an intelligent mother, who wouldn't be a public embarrassment; a loving, sexy mother who didn't drive her husbands away; a young and pretty mother, a fertile mother who could produce more than one child – siblings to share the burden.

She switched the computer off. No point trying to work. Better to go to bed, set the alarm for five and have another crack at the report first thing tomorrow.

'Brilliant presentation, Jude!' Tom grinned. 'We're in with a chance now, thanks to all your hard work.'

She gave a self-deprecating shrug, although Tom wasn't one to use words like brilliant lightly.

'In fact, why not push off early, for a change? You've been putting in such long hours I've sometimes wondered why you don't camp out here permanently and be done with it.'

She laughed. 'OK. I just need to get the final figures on this spreadsheet.'

It was 6.30 when she finally left the office, but the evening was still surprisingly warm – close and muggy, with a hint of thunder in the air. On the way home she stopped to buy some steak and strawberries – her first proper meal in weeks. If the weather held, she'd have it on the balcony with a celebratory glass of wine.

But as she let herself into the flat, she heard a familiar voice.

'. . . you're messing Ray about, Tina. He likes to go fishing Sundays, and until he knows when you're coming, he can't make any plans. And I'll have you know I've paid him for those plants, so if you're not coming, I'll have wasted all that money. I don't know what you're playing at, but . . .'

She dumped her things on the sofa and snatched up the receiver. 'Now listen to me, Mrs Wright . . .'

'Who's that?' The voice was startled now, defensive.

'It's no concern of yours, Mrs Wright. But I've been wanting to speak to you—'

'Miss Wright if you don't mind. And where's Tina, I'd like to know.'

'I'm afraid she's—'

'Can you get her for me, please?'

163

'She's not here. As I was about to tell you when you so rudely interrupted . . . I'm sorry but it *was* rude . . . No, I'm not expecting her back soon. But she left a message for you. She's not coming this Sunday, or the next, for that matter. And she won't be putting your plants in – ever . . . No, wait, there's more. She says she's not your unpaid maid of all work, so can you just stop pestering her and stand on your own two feet for a change. And it's no good saying you're ill. Lots of people are ill – some a damned sight worse than you, but they don't just fall apart and expect somebody else to pick up the pieces . . . Look, if you keep shouting down the phone, I can't give you the rest of the message . . . It doesn't sound like Tina? Well, I'm sorry – those were her exact words. I wrote them down so I'd remember . . . Hang on – there's one last thing. She said if you hadn't driven away three perfectly good husbands, you might still have someone around now to give you a hand. Goodbye.'

She slammed the phone down and sank trembling into a chair. Whatever had she done? Mothers were always right; daughters always wrong. Never in her life had she so much as raised her voice to her mother, let alone been so unforgivably rude. All her pleasure at today's success was draining away like water down the plughole. And in any case, what did brilliant presentations matter? Her mother disapproved of working women; she had been 'cheated of a son-in-law and grandchildren' by her only daughter's selfishness.

The steak and strawberries, now bleeding through their bags on to the sofa, seemed to compound the accusation. It was selfish to buy little treats with no intention of sharing them, and to avoid compromise and confrontation by living on one's own. She dumped the food in the bin, grabbed her bag and fled from the flat. The phone might ring again at any moment. Like a murderer she expected retribution – punishment for matricide.

She returned well after midnight, having driven aimless miles. Yet even now, sleep wouldn't come. Every time she closed her eyes, vivid images slipped in under her eyelids: her mother slumped in a chair in an old dressing-gown and flip-flops, unable to get dressed; her mother with livid bruises on her arms, pretending she'd banged into a door; her mother fighting for breath in the throes of an asthma attack . . .

Finally abandoning all attempts at sleep, she got up and had a shower, then set about her long-postponed jobs – letters, e-mails, laundry, clearing up.

As she put clean sheets on the bed, she recalled wash-days in her childhood: holey sheets and pillow-cases draped over the radiator; damp vests and towels steaming in front of the gas fire. There was no room in the bedsit for a washing-machine (even if they could have afforded one), and without a garden, nowhere to put a clothes-line. As a child she never asked friends home. The other girls had proper houses, and proper fathers, and their mothers wore nice clothes and served roast beef and apple pie for Sunday lunch, not tinned spaghetti hoops. Still, if nothing else, those joyless years had taught her self-sufficiency. In adult life she was never lonely, only grateful to be solvent and in charge of her own fate.

By eight o'clock the whole flat was clean and tidy and she'd caught up with her correspondence at last. She rewarded herself with a quick bowl of cornflakes before driving to the garden centre. The array of flowers and shrubs was daunting, but thanks to Ray she knew exactly what to ask for, and if she could just find a helpful assistant . . .

In less than an hour she was home again, the boot of the car packed with trays of plants. Now all she needed was the address.

The local phone directory contained five full pages of Wrights. Well, at least she could narrow it down to Ps and Ms. No Peggy was actually listed, and only one Margaret, whom she rang immediately – a shy, soft-spoken lady with a slight Scots burr. Next she tried the first of the Ms – a Michael Wright, who was annoyed at being disturbed so early on a Saturday. There was no reply from the second, and the third and fourth were also men. After a dozen more failures she was beginning to lose hope. The plants were ready and waiting in the car, and as Peggy had pointed out, they wouldn't survive for long in the heat. It was already the high seventies – unusual for mid-May.

Of course, Peggy might just be a nickname or short for something else. The only solution was to work through every single Wright, regardless of initials. Which was not only time-consuming but thoroughly disagreeable, since most of the responses were bad-tempered or suspicious. And then halfway down the second page it struck her that Peggy might not be local at all – she could have been calling from anywhere – and it was hardly feasible to contact every Wright in the country.

In despair, she replaced the directory, and then suddenly the phone rang. Oh God! she thought – it's *her*. Or Ray, perhaps, dragooned into ringing on her behalf. Best not to pick it up. Except if she wanted to make amends, she must have an address . . .

'Yes, hello? . . . Oh, *Susanna*! Sorry – I was expecting someone else . . . Yes, I know it's been engaged for hours . . . No, I'm awfully sorry, not this week. I'm up to my eyes . . . Look, can I ring you back later?'

As if spurred into action by Susanna's voice, she went down to the car again and after a quick inspection of the plants, got in and started the engine. At the end of the road she turned left and left again, then accelerated up the hill towards the motorway, prepared for a long, hot drive.

She carried the plants in relays, one tray at a time, making a final trip for the fork and trowel and the Growmore. The place appeared to be deserted, probably due to the stifling heat. On a day like this sensible people stayed indoors.

Kneeling on the rough grass, she was overcome with a deep sense of shame. The grave was choked with impertinent weeds: stinging nettles, dock leaves, meandering snares of convolvulus. Even its position at the back end of the cemetery, near the dustbins and the rubbish dump, seemed an added affront. She hadn't noticed at the time of the burial, being too consumed with guilt: her mother had died alone while she, the callous daughter, attended an international marketing conference in Amsterdam.

The adjoining graves gave her further cause for shame. The one to the left was bordered with a neat little box hedge, enclosing a trio of rosebushes in copious pink bloom, while on the right stood a vase of madonna lilies, dewy fresh. In death, as in life, her mother was the odd one out, the poor relation, lowering the tone. And the inscription on her headstone, limited to name and dates, seemed paltry in comparison with the elaborate tributes of its neighbours: 'Deeply loved and sorely missed', 'A most beloved husband', 'A woman of great courage' . . .

Yet her mother *had* been courageous, surviving against the odds – defenceless and alone, asthmatic, often depressed. And was she really to blame? After all, she'd had no education, no decent start in life, no mother of her own, for heaven's sake. And with such limited resources, it was hardly surprising that she had stumbled through a

series of bad relationships – men who had abused and then abandoned her.

Seizing the nettles with her bare hands, she wrenched them out and
flung them on the rubbish tip. 'Cruel aggressive shits!' she shouted.
'Hitting a woman when she's down.' Then she attacked the convolvulus, her puny fork buckling in the hard, unyielding ground. She persevered, although the roots kept snapping, and finally she set about the
dock leaves, with a strength fuelled by searing rage. 'She's rid of you
at last, you bullies! Now she's free to breathe.'

Her nettle-stung hands had come up in itchy bumps, but she
ignored the pain and continued jabbing with her fork, determined to
create here for her mother the only garden she had ever had. After
grubbing out the remaining weeds and loosening the stubborn soil,
she dug a series of small holes around the grave. Then tenderly she
slipped the plants in – begonias, lobelia, zinnias, pansies, marigolds –
firming the earth around each one and sprinkling it with fertilizer.
Sitting back on her haunches, she appraised the overall effect. Yes, the
discreet pink of the begonias was well balanced by the orange shout
of the marigolds, and the pansies' smiling faces contrasted in their
turn with the fat cushions of dwarf zinnias. But the poor things were
all drooping in the heat. She remembered seeing a cluster of watering
cans on her way from the car, so she went to fetch one and gave the
plants a good soaking. On returning the can, she spotted a pile of
broken flower-pots, and picked out a handful of shards to make an
edging round the grave. It was a credit to its neighbours now –
spruced up and colourful. There were masses of plants left over,
though, and three-quarters of a bag of Growmore.

Wiping the sweat from her forehead, she surveyed the stretch of
ground between the grave and the rubbish dump. If she cleared that
too and planted it with flowers, her mother would have a more exten-
sive garden to look out on – rather different from the bare brick wall
that had been their only view from the bedsit.

But it would be punishing labour without a proper spade and fork.
The grass was coarse and tangled, and had been colonized by cow
parsley and defiant-looking thistles. And in any case, planting flowers
on open ground might well be forbidden. There was no one to ask,
though; no one in sight at all except an old man sitting on a bench,
apparently lost in thought. Might it not be better to call a halt and
embark on the long trek home? If she left straight away she could just

167

about fit in her usual Saturday jobs – shopping, ironing, catching up with phone-calls.

No, the jobs could wait. She owed it to her mother to make her final resting-place as congenial as possible. A few hours' gardening, however strenuous, was small recompense for the years of hardship bringing up a child with very little money and no emotional support.

Armed with the fork again, she began her onslaught, hacking at the cow parsley, slashing down the thistles. This was her tribute – not carved in Gothic script on marble, but hewn with smarting hands in stony soil. Soon her shirt was sticking to her back and her knees were covered in grazes, but sweat and toil were symbols of devotion. Broken fingernails signified 'Deeply loved', grubby hands meant 'Sorely missed', and grazed knees were bent in honour of 'A woman of great courage'.

The sun beat down, burning her neck and shoulders, but she persevered until every weed and flint had been prised out.

Only then did she allow herself a break, standing up and stretching to ease her aching muscles, before she made a start on the planting. She grouped the remaining flowers in little clumps of colour – orange, scarlet, purple, pink and blue – fanning out in a wide arc. Her knees were raw and her skin was sore and reddened, but now at least the hardest part was done. On future visits she would only have to tidy up and water, until the autumn, of course. Then (with more advice from the garden centre) she would replace these plants with new ones, evergreens perhaps. It would all take time – but time would no longer be a problem, because she was going to give in her notice. The decision was startling, even shocking, yet it suddenly seemed the obvious thing to do. She hadn't realized till today how oppressive and thankless her job was. It had stopped her thinking – except about work – stopped her living, for God's sake; a form of slavery, consuming her heart and soul. (It even intruded into her dreams, where she was struggling with impossible deadlines, or locked in ghostly offices at meetings doomed to drone on for all eternity.) She and her mother were at opposite extremes; her mother a drifter, she a workaholic. Yet neither had found joy or satisfaction.

Now, though, she had been shown a truth: it was within her power to break the chains. Purposefully she walked over to a tree and lay down on the grass. The cemetery was fringed with trees, but she simply hadn't seen them. Or perhaps they had materialized only at this precise moment because, for once, she was aware of something beyond a computer screen or balance sheet. Like a blind person with sight restored, she feasted her eyes on the lush sheen of dappled leaves. How could she not have noticed so jubilant a green, or the way the branches grew, dividing and dividing into a tracery of twigs? And the sky – had she ever really looked at it before? Certainly not long enough to register its nuances of blue or white or grey. Yet gazing up at that dazzling vastness could occupy a lifetime. The clouds were gently expanding, like giant celestial soufflés, and their languid motion seemed to underline the folly of her own stress-filled existence. If clouds could idle their days away, so could she.

Birds twittered in the branches, hailing the start of summer. They must have been singing all her life, but she'd been too busy to listen. Were they thrushes? Blackbirds? Robins? She had no idea. Birds, like clouds and gardens, were unfamiliar territory. But that could change. It *would* change.

She closed her eyes. The tree's green embrace was deliciously refreshing. And time was self-renewing, like the birdsong, making moment after moment a glorious perpetuity.

'Rest in peace,' she whispered to her mother.

'Rest in peace,' she repeated, to herself.

Ex

'Mum?'

'Oh, hello, darling! How nice to—'

'Mum, listen – we've changed our minds.'

'Again?'

'Yes.' An embarrassed laugh. 'We've decided to do things properly – you know, a white wedding, with both families there.'

Beth was suddenly floundering in acres of white tulle, choking on mouthfuls of confetti. 'I . . . I thought you said Mark's parents weren't on speaking terms?'

'No, they're not, but that's the point. He thinks it's a good way of bringing them together, and . . .' – a pause – 'you and Dad too.'

The tulle frayed to rags; the wedding cake collapsed into a debris of dark crumbs. 'Fiona, your father won't come over. You know what he's like. And anyway, he swore he'd never make that flight again.'

'He's *here*, Mum.'

Involuntarily she tensed, as if at any moment he might saunter into the hall. 'What do you mean, "here"?'

'London. He's left his job and sold the place in Adelaide, and bought a flat in Belsize Park.'

As ten thousand miles shrank to five, Beth felt physically besieged. Robert's deep, commanding voice was virtually within earshot now. 'But . . . but why didn't you tell me?'

'I didn't know. Well, not until last week. He phoned me out of the blue and said he was in England. I nearly died of shock! Anyway, I told him about Mark and the wedding and everything, and he invited us both over.'

'You mean you've . . . seen him?' Awful to be jealous. Any decent mother would want her daughter to re-establish contact.

'Yes. And Mum, I know you'll find this hard, but he's . . . he's married again. In fact that's why he came over. The new wife didn't fancy staying in Australia. Mum . . . Are you OK?'

With infinite care, she untwisted the kinked phone-cord, trying to focus on her breathing.

'She's nice, Mum – honestly. And really good for Dad. He's much calmer now, and less scratchy and . . .'

Stop – don't say any more.

Too late. The new wife had already burst into the flat – no, several self-contradictory wives: cool yet sultry, slender yet voluptuous, but all impossibly pretty, impossibly young. 'What's her name?'

'Juliet.'

Well, naturally. Romeo and Juliet. Not a soppy name like Beth. Beths got dumped.

'In fact it was her who gave us the idea. She said it seemed a shame to have such a low-key wedding, and if we wanted to splash out a bit, she and Dad would be happy to chip in. Then we got talking about my dress, and Dad said if he was going to lead me down the aisle he didn't want me disgracing him in some old cast-off from a charity shop.'

No, of course, nothing less than a designer dress would do for Robert's daughter. A pity, though, he hadn't shown such generosity while she was growing up. These last twenty years he had contributed practically nothing except the odd unsuitable present – a pink satin party frock, when Fiona lived and died in jeans, a diamond-studded child-size watch, which they'd been forced to sell to keep them in food and clothes. 'And . . . and you *want* him to lead you down the aisle?'

'Oh, yes! I mean, obviously it wasn't feasible before. But now . . .'

Typical of Robert to absent himself from his daughter's life, conveniently missing the toddler tantrums, chickenpox, school runs and teenage angst, only to swan in for the wedding.

'And Mum, there's something else. I've a favour to ask. Promise you'll say yes.'

'Depends what it is.'

'Well, you won't like it much, I know. But Mark and I want you to go and see Dad – to make your peace and meet Juliet and everything – before October the third. So that on the day no one's picking quarrels, or trying to settle old scores.'

172

'Except Mark's parents, you mean.'

'No, we're asking them to do the same. It is our big day, after all. I had a chat with Juliet about it, and she said she'd phone and invite you for a meal.'

'I can't wait.'

'Oh, Mum, *please*. Say you'll go, and be nice, and make an effort.'

She hesitated only long enough to kick Juliet in the teeth – perfect white film-star teeth, gleaming in a sensuous mouth. 'OK,' she said. 'I promise.'

'Ah, Beth! Come in!'

Stiff as an automaton she stepped into the hall, stammering out a greeting like an abashed and tongue-tied child. Astounding that after all this time Robert had such power to arouse her – to lust, resentment, trepidation, fury. His hair was still arrogantly black. Surely it wasn't dyed? Or did his masterful control extend even to his physical attributes and his hair dared not defy him by turning grey?

'How are you?'

'Pretty well.' She had forgotten just how tall he was, so that she was forced to look up at him if she wanted to see his eyes (molasses-dark, but wary now, as if unsure of her reaction). His deep tan was a shock; the years of unstinting sun must have permanently darkened his skin. There was no trace of an Australian accent, though, she noted with surprise.

'It's been . . . quite some time,' he murmured, deliberately avoiding her gaze.

'Yes.' Nineteen and three-quarter years. The few divorcees she knew saw their exes on a regular basis – or at least their children did. The court laid down visiting rights and drew up maintenance orders, but Robert, of course, was above the law.

'Can I take your coat?'

Unbelievable – such banalities from a man who'd once made passionate love to her. It would be better if he didn't talk at all. She needed silence to drink him in, see how he had changed. His clothes were less conventional than in her day; more stylish altogether. Perhaps Juliet had chosen the soft grey moleskin trousers and that expensive-looking suede jerkin the colour of wet sand. And was it her place rather than his? He didn't seem quite at home in this flamboyantly bright flat, over-stuffed with plants and pictures.

173

Somehow they'd reached the sitting-room, although she was amazed her legs still functioned. He had affected every system of her body: digestion, muscles, heart.

'Do sit down.'

She sat. The paintings on the walls blazed and flared around her – vibrant abstracts in brilliant reds and yellows. 'I . . . I don't remember you being interested in art?'

He laughed. 'That's Juliet's work. She's a painter.'

Envy gnawed. Not only beautiful, talented too.

'She won't be long, by the way. Her gallery phoned just as you arrived. They've offered her a new show in the spring, so there's lots to organize.'

Should she say congratulations? No – Juliet could go to hell. Besides, these few moments alone with Robert might be her only chance of asking him the questions that had troubled her for years: what exactly had gone wrong in their marriage and why he had walked out. Yet she continued to sit in silence, appalled at the gulf between them when once they'd been so intimate. She had met Robert as a boy of eighteen; seen him in the most vulnerable states – sick, drunk, weeping, naked – but now he was wearing a shield and breastplate impossible to pierce.

'I hear you're working at Westlakes. Fiona said you've been promoted.'

'Yes,' she said impassively. A tin-pot job in a leisure centre could hardly compare with the life of an artist. 'At least it keeps me off the streets,' she added, with a forced laugh.

He cleared his throat as if about to say something else, then appeared to think better of it. She noticed that his fists were clenched and wondered what *he* was feeling – apprehension, guilt, regret, maybe even a grudging approval? She had spent enough time on her appearance, for heaven's sake, although she wasn't proud of the fact. Any self-respecting woman wouldn't give a damn about an errant ex-husband's opinion.

'Ah, here she is now.'

The door opened and in walked a tall, solid, untidy-looking woman, face devoid of make-up, mid-brown hair escaping from its chignon. She wasn't young – fortyish – nor particularly attractive. Her attire, though, was unusual and certainly artistic: a long, flow-ing, silky caftan thing in shades of umber and burnt orange, and chunky amber beads the size of golfballs.

Rising to her feet, Beth arranged her features in the semblance of a smile. But before she knew it, Juliet had advanced on her and clasped her in a hug. She stood ramrod-stiff, pressed painfully against the beads. Why the hell was this woman embracing her?

'It's so good to meet you,' Juliet said, releasing her at last.

'Yes. Well . . . er, thank you for inviting me.'

'It's a pleasure. Besides, I fell in love with your gorgeous daughter. She's such a poppet, isn't she?'

The ingratiation was sickening. Why not stop pretending and admit they loathed each other's guts?

'Beth, what can I get you to drink?' Robert was lining up various bottles on the sideboard. 'Gin, Scotch, sherry, vodka . . .? Or there's wine if you prefer.'

'Yes, wine, please.' Spirits could be lethal, and for Fiona's sake she was determined to stay in control. 'A glass of white would be lovely.' Again, the formality seemed grotesque. *Love* me, her inner voice was pleading. Hold me, kiss me, tell me it was all a terrible mistake.

As he handed her the glass, she noticed the dark hairs on his wrist, and instantly pictured the hair on his body: coarse crinkly whorls on his chest, soft dark fuzz on his back, the black exuberance of his pubic hair – all forbidden territory now, barred to her touch for ever.

Juliet flopped into a chair, the caftan straining over her hips. What on earth did Robert see in her? She definitely wasn't his type, neither submissive nor quiet. Her voice was as loud as his, and she was still babbling on about 'darling Fiona' and 'adorable Mark'. If he had settled for a less than stunning new wife, either he was losing his powers (unlikely – he still gave off a disturbing sexual charge) or Juliet herself was dynamite in bed.

She took a gulp of wine, reliving his first kiss. He had cupped her face in his hands and looked at her intently, as if he were seeking her very essence in the blue depths of her eyes. Then, with a gently exploring finger, he had traced the outline of her lips, running the same finger along the inside of her teeth, before giving her a series of teasing little bites. And those were just the preliminaries . . . The full explosion of his mouth had sent shock-waves through her body, right down to her feet. 'I . . . I'm sorry, Juliet – what did you say?'

'We thought we'd take Fiona to di Monzi's – you know, for her dress.'

'We' hurt. She and Robert had once been 'we'. Anyway, surely it was a mother's prerogative to help choose her daughter's wedding dress. (Not that she and Fiona would have gone anywhere near di Monzi's, where you'd probably pay £30 just for a pair of tights.) 'Don't you think it's rather extravagant to spend such a lot on a dress she'll never wear again? I mean, they need so many other things, like furniture and sheets and—'

'Oh, Beth, come on! Where's your romantic streak? She's just got to have the dress of her dreams.'

Which is what *you* had, I suppose, Beth thought, seething at the vision of this graceless, broad-beamed woman poncing about in ivory satin with a tiara and a sweeping train. There were no wedding photos around, thank God – no photos of any kind. Perhaps they'd been tactful enough to remove them. It was surprising, really, that Robert hadn't remarried years before. For close on two decades she had dreaded the prospect of him exchanging vows with some malleable nymphet.

'And we wondered about Hamilton House for the reception. The grounds are absolutely fantastic.'

'Oh, really?' Juliet had met Fiona precisely once, yet was now dictating the arrangements. Maybe *she* should simply opt out, spend the wedding day catching up with chores at home and let Juliet assume the role of mother of the bride.

'Anyway, why don't we discuss it over dinner? It's all ready, if you are.'

'I'll . . . just wash my hands.' She needed a moment to compose herself, stem the tide of anger.

'Of course. The loo's along there – second door on the right.'

The first door on the right was half open. She peered in at a huge double bed – flagrant, obscenely smug; saw their naked bodies, thrashing about on the dishevelled satin sheets. First Juliet was on top, then Robert, then they were both kneeling, then lying stomach to back, like spoons. After all these years (and women) he was bound to have learned a host of new techniques – positions she couldn't begin to imagine; refinements she'd never enjoy. Juliet, no doubt, would be a virtuoso, inspiring him with her love of romance, their every encounter throbbing with artistic flair.

'Beth, are you OK?' Robert called.

'Yes . . . coming.' She scuttled back to the sitting-room, her cheeks on fire, beads of perspiration snailing between her breasts.

Juliet led the way into the kitchen, which had a separate dining area with a scrubbed pine table set with orange place-mats. If orange was the colour of happiness then Robert and Juliet must be near-ecstatic. The walls were painted marigold, a set of orange mugs hung on the dresser, and in the corner stood a massive vase of orange paper flowers.

As Robert held the chair for her, she fought an urge to hit him – or thrust her tongue deep inside his mouth. She could already taste the tang of his whisky on her lips, feel the dangerous contours of his teeth. She fixed her eyes on the orange linen napkins, two in wooden napkin-rings, hers neatly folded in a square. Didn't that say it all – that she was just the visitor, soon to be turfed out. Angrily she spread the offending napkin on her lap. It was so pretentious anyway. At home she used a piece of kitchen towel.

Juliet placed a heart-shaped dish of butter on the table and a basket of crusty bread. 'This is home-made, by the way. It's olive and sun-dried tomato – a new recipe I thought I'd try.'

'Lovely,' murmured Beth. Was there no end to the wretched woman's talents? Artist, wedding consultant, sexual athlete and now domestic goddess.

'Robert, could you pour the wine, darling, while I serve the first course?'

Darling . . . Christ, she was going to lose it – scream, sob, rush out of the room.

While he refilled the glasses, Juliet set the plates out. On each sat a perfect circle of fried goat's cheese, melting on to a bed of fresh green leaves. 'I made this too,' she smiled, passing Beth a jar of chutney. 'It's apricot and orange.'

More bloody happiness. Beth took a brimming spoonful. 'You shouldn't have gone to so much trouble.'

'Oh, it isn't any trouble. I love cooking, don't I, Robert?'

He had the grace to look embarrassed, probably remembering *her* meals – sad, rushed affairs, often out of tins. Well, she'd been young and inexperienced then, and trying to juggle a baby and a job. What if *Juliet* were pregnant, she thought with rising panic. The only winning card she held was that she had borne this man a child. He had been there at the birth, lain beside her afterwards cradling his new daughter, intrigued by the contrast between his large, long-

177

fingered hand and Fiona's tiny, dainty one. She remembered her post-birth smile – a never-before-in-her-life smile that embraced the whole ward, the whole world.

He was helping himself to butter from the repellent heart-shaped dish. It was all she could do not to snatch it up and hurl it to the floor.

Behave, she told herself. You love Fiona; she's the one who matters.

She swallowed a mouthful of goat's cheese, its strong, gamey taste perfectly balanced by the sweetness of the chutney. 'Delicious,' she said, aware that jealousy had driven out good manners. She should be asking Juliet about her work, her background, her life before Robert, their plans for the future. Yet the words stuck in her throat, along with the delectable, loathsome bread. The only future she could foresee was later tonight when they had closed the door behind her. They would rush at each other, hungry mouths and bodies meeting, grind her into oblivion – Fiona's scatty mother, who wore clothes from Oxfam and couldn't cook, or fuck . . .

Well, she *wouldn't* leave. She'd stay and stay and stay – all night, and all tomorrow and the next day, and the next, the next, the next . . .

'More bread?' asked Juliet, offering her the basket.

'Thank you.' She took the largest piece. She'd have more of everything, second and third helpings, endless cups of coffee . . . By spinning the meal out for eternity, she would prevent these odious newlyweds from ever making love again.

She woke with a start, to the sound of a siren. Of course – they had come to get her. They would lock her up for life. No hope of mercy. She had shot Robert through the heart.

She'd *had* to do it, to stop him walking Fiona down the aisle. To stop Juliet muscling in and taking over the whole wedding.

The siren shrieked its warning. Shouldn't they be here by now – breaking down the door and charging in, clamping her in handcuffs?

She groped for the bedside lamp and switched it on. No one there. Only a narrow beam of sunlight filtering through the curtains – an accusing finger pointing at the criminal in the bed. The siren-phone was shrilling on and on. She picked up the receiver, croaked a terrified 'Hello?'

'Mum, it's me. What's wrong?'

'N. . .nothing.'

'You sound a bit weird.'

She blinked. Her head was full of dense grey sticky stuff. 'I was asleep. I . . . I think.'

'*Asleep*? It's three o'clock.'

'In the morning?'

'No, you nut! The afternoon.'

It had been three when she'd arrived back from Robert's. And for ages after that she'd sat staring at the wall, before finally gulping down some sleeping pills. 'I . . . I had this ghastly dream . . .' *Was* it a dream? The details were so vivid – her hand shaking as she pulled the trigger, the violent kickback practically knocking her over, the sickening thud as his body fell, Juliet's unearthly screams . . .

'Mum?'

'Yes?'

'Do you want me to come round?'

'No. *No*. Of course not.' Fiona mustn't find out. She would never recover, ever.

'Well, if you're sure you're OK, Mum, I really need to speak to you. It's about the wedding. I know you'll go berserk if we change things yet again, but Mark's parents are being a real pain. Neither of them will come if the other one's there, but we can't invite her without him or him without her . . . so we're thinking of getting married abroad.'

It *wasn't* a dream. She had made the decision last night while driving home, planned it down to the smallest detail – how to get the gun, what excuse she'd give for returning, where she'd hide the—

'I mean just the two of us, with no relatives at all. Mark likes the idea, but I'm worried about you, Mum. It seems so awful not to have you there. Of course we could have a party afterwards, as soon as we get back . . .'

What had happened to the gun, though? And the body? And had no one heard the shot and alerted the police?

Still clutching the phone, she wormed herself out of the duvet, crept to the window and peered up and down the street. Yes, there it was – a patrol car, parked at the far end. They were waiting for her, obviously. As soon as she came out, they'd pounce, brandishing the arrest warrant . . .

'We've found a fantastic deal in Sri Lanka. They lay on everything – marriage licence, registrar, wedding cake, bouquet. And for thirty quid extra, you can even hire an elephant to take you to the ceremony

... *Mum*? Are you listening?'

'Mm.' Her ears strained to hear the faintest sound. They were play-ing cat and mouse with her – it was just a matter of time now.

'Well, what do you think?'

Yes, the car had begun to move. She could see the two figures clearly: the driver dark and swarthy, and a female officer beside him. The car was creeping towards her house, inch by treacherous inch.

'I want you to be honest, Mum. Would you *mind* not being there?'

'No,' she said, 'I wouldn't mind.' Putting the phone down for a moment, she pulled a sweater over her nightshirt, then struggled into her jeans. She would offer no resistance, but simply go along with them. What was done was done – and done with the best of motives: to spare her daughter pain. She picked up the receiver again, listening now for the footsteps on the stairs. 'To tell the truth, Fiona, it would suit me very well. You see, I ... I may not be around in October.'

Bella

'Happy birthday, Nan!' Ronnie leaned over the bed and gave his wife a kiss. 'Your present's downstairs. It was too bulky to bring up.'

Bulky? Could it be a new washing machine? Theirs was ten years old and tended to stick on the spin cycle. (Actually, she'd been hoping for a gold bracelet – the one they'd seen in Samuels window.)

'Come on then!' Ronnie held out her dressing-gown – ancient, too, the pink candlewick nearly worn through at the elbows.

He led the way downstairs, not into the kitchen but towards the sitting-room. 'Shut your eyes,' he ordered, pausing outside the door.

Obediently she held his arm while he shepherded her through.

'OK – now you can look.'

She stared open-mouthed. Bang in the centre of the room was a bird-cage on a metal stand. Inside, a small yellow bird sat trembling on a perch.

'Meet Bella!' Ronnie announced. 'Bella the budgie. I thought she'd be company for you when I'm out.'

A bird – company? To tell the truth, she had never been keen on pets – the mess, the extra work, sometimes even the risk of infection. Only last month, Amanda Thorpe had caught something very nasty from her spaniel.

'Well, aren't you pleased?'

'Y. . .yes, of course. Thank you, Ronnie.'

'I thought you'd like her. It was Pete at work who gave me the idea. He and Nadine have a budgie and they've taught it to speak. It chatters nineteen to the dozen now, and he says there's never a dull moment. Mind you, his is a male and the males are better talkers. Unlike the human species.' Ronnie gave his throaty laugh. 'But I knew you'd prefer a female, somehow. Was I right?'

'Er, yes.' A preference for male or female budgerigars was not a subject she had given much thought. Now a choice of *washing machine*, on the other hand . . .

'The poor thing's a bit nervous at the moment. Only natural, really – she needs time to get used to her surroundings. And I expect she's feeling lonely. At the pet shop she was in a cage with a dozen other birds.'

'Yes, I suppose . . .'

'While I'm at work, maybe you could talk to her, so she gets used to the sound of your voice.'

'But Ronnie, I'm up to my eyes today. I promised to make a batch of sponge cakes for the fête.'

'Take the cage into the kitchen, then.'

'I'm not sure it's very hygienic, is it? And anyway, after that I'd planned to spring-clean upstairs.'

'Can't it wait?'

'Not really.'

'Well, leave the radio on down here. And make sure it's a talking programme – Pete says they like the sound of human voices. Oh, and don't use any aerosol sprays. The fumes are bad for them.'

'But—'

'Goodness, I must get dressed! It's half past seven already. Don't bother cooking breakfast – I'll just have cereal today. The earlier I get in, the earlier I can leave.'

She brightened. 'We're going out tonight, you mean?' Perhaps he'd booked a table at Domingo's, even ordered a birthday cake. She'd get a wish if she blew all the candles out at once. *I wish Ronnie would retire. I wish his mother would move into a nursing home. I wish . . .*

'No, I'm afraid we can't leave Bella alone – not her first evening with us.'

'Oh . . . I see. Well, I'd better cook, as usual, then. What do you fancy?'

'How about steak and kidney pie? And maybe you could do some sort of pudding with the rhubarb. There's a hell of a lot needs picking.'

'And what about Bella? Should I feed her?'

'Don't worry, I've already put some bird-seed in her tray. You could cut up an apple, though, and give it to her mid-morning. I'm sure she'd like that, wouldn't you, my beauty?' And blowing the bird a kiss, he disappeared upstairs.

She pushed a piece of apple through the bars of the cage. The bird shrank into the furthest corner, its eyes glittering with fear. 'It's all right, Bella,' she whispered, 'I won't hurt you.' The poor cowering creature made her feel uncomfortable. It seemed to be watching her all the time, judging her, even. She didn't have Ronnie's sociable nature – he could talk to anyone and everyone, birds and animals included. But she found conversation rather a trial, and was thrown at times by unfamiliar words. 'Exiguous', for example, which she'd heard on the News last night. Or 'heinous', which she couldn't even look up in the dictionary because she wasn't sure how to spell it. And with Ronnie out at his Furniture Restoration class, she had nobody to ask.

'Heinous,' she murmured to Bella. 'Do *you* know what it means?'

No reaction. Perhaps it preferred men's voices. Switching on the radio, she managed to find a discussion programme – a group of earnest scientists debating environmental pollution. But the bird looked more startled than ever and fluttered pathetically around its cage, blundering into the bars. 'Bella, please calm down,' she begged, 'or you'll hurt yourself. The radio's just to keep you company while I'm in the kitchen.'

Another frantic flurry. Well, perhaps global warming wasn't an ideal choice. She re-tuned to the Daily Service, hoping the creature would respond to a little spiritual uplift, even a rousing hymn or two. And if religion didn't do the trick, too bad. She had half-a-dozen sponge cakes to make, as well as a house to clean and rhubarb to pick, and she couldn't spend all day baby-sitting a budgie.

'Hello, dear, I'm home!'

Still in her apron, she hurried out to the hall.

'Well, did you have a nice birthday?' he asked, giving her the usual peck on the cheek. (Ronnie's greetings were invariably brief, as if he had other, more important things on his mind.)

'Yes, thank you. Not too bad.' She hadn't even washed the kitchen floor, let alone begun the cleaning upstairs. The table was unlaid, the rhubarb still uncooked and the sink full of dirty cake tins. But Ronnie wasn't interested in housework – and wasn't listening anyway.

'How's Bella?' he asked, already halfway into the sitting-room.

'Well, I've been trying to keep her amused but she seems a bit . . . unhappy.'

'Ah, there's my girl!' he said in a low, coaxing voice as he tiptoed over to the cage. 'Have you missed your Dadda?'

The bird's response was remarkable. On hearing Ronnie's cooing tones, it instantly perked up, cocking its head to one side and listening, enthralled. With *her* it had just looked frightened or forlorn.

'Who's a pretty girl, then?' Ronnie continued flirtatiously. 'Beautiful, like your name.'

'Did you choose the name?' Nan hung back in the doorway, not wanting to intrude. The bird was now preening itself, as if solely for Ronnie's benefit. They seemed to be in their own private world.

He nodded. 'It suits her, don't you think?'

'Mm.' Her own name didn't suit her at all, with its overtones of 'grandmother' – incongruous when they hadn't any children. She'd been christened Ann, but that was no more glamorous, just the same three letters rearranged.

'And I chose *her* carefully, too. Pete gave me some tips. He said to look for a nice plump chest, strong, straight legs and bright eyes.'

Was that how he'd chosen *her*, she wondered, when they'd first met a lifetime ago? If he'd been on the look-out for a nice plump chest and good legs, he must be sorely disappointed now. Her bosom had shrunk, her legs were no longer strong, and as for her eyes, did he ever notice them behind her glasses?

'Now, my sweet . . .' It was the bird he was addressing as he delved into his briefcase. 'Dadda's bought you some presents.' He drew out a plastic mirror with a little silver bell attached, and a sort of lumpy brown stick. Opening the door of the cage, he fixed both items to the bars. Far from being upset by this intrusion, Bella watched with interest, and was soon studying herself in the mirror and making excited little tweeting noises.

'She's so *quick*,' he said with pride. 'She thinks it's another bird, you see.'

'And what's the brown thing?'

'A honey and millet treat-bar. They love sweet things, Pete says.'

She loved sweet things too, and it was her birthday, after all. If he'd had time to stop at the pet shop, couldn't he have called in at Marshall's and bought her a box of chocolates? Or perhaps a bunch of flowers. He had last bought her flowers eleven years ago, after her hysterectomy – a magnificent bouquet. She had saved the pink satin ribbon and kept it all this time in her underwear drawer, along with the small white card. 'Darling Nan', he had written on the card, and she would never throw away a 'darling'.

'Well, I'd better get on with the meal. I'm afraid I'm a bit behind-hand.'

'Don't worry. Bella and I can be getting to know each other.'

On her way out she stole a glance at the bird, which was now gazing at Ronnie with what could only be described as devotion. It was the same with people – they liked to be around him, whereas her they could take or leave. Even at school she used to dread the times when they were told to get into pairs. She always seemed to be the one left over.

'Do you think you could set the table, dear?' she called.

He didn't hear. He was busy telling Bella what a precious, lovely girl she was.

'Ronnie, it's awfully hot in here with the windows shut.'

'Yes, I know. But if we're going to let Bella out, we must be absolutely sure she's safe. In fact, I'd better draw the curtains, too. We don't want her crashing into the glass.'

'But why are we letting it out? Can't it stay in its cage?'

'It's "her", Nan, not "it". I keep telling you.'

'Well, why can't *she* stay in *her* cage?'

'A change will do her good. And it's the best way to tame them, Pete says. His little Bertram sits on his head and even preens his hair – what little he's got left!' Ronnie's hand went automatically to his own thick silver mane. 'Now, let's see . . . we'd better remove the plants, in case any of them are poisonous. *And* the tea things – we don't want Bella perching on a cup and burning her toes.'

Wearily Nan fetched a tray and took the offending items out to the kitchen. Then, opening the back door, she breathed in a lungful of fresh air. They had planned, pre-Bella, to spend the bank holiday weekend in Scarborough. She tried to imagine the sea breeze on her face, the cool kiss of the waves frothing across her bare feet. But up loomed the familiar DANGER sign, warning of treacherous currents. As a child of three, on holiday, she had very nearly drowned.

Back in the sitting-room, she found Ronnie kneeling in front of the fireplace. 'I thought I'd block this, too. We don't want her disappearing up the chimney. And we must get rid of the ornaments. She could do herself an injury if she knocked one of them over.'

At this rate the house would soon be reduced to a cage itself, containing only a plastic mirror, a seed-dish, a treat-bar and a rope ladder – although a rope ladder might be useful as a means of escape. Perhaps she could go to the coast on her own. Ronnie wouldn't mind (or even notice). He had more than enough to occupy himself over the three-day break – studying the brochures from the Budgerigar Society, giving the bird more speech lessons, and restructuring the garden. He had designed a completely new layout, to turn the whole thing into a food-supply for Bella. He had already sowed canary seed, which would produce succulent fresh green seed-heads in five or six months' time, and he was planning a mammoth planting in the spring – spinach-beet, sweet corn, celery and carrots (all budgie favourites, apparently).

'You must promise me, Nan,' he said, still on his hands and knees, stuffing her best brocaded cushions into the fireplace, 'never, ever to let Bella out of her cage unless I'm here to supervise. There are so many hazards, and the phone might ring or something and distract you, and Bella could escape. And that's the last we'd ever see of her. She'd be totally disoriented, and never find suitable food. In fact, I hate to say it but I doubt if she'd last two minutes in the wild, what with cats and dogs and foxes on the prowl. Even other birds could gang up on her and kill her.'

Why should he imagine she would have any intention of letting Bella out? She was already worried about bird-droppings on the carpet or the furniture. You could hardly put a budgie in a nappy.

Having finally satisfied himself that the fireplace was secure, Ronnie scurried into the kitchen and returned with a couple of tea-towels. 'For the mirror,' he explained. 'So she doesn't get confused and fly into it.' Clambering on to a chair, he fixed the tea-towels in place, then turned to survey the room. 'D'you know, I think I might build her a new cage – a nice big one so she has lots of space to fly around without all this palaver.'

'It seems an awful waste of money, when you've just shelled out for this one.'

'Yes, ninety-seven quid.'

'*How* much?'

'Ninety-six pounds ninety-nine. Cages don't come cheap, you know.'

186

'Ronnie, I can't believe it! Nearly a hundred pounds on a . . . a bird-cage?'

He looked genuinely hurt. 'It was your birthday present, Nan.'

He could have bought her the gold bracelet *and* a new dressing-gown *and* every box of chocolates in the shop.

'I'll build the cage myself, then it won't cost more than the price of the wood and a few metres of wire mesh. And I could fit a sliding tray on the bottom, to make it easy to clean.'

'But you're so busy as it is.'

'Not too busy to make Bella a lovely new home. Isn't that right, my precious?' He put his finger through the bars and tenderly stroked the yellow feathers. 'Now, sugar-plum, I think we're ready for your little fly-around. Let's open your door – that's it. Hop on to my finger, like I taught you yesterday . . . Clever girl! Hold tight – this time I'm going to lift you out of the cage . . . Gently does it . . . Nan, don't make any sudden movements, will you. Whatever happens we mustn't frighten her.'

Nan sat stone-still in her chair, wondering how long the little fly-around might take. She couldn't even read the paper – with the curtains drawn it was too dark to see the print.

'Oh, look, Nan!' Ronnie gave a triumphant smile. Bella had perched on his shoulder. 'Isn't she brilliant?'

'Mm.' The animal magnetism between them certainly didn't extend to her. If she so much as approached the cage, Bella showed signs of distress, although she spent far more time with the creature than he did. Why was it so hostile? She had never raised her voice to it, and spent ages preparing its food: grating carrots, removing pips from grapes, collecting chickweed and groundsel from the common, and washing all the green stuff in several changes of water to get rid of pesticides.

'It's odd, though, Nan – she doesn't seem to want to fly.'

'Well, can't we put it back, then? – sorry, *her*. Then we can go out for a breath of air. We ought to make the most of this sunshine. They've forecast rain for tomorrow.'

'Nan, she's on my *shoulder*,' he said in an excited whisper. 'That's terrific progress. It would be crazy to put her back when she's just beginning to show more trust in us.'

'In you.'

'What did you say?'

'She doesn't trust *me*.'

'She will in time. She probably realises you're a bit nervous of her. Budgies are very sensitive, you know. You need patience, that's all. Actually, now she's out of her cage, I think I'll weigh her. I'm worried she may be getting a little on the fat side. I was reading last week that birds can develop diabetes.'

Nan mopped the perspiration from her forehead. The heat was almost unbearable. 'And how do you propose to weigh a budgerigar?'

'Oh, you just pop them on the kitchen scales.'

She rose to her feet indignantly. 'Ronnie, those scales are for weighing food, not livestock.'

'Shh! Don't raise your voice – you'll frighten her. And there's no problem anyway. I'll line the bowl with a piece of kitchen towel.'

'That's not enough to prevent germs. It might have mites or fleas or something.'

'*She*.'

If he corrected her once more, she was sure she'd scream. Every time he referred to Bella as 'she', the bird became more threatening: a black-eyed beauty with fluffy golden hair – lively, affectionate, amusing and intelligent: all the words he used to describe his new young love.

'Look, if you're going to make such a song and dance, I'll cover the damned scales with clingfilm. In fact, *you'd* better do it. I don't want to scare her off my shoulder.'

She marched into the kitchen. Even here there was no escaping budgerigars. Ronnie had built a special shelf for his growing collection of bird books: *The Complete Cage and Aviary Handbook, Looking After Pet Birds, The World of Budgerigars, Handy Tips for Budgerigar Breeders* . . .

Breeders? Her failure to have children had been a dreadful sadness for them both. After her hysterectomy she had cried for days on end. If the bird produced a brood of chicks, she didn't think she'd be able to bear it – Ronnie acting the proud father, fussing round the cage, showering the 'clever, precious Mum' with praises.

She opened the fridge to take out the cod steaks, only to slam it shut again. Supper tonight would be bread and cheese. Why go to the trouble of cooking for a husband who was besotted with another female?

*

'Yes, I'll take it, please. Is a cheque all right?'

'Certainly, madam. Could you make it out to Felicia Fashions.'

Ninety-six pounds ninety-nine, she wrote – a wicked amount to spend on a dress. But it was a floaty chiffon creation in a glorious shade of yellow, and the fact that it was exactly the same price as the bird-cage was surely not insignificant.

Tonight, things were going to change. Ronnie had made a good start by actually remembering their wedding anniversary (and the correct number – forty-two years) and had even booked a table at Domingo's. And she was determined to be a credit to him, with a new dress and a new hairstyle. Since he was attracted to fluffy blondes, she had decided to go along with it, and had spent the morning having a perm and highlights. It was up to her, she realized now, to try to reawaken his interest rather than just sitting back and letting Bella reign supreme.

As soon as she got home she went upstairs to change (first shutting the sitting-room door to muffle the cheepings and twitterings). Then she sat for a good hour at the mirror, applying her new make-up. She had let the girl at Hammonds advise her – a light-reflecting foundation to give radiance to the skin, a hint of blusher, a subtle pink-toned lipstick and beige gloss on the eyelids. As the girl had said, when you reached a certain age, you had to give nature a helping hand.

At seven o'clock precisely she heard Ronnie's key in the door. Another good sign – he was dead on time.

'Happy anniversary, darling! Wow, you do look nice! What a gorgeous dress! And your hair – it's different.'

'Do you like it?' she asked anxiously.

'I love it. It's not our *golden* wedding, is it?' He laughed at his own joke. 'No, honestly, the colour really suits you.'

She wanted to hug herself with pleasure. 'I'd like to get off fairly soon, darling, if that's all right?'

'Yes, fine. I'll just have a quick wash and brush-up. And say hello to Bella, of course. How is she?' He bounded into the sitting-room. 'Dadda's home, my treasure. Are you going to give me a kiss and—?' He broke off. 'Oh, my God!'

'What's the matter?'

'Her eyes . . . *look* – they're inflamed. The left one's terribly red. Surely you noticed, Nan?'

'I . . . I haven't been here much today.'

'But you must have seen it when you gave her lunch?'

'I, er, didn't give her lunch.'

'What d'you mean?'

'I told you, Ronnie, I wasn't here. But I left her plenty of food before I went out. And there's still masses in her seed-tray so she can't be exactly starving.'

'But don't you see, that's a bad sign. If she's off her food she may be running a temperature. I'd better phone the vet.'

'They won't be there at this hour.'

'Yes, they will. Thursday's their late night.'

'But what about our dinner?'

'Nan, surely you wouldn't be so callous as to leave a poor sick bird on its own while we go out and pig ourselves? . . . Hello? This is Mr Simpson, 7 Hogarth Road. It's an emergency . . . A budgie – still very young . . . It's difficult to say, but I'd guess an eye infection. Could you fit us in if we came over right away? . . . You could. Thank God. We'll be with you in ten minutes.'

'Bel-la, Bel-la, Bel-la, Bel-la, Bel-la, Bel-lissi-ma.'

Nan's knitting needles came to an exasperated halt. If only Ronnie would accept that the bird *wasn't* going to learn its name, however many thousands of times he repeated it . . . Silence was now a luxury that could only be enjoyed at night, when Bella's continual cheepings stopped, and the tinkling of those stupid little bells. It had amassed more toys than the most pampered child in the land, and as for the new cage, it dominated the room, spilling seed-husks, grit and feathers on to the carpet. Actually it was a wonder Ronnie didn't dispense with the cage altogether. The bird spent so much time perched on his head or hand or lap or shoulder, he might as well go the whole hog and take it to bed with him. She could sleep in the spare room – or the cage.

'All right, sweetheart, lesson over! Time for your bath.'

As he went to fill the spray-bottle she had a sudden vision of him and Bella sharing a bubble bath, Bella's 'plump chest' and 'strong straight legs' nestling up to his naked limbs. Abruptly she took up her knitting again, clicking the needles with unnecessary force. Her wishes had all come true, alas. Ronnie had retired, his mother was safely installed in a nursing home and he had given up his evening classes, yet she had less of his attention than ever. He had become obsessed with entering Bella for every local show, and would drive all over the county in a quest to win rosettes. She was not included. And holidays were out of the question, since he refused to leave his precious bird with anyone, for fear it might fall ill. (The eye infection had shaken him, despite the fact that it had cleared up overnight.) He wouldn't even trust Pete and Nadine to look after Bella properly – they were bound to favour Bertram, he said, and his poor darling would feel left out. Besides, there wasn't a lot of money to spare, what with pet insurance, vet's bills and his mounting petrol consumption.

'Don't make a mess of the sink,' she called, knowing she was wasting her breath. Ronnie and Bella in tandem made a mess of everything. Anyway he couldn't hear – he was crooning his usual endearments: honey-baby, cherub, sweetling, angel, jewel. Not in forty-two years had he ever used such terms to *her*.

Eventually he returned with a damp, self-satisfied Bella snuggled into the crook of his arm.

'If you put her back in her cage, perhaps we could have lunch – or should I say tea? It's nearly three o'clock.'

'Oh, didn't I tell you, Nan? – I'm going out.'

'No, you didn't tell me. In fact you asked if we could have shepherd's pie. Which I've made.'

'I'm sorry, dear, honestly. Ted rang half an hour ago and invited me to see his new aviary.'

'Well, I'll just have to save it for supper. But it won't be as nice. It's overcooked as it is.'

'I'm terribly sorry but I'm out this evening, too. Michael Murray's giving a talk at the Budgie Club and I really don't want to miss it. It's about budgerigars' prehistoric ancestors. Apparently they've discovered some fossils in Australia that date back four million years. Amazing, isn't it? And Michael's absolutely brilliant – what he doesn't know about budgie history isn't worth knowing.'

She watched, unspeaking, as her husband went through the elaborate procedure of putting the bird back in its cage, softly caressing its neck and chest, and bestowing an impassioned kiss on its head before he closed the door.

'You'll have Bella for company, Nan. In fact, you might try giving her another lesson. The more we repeat her name, the more likely she is to get the idea, then one of these days she'll surprise us and suddenly say it herself.'

In silence she consulted her knitting pattern – another sweater for him.

'You seem a bit down, love. Are you OK?'

'Yes, fine.'

'Won't the shepherd's pie keep for tomorrow?'

'I expect so.'

With a sigh she abandoned the knitting and went out to the kitchen to turn the oven off. Even there she could hear him though: 'Goodbye, my darling precious girl! Dadda loves you so so much. Kiss-kiss, kiss-kiss, kiss-kiss . . .'

'Shut *up*,' she muttered under her breath as the bird bashed the plastic ladder with its beak. It seemed to be deliberately annoying her by making as much noise and mess as possible. Earlier, it had ripped a fir-cone to shreds, scattering the debris on the floor. In fact, the carpet was a disgrace, stained from continual bird-droppings and water-marked where she had tried to clean them off. And the wretched creature had even gnawed the edges of the furniture and chewed strips off the wallpaper with its destructive little beak.

At least when Ronnie was out, it stayed put in its cage, although there was still little chance of peace. Its non-stop tweet-tweet-tweet nearly drove her to distraction, not to mention the racket from bells and balls and the string of empty cotton reels. Ronnie talked glibly about it being company, but in fact her life was lonelier than ever. She was a prisoner in a cell, with a stupid little bird for jailer; her every movement subjected to its sharp reproachful gaze. As now, when she had just sat down for five minutes with a cup of tea and a ginger nut.

'OK, OK, I'll get you something too.' She stomped out to the kitchen to cut up a couple of grapes, but when she opened the cage to put them in the food-pot, the bird gave her a vicious nip. She slammed the door shut again and sat nursing her injured finger. Bella had bitten her yesterday, too, and the day before. She hadn't said a word to Ronnie but she knew the reason – pure jealousy. Bella might monopolize his attention for hours of every day, but *she* was still his wife. She shared his bed, wore his ring, had seen him age from a lanky, dark-haired lad to a solid, greying sixty-six-year-old. And most important of all, they had sworn solemn marriage vows – for richer, for poorer, for better, for worse – whereas Bella was just an interloper who, in the end, could only do him harm. Already she was concerned about his health. He spent far too long cooped up in the car; he'd lost half a stone, on account of the many meals he'd missed, and yesterday he'd strained his back moving the load of wood he'd bought to build a yet bigger cage. So if she truly cared for him, she must put a stop to this impossible situation before it led to tragedy.

She approached the bird once more. 'Bel-la,' she said, lapsing unconsciously into his singsong tone. 'I'm sorry to have to do this, but it's for Ronnie's sake, and I know how much you love him.'

'Bel-la,' said the bird.

She gasped. Had she dreamt it?

'Bel-la,' it repeated.

She stood, transfixed. Ronnie would be ecstatic. But this victory would make him more determined than ever to teach his lady-love new words. *She* would be ignored while they triumphed through the alphabet together. It might even learn love-talk and start responding directly to Ronnie's 'sweetling', 'treasure' and 'jewel'. She, his lawful wedded wife, would never get a word in, never make herself heard. And as the creature's skill increased, Ronnie was bound to enter it for more and more events. There was no end to the classes and categories – Best Young Bird, Best-Beloved Life Companion, Most Attractive Female, Most Adored . . . She was fit only for the Discarded Wife and Divorcée class. The bird might even outlast her, for heaven's sake. He had told her once they could live ten years or more.

No – any lingering doubts she might have had were now utterly dispelled. She was duty-bound to take action in the name of morality, if nothing else.

She strode into the kitchen and cut up a ripe kiwi fruit (Bella's all-time favourite), then returning to the sitting-room, she opened the windows as wide as they would go. The bird's black eyes watched inquisitively as she laid a tempting trail of kiwi slices along the back of the sofa, from there to the top of the bureau, and finally to the windowsill.

'Bella,' she said, her voice cracking with emotion, 'I'd hate you to come to any harm. I pray that you'll be safe from cats and dogs and foxes on the prowl. I hope you'll find some food. Believe me, I want you to survive. But if you stay here any longer, it won't be good for Ronnie. And because we both love him, he has to be our first concern.'

The bird cocked its head to one side. It seemed to understand, thank the Lord, knew what it must do.

'Good luck,' she murmured huskily and, stepping forward, she opened the cage door.

Away-Day

With difficulty, Miss Feltham alighted from the train, negotiating the wide black void between the step and the platform. In her day, the step had been lower, just as the trains had been cleaner and quieter. She had spent most of the journey listening to one-sided conversations. The man opposite had made seven phone-calls between Charing Cross and Ashford. By now, she felt she knew him: his sinus trouble, his mother in Crouch End, his planned trip to Marbella, his dislike of nylon shirts. She smiled as he hurried past her on the platform, but he didn't seem to see her. He was on the phone again.

Emerging from the station, she walked down towards the sea. She couldn't smell it yet, only the reek of frying onions. Perhaps it was foolish to have come on a bank holiday. With her slow, unsteady progress she was a hindrance to other people – young couples walking entwined, practically devouring each other in public; families with push-chairs, or toddlers darting all over the place.

'Hello,' she imagined saying. 'Yes, reasonably well, thank you. Lovely weather, isn't it?'

A little too hot, in truth. The sun smirked at her lisle stockings and chunky cardigan. Still, best to be prepared.

Suddenly she stopped. She could see it now – valiant blue and vast, stretching away, away, to France. (They should never have built the Tunnel. England was an island and she for one was proud of the fact.)

How busy and eager the waves were, pounding in, swishing back, up and back, up and back, all day, all night, all day. No empty hours, no silence.

The promenade was lined with stalls selling ice-cream and souvenirs. One was just a makeshift booth, manned by a tiny, gnarled old fellow dressed in a shiny blazer and a lopsided red bow-tie. Beside him was a hand-crayoned sign: 'I'll guess your age. Price 50p. If I'm wrong, even by a year, you win a prize.' She hesitated. 50p would buy a cup of tea, or pay for the hire of a deck-chair. But people were always saying she looked much younger than her years. It would be nice to win a prize . . .

She joined the queue. There were two young girls, teenagers most probably, although it was so hard to tell these days. They wore skimpy tops that showed their stomachs and peculiar clumpy shoes. Behind them stood a middle-aged couple in matching baseball caps.

'Yes, dead right!' she heard the girls exclaim. 'However did you know?'

'Practice,' smiled the little man. *He* was no spring chicken. Not as old as her, of course – no one was as old as her – but wrinkled like a walnut shell, with bowed shoulders and thinning grey hair.

The middle-aged couple turned away, sour-faced. 'You said I don't look forty-eight, Clive,' the woman snapped.

'How was I to know?' her husband muttered. 'Flaming waste of money, if you ask me.'

Her turn now. She handed over the coins and the wizened little man fixed her with an unwavering stare, as if his eyes could penetrate her skull, her very soul. No man had ever gazed at her like that before, and as time passed – whole minutes, it seemed – she felt a blush suffuse her, spreading even to the soles of her feet. Finally he scribbled something on his notepad and covered it with his thumb. 'And how old *are* you?' he asked.

He was cheating, obviously. Whatever age she told him, he would pretend that's what he'd guessed. 'Ninety-one,' she retorted in a defiant tone.

His eyes widened. 'Good gracious! I was *miles* out.' He removed his thumb from the pad and showed her the figure he had written: seventy-four.

Astounding. Thirteen years gone at a stroke. She was a youngster in her seventies again. She still lived in the cottage; still had all four dogs; still dug the garden, mowed the lawn.

'And here's your prize.' The man ducked below the table top to pick up a small silvery object – a key-ring with a tiny globe attached.

She closed her fingers round it; the whole world in her hand. She had never travelled (impossible with dogs) but now she was abroad at last – a tropical sun blazing down, and a group of dark-skinned men in turbans strolling past.

In a happy daze she set off towards the pier. On the beach, scores of bodies were stretched out on towels, exposing naked flesh. Some of the women had even removed their tops, and lay face-up, revealing their breasts. When *she* was a girl, she'd been encased in layers of clothing: liberty bodice, woollen vest, starched white petticoats, voluminous pink bloomers that came up above the waist and down below the knee. She unbuttoned her cardigan and slowly took it off, smiling with pleasure as warm air caressed her arms.

Postcards, she thought. She must send a sea-view to all her friends. 'Having a lovely time. Wish you were here.' If she was only seventy-four, they would still be at their old addresses, not in coffins in the cemetery. And there would be money in her Post Office account, not yet swallowed up by Eldon Court.

At the pier, she paid her entrance fee, staring down at the cracks between the boards, thrilled to see the long glistening lines of water. Sea beneath her and all around her, rippling and white-flecked. She was on a boat, cruising from tropical island to tropical island, the band playing a romantic waltz, the chef preparing a five-course banquet.

Yes, she could do with something to eat. Before setting off this morning she'd had only a cup of tea and an osborne biscuit. (Breakfast was served later on bank holidays, and sometimes didn't arrive at all.)

'Would you mind if I joined you?' she asked a heavy-jowled man, wearing what appeared to be his vest. It was the only empty seat.

He shook his head, unable to speak with a mouth full of chips. He was eating them from a small white plastic tray, dunking each in ketchup before cramming it into his mouth with barely a pause before the next one.

She was about to order soup and a roll, then changed her mind. 'A portion of chips, please, dear,' she told the waitress. At Eldon Court it was always boiled or mashed.

The waitress returned with an identical tray, piled with luscious fat chips. Excitedly, she prodded one with the plastic fork, spearing the white floury flesh beneath the golden coating. She reached for the ketchup container – a plump red plastic tomato with a nozzle at the top – and squeezed out her initials, two Fs. She had been christened Freda after her father, Frederick, although he had never liked her much.

She bit into a chip, relishing the glorious greasy taste. Glancing up, she caught sight of the blue expanse again, sparkling outside the windows of the café. Where was their next port of call – Miami? Honolulu?

She span out the chips as long as she could. The man had finished eating and was flicking through the *Daily Mirror*. There were bristly dark hairs on the backs of his hands, a tiny clump sprouting on each finger. She was cruising with her gentleman friend. At any moment he would speak to her, suggest they took a stroll on deck.

'Yes, I'd love to,' she fluttered, rising to her feet. (She pocketed the plastic fork as a souvenir – although she would have to hide it in her bedside drawer. Anything you left about was stolen.)

Outside, she feasted on the colours: pink whorls of candyfloss, purple flowers splashed across a man's Hawaiian shirt, gold and scarlet cockerels on the children's roundabout. At Eldon Court everything was beige.

Her nose twitched with a clash of smells: hot doughnuts, shellfish, vinegar. And there was a cacophony of sounds as well: the jaunty carousel music vying with the thudding beat booming from a neon-lit arcade.

She reached the end of the pier and stood gazing out to infinity, watching a blue-sailed yacht tacking in the wind. As a child she had lived in Walsall, where the sea was just a word. But now the world had become a playground with no work, no rules, no Matron. Everyone was carefree – swimming, boating, water-skiing. And looking back towards the town, she could see the lights of a fun-fair. She imagined whooshing down the helter-skelter, shrieking with excitement; soaring in a swingboat higher than the sun.

On the hill beyond were dozens of hotels, their icing-sugar whiteness belying the dirty weekends they had witnessed in the past. She remembered her friend Maisie stealing away for a seaside 'honeymoon' with her young man, Arthur Wainwright. Maisie had bought a Woolworth's ring, which she was careful to display while Arthur booked them in as Mr and Mrs Smith.

She had never had a young man, or a ring; never been plucked from naïve spinsterhood and turned into adventurous Mrs Smith.

Dawdling back along the pier, she came upon a kiosk selling rock. Sticks of every size and colour were arrayed beguilingly, each imprinted with tiny red letters that lasted until the final lick. If rock had different names inside – not Brighton or Bournemouth or Blackpool, but 'youth' and 'health' and 'friendship' – then might those things last longer?

She ambled on to the next kiosk and studied the pictures of the ice-creams: Mivvis, Magnums, Oyster Shells, Cornettos. In her day it had been plain vanilla and you ate it at the table from a dish.

'Yes, can I help you, love?'

'A tutti frutti, please.' She liked the name – exotic again – and the intriguing little fruity pieces nestling in the rich smoothness of the ice-cream. She didn't eat the last inch of the cornet, but wrapped it in her handkerchief and put it in her bag. Another souvenir.

The bag was an encumbrance. Dare she leave it somewhere? Then she could take her shoes and stockings off and paddle in the sea.

She found a ladies' lavatory, gloomy-dark and smelly after the bracing glare outside. Sitting on the toilet seat, she unfastened her suspenders and removed her lace-up shoes. It took some time – even at seventy-four she had arthritis – but it was worth the effort. A wonderful sensation: bare feet on hot sand.

Picking her way through the sun-worshippers, she ventured to the sea's edge. A wavelet frilled across her crooked toes, joltingly cold. A child ran past, splashing her unknowingly. She laughed to feel the water against her legs. Her limbs had been confined so long, they'd gone grey-pale, like grubs, but now they were untrammelled, exposed to light and air. With every step, she lost another decade. Sixty-four; fifty-four; a slip of a thing in her twenties; a little girl of ten. She stooped to pick up a shell, and put it in her pocket. Hidden treasure. And when she found a discarded pail, still serviceable despite its missing handle, it gave her an idea: now she could make sand pies.

Having lowered herself cautiously to a sitting position, she scrabbled up some damp sand with her fingers, packed it into the pail and pressed it down. Her father smiled in approval. 'Clever girl!' he said, as she turned out a perfect pie and placed the shell on top as the finishing touch. 'Is that for Daddy?'

'Yes,' she whispered, feeling his strong arms around her, his cheek rough against her own.

She made another pie, and another; turned out a whole batch. With every one she felt more independent. Now she had food in the larder, money in the bank – and company, it seemed. Half a dozen children had gathered to watch, and were staring at her wonder-ingly.

She closed her eyes. Not that she was tired – you didn't get tired at seventy-four – but a nap would be delightful. Naps were difficult at Eldon Court; someone was always barging in, to give you pills you didn't want.

When she woke, the children had gone. There were fewer people altogether, and the sun was less cocksure. Her back ached and she had cramp in her legs. The holiday was over – time to catch her train.

Reluctantly she hauled herself to her feet and returned to the ladies' toilet, where her bag was still hanging on the hook behind the door. Not bothering to put on her stockings, she wriggled her bare feet into the shoes. The nurses would be cross: her feet were sandy and she'd spilt ice-cream down her dress. Nor had she told them where she was. You weren't supposed to go out on your own, so she had slipped away when nobody was looking. She hated being cooped up in Eldon Gaol.

The promenade seemed longer than before, and the sea had turned from blue to sullen-grey. Her shoes were chafing and her legs felt cold and clammy.

At last she reached the Guess Your Age booth, but the wrinkled old fellow had gone. In his place was a much younger person, although of identical height and build. His skin was smooth, his hair thick and brown, his posture upright, not stooped. Perhaps it was the old man's son; they were uncannily alike in face and feature, and even wearing the same clothes, except that this man's blazer was crisp and new, and his red bow-tie sat smartly to atten-tion. He waved a hand in greeting – a hand unblemished by age-spots.

'So how's my young lady?' he smiled.

For some moments she stood there, dumbfounded, blushing scarlet as his eyes searched the depths of hers again.

'I . . . I'm very well,' she stammered. 'In fact,' she added daringly,

'I've decided to stay – for the night. I'm looking for a hotel and I wonder, could you help?' Still he held her gaze and, thus encouraged, she stepped a little closer. 'Something tells me that your name is Mr . . . Smith.'

Hot Ice-Cream

'Rain, rain, go away. Come again another day . . .'

As a child, Irma had always believed it would go away, if she told it firmly enough. She stared out at the downpour drumming against the windowpane. As a child, she had believed a lot of things. She glanced at her watch – still only noon. Another seven hours before Martin's key turned in the lock and they commiserated with each other about the weather (the wettest September in eleven years, except they had used that statistic already, over breakfast), and exchanged details of their day. She wouldn't include the last half-hour, which she had passed in watching raindrops seep slowly, slowly, through a tiny crack in the window-frame, hover for a few seconds, shivering and swelling, then plop down on to her desk. She mopped up the wet with a sheet of blotting paper – the back-to-front record of her work streaking into blue tears.

There would be more havoc in the garden. Rain was scything petals from the last bedraggled roses and battering Martin's precious white hydrangeas. It had bruised the lupins and flung them horizontal, and was whipping furious circles into every puddle on the path. She envied its energy and sheer determination – just the qualities she needed to meet this evening's deadline.

In defiance of the White-Bearded Computer In The Sky, she poured herself a sherry. The W.B.C. kept a record of all her lapses – the manzanillas, amontillados, kettle-watching, crossword puzzles, doodlings in the margin – and sent a print-out to Martin at the end of every month, like a celestial bank statement, always in the red.

Taking the glass to her desk, she spread her work-sheets out. She was writing a brochure for a local advertising agency, on domestic and

203

industrial fire extinguishers. Not the most enthralling of subjects, but since going freelance she accepted any job available. One week it might be a twelve-blade cylinder lawnmower; the next baby food or foot deodorant. She read back her opening paragraph:

'WHOLE FACTORY GOES UP IN SMOKE! FAMILY OF FOUR WIPED OUT IN HORROR BLAZE! – *How many times have you read headlines like those?*'

Start with a forceful lead-in – that was the idea, to encourage people to read on. '*It could never happen to you . . . or* could *it? There are over 300,000 calls each year to the London Fire Brigade alone, 400,000 to—*'

The doorbell was ringing, but she decided to ignore it. She didn't love Jesus, nor did she want to be interrogated about margarine or detergent. It rang again, louder. Muttering to herself, she marched along the hall. If it was that man selling brushes, he could . . .

It was someone half his size – a child, she assumed at first, from the back view: long red cycling cape, scarlet wellingtons, waist-length hair dripping in dark rat's-tails. But as the figure turned to face her, she realized it was a woman – barely five foot in height, but with a disarming smile and striking grey-green eyes.

'Does Martin still live here?'

'Martin? Yes, but—'

'Thank God! I'm drenched. Can I come in?'

'Well, I'm very busy at the moment. Perhaps you could explain what—?'

'I'd rather explain to Martin. I'm an old friend of his, you see.' The girl edged closer, tossing back a sodden strand of hair. 'You must be the wife. Nice to meet you. I'm Scottie.'

Irma could hardly ignore the damp paw thrust at her. She shook it briefly, keeping her other hand firmly on the door. 'I'm afraid he won't be back till this evening.'

'That's OK. I'll wait.' Scottie ducked under Irma's arm and pushed past her into the hall.

'What the hell d'you think you're doing?' At once she regretted her harsh tone. If this girl did know Martin, she ought at least to be civil. Yet he had never mentioned a Scottie. One would hardly forget a name like that – a dog's name or a nickname – and sounding more male than female. 'Look, I don't want to seem rude, but it really would be better if you came back later on.'

'And face those floods again? No fear!' Scottie was already

wrestling her way out of the voluminous cycling cape, her voice muffled beneath its folds. 'I'm on my bike and it's a real sod in this weather.' Emerging at last, she shook the cape vigorously, showering Irma with raindrops, then tossed it over the hat-stand. She sauntered down the hall, stopping to look at the print of Dürer's *Hare*. 'Nice place you've got here. I like the bunny.' Abruptly she bent over from the waist, so that her sheet of hair hung almost to the floor. Seizing it with both hands, she wrung it out like washing, the resultant trickles of water soaking into the Persian rug. 'Be an angel and lend me a towel.'

Irma fumed into the kitchen. This 'old' friend of Martin's didn't look a day over twenty, with her freckled face and her fraying jeans. Yet there were mature hips beneath the denim, and the two red hearts appliquéd on her sweater were pushed out by the curve of her breasts. She herself went upwards rather than out. As a child she had been tall for her age and gawky, and had prayed to the stern grey God at Sunday School for an Alice-in-Wonderland 'Drink Me' potion to make her petite and inconspicuous. He hadn't heard.

She got out her oldest kitchen towel and took it into the hall, only to discover that Scottie had disappeared. Tracking her down to the sitting-room, she found her ensconced on the sofa, tugging off her boots. Her feet, bare of socks, were small and podgy, with dirty toenails and a plaster on the left heel half-covering a blister. Had Martin seen those feet – so pink and plump and naked? 'How well did you know my husband?' she asked tersely.

'Oh, very well. We were soul-mates, you could say. We shared a cottage in Falmouth and Martin used to paint. You know – water-colours and stuff.'

'*Paint?*' Martin had no time for hobbies.

'Yeah. He was really talented. He made sculptures out of drift-wood, and collages with shells and bits of paper. We worked on a mural together once. I did the bottom part, as far as I could reach, and he did the rest. For the very top he had to use a ladder.'

Irma sank into a chair. She had never seen Martin up a ladder. He was so much an extension of his desk, Angle-poised over his work, absorbed in his writing (or improving or criticizing hers) until he finally clicked off at midnight and straightened out again, in bed.

'And I helped him with a collage called "Spirit of the Sea" that won first prize in a local art show. He said without me it wouldn't have stood a chance because I was the inspiration.'

Irma gripped the arm of her chair. 'It sounds as if you should have married him, if you had so much in common.'

'Well, we did discuss it sometimes. But it was the kids, you see. I've got four – they're still just babies, really – and Marty couldn't cope.'

Marty. Babies. Four. Martin regarded children as messy, unpredictable and a positive encumbrance. Had he only married her on the rebound from a cuddly artist's model with a cottageful of Cornish nappies? She looked again at Scottie. So those voluptuous hips and breasts had worked hard for their living, giving birth, giving suck . . .

Go away, she muttered under her breath. There was work to do, a timetable to follow. She didn't stop until the dot of one o'clock, and then only briefly, for a couple of Ryvitas and a tiny cube of cheese. She broke again at four and drank a cup of (sugarless) tea while preparing Martin's dinner, then back to her desk till six, when she would light the oven and lay the table, ready for his return. Admittedly there were lapses, like this morning, but usually just minor ones, and always redeemed by weekend overtime. Martin would expect to read the completed brochure tonight, so that he could do his customary editing – tone down her adjectives, sharpen her prose-style – but this unforeseen invasion could disrupt the entire day.

Scottie finished drying her hair and unceremoniously dropped the towel on the floor. 'I'd love a coffee if you're making one.'

I'm *not*.

'And a few biscuits would be great. I'm starving! I usually have dinner with the kids about this time, but I've parked them with friends today. Funny – I feel sort of naked without them all in tow.'

Irma trailed back to the kitchen, annoyed with herself as much as Scottie. Why couldn't she tell the girl to get lost? She stood at the window, watching the still merciless rain cascading over the edges of the bird-bath. Yellow leaves were showering from the apple trees, making blight-stains on the sodden lawn. The gutter on the shed had sprung a leak and a fierce retort of water gushed into the seething drain below.

'Bread and cheese would be better still.'

She jumped. Scottie had followed her into the kitchen, making splodgy footprints on the quarry tiles. 'We, er, don't eat bread.'

'Don't eat *bread*? How on earth d'you survive? We must get through fifteen loaves a week.'

Irma kept her back turned. The numbers were mounting. Four children, fifteen loaves, forty sticky fingers. Plastic ducks overflowing the bath, driftwood sculptures on the mantelpiece. Milk, honey, Mother's Pride. 'Martin prefers Ryvita. It's more digestible. Anyway, he has to watch his weight.'

'Marty? He was always as thin as a rake. We used to go out some-times for a six-course Chinese meal and order the most fattening things on the menu – crispy duck and dumplings and sweet and sour pork and spring rolls, and banana fritters for afters, with syrup and ice-cream – and he didn't put on an ounce. I suppose he burns his food up fast. Lucky blighter!'

Irma steadied herself against the window-frame. Martin never ate fritters of any description and had an aversion to Chinese restaurants, disliking both the décor and the food. And if he was still reasonably slim it was because he *worked* at it – as indeed did she. If she weak-ened and bought a bar of chocolate, the W.B.C. had noted every detail before she had taken a single bite.

'OK, Ryvita'll do.' Scottie dragged a stool up to the kitchen table. 'Where's the cheese?'

Irma didn't answer. This uncouth girl had more or less invited herself to lunch, and at only ten past twelve. Well, at least they would stick to the rationing. Martin was right – you had to count the calo-ries and maintain a rigorous control. She doled out two Ryvitas each, then opened the fridge to get the low-fat ricotta.

Scottie jumped up, to investigate. 'Weird cheese! And who's the wine for?'

'Don't touch that! We're expecting guests tomorrow.'

'Oh, come on, let's have it now. Wine's meant for drinking, not keeping. That's what Marty says.'

'Look, Scottie . . .' The name stuck in her throat, like the Ryvita. 'I'm beginning to wonder if we're talking about the same Martin.'

' 'Course. He gave me this address, didn't he?'

Why had he given her the address? And where was Scottie's husband (if she had one)? When had she first met Martin? And, more worrying, who had fathered all those babies? Impulsively she seized the Chablis from the fridge and practically hurled it into Scottie's lap. 'There's a corkscrew in that drawer there.'

The sudden silence was filled with the snigger of the rain.

Scottie found the corkscrew, and after mangling the cork and jabbing her thumb, finally sloshed wine into two coffee mugs. 'Cheers!' she said. 'Here's to Marty.' Mug in hand, she started wandering round the kitchen, like an estate agent on a tour of inspection. 'You're not exactly short of space here,' she observed. '*Or* fancy gadgets,' she added, prodding the electric juicer.

Irma surveyed the room as if it belonged to someone else. Automatic everything – washing, drying, cleaning, chopping, coffee-making. Some machines hadn't been invented yet, but she would buy them when they had – machines for eating and conversing, and for turfing people out. It was safer on your own. Sometimes she left the answerphone on, even when she wasn't working, to hear Martin's stern recorded voice announcing to all callers that they were 'unavailable'.

'I could do with one of these,' said Scottie, patting the dishwasher, like a dog. 'I don't bother to wash up until we're completely out of cups and plates, but still . . .' She held up her hands for Irma to see. They looked years older than the rest of her, criss-crossed with tiny lines, the nails broken or bitten, the fingers roughened, red.

That's what babies did to you, presumably. Irma examined her own hands: the nails discreetly varnished, the fingers smooth and cosseted. She and Martin had never had a cat or a dog, let alone a baby. Disconsolately she picked up her mug and took a long, slow draught of wine.

Scottie's tour had now brought her to the freezer. Without a moment's hesitation she opened it and peered inside. 'Why have such a big one and leave it three-quarters empty? Mind you, what's here looks pretty pukka – Dover sole and duck breasts and Häagen-Dazs ice-cream.'

'*Shut* that!' Irma snapped. 'I don't want things defrosting.' Snooping was extremely rude. A kitchen was as private as a bedroom – more so. She hated being judged. If she bought luxuries or sweet things, it didn't mean she would necessarily eat them. Sometimes it was just a test of self-control, like medieval saints who invited naked virgins into their beds and then spent the night reading sacred texts. The ice-creams were her untouched naked virgins.

But Scottie was already taking out a carton. '"Royal vanilla pecan" – never heard of it. My favourite's chocolate chip.'

'Will you kindly put that back. And d'you want the Ryvitas or not?'

'Strawberry, too. Great! Chuck us a saucepan over, will you? I prefer it hot.'

'*Hot*? Ice-cream?' Bemused as much by Scottie's insolence as by her peculiar eating habits, Irma sought comfort in the wine once more.

'Sure. It's yummy. Heating brings out the taste. Marty used to love it. In fact, make that three pans. If you've never had it, you should try several different flavours. The kids like them all mixed up together. You get some smashing colour effects. But we'll start with one at a time.' Scottie dolloped chocolate chip into the largest saucepan, and strawberry into the second. She prised open the vanilla pecan and scooped some up in her fingers to sample. Evidently it passed muster, as she then spooned a generous quantity into the remaining pan, and put all three pans on the hob.

Irma watched, in a daze. Part of her was still working on auto-pilot, composing sentences in her head. '*Fire in the kitchen accounts for a shattering loss of life and property. Our portable dry-powder extinguisher has been designed to cope instantly and efficiently with all risks from . . . from . . .*' From *what?* The wine had gone straight through her empty stomach to her legs, leaving her dizzy and disoriented. Yet when she looked, her mug was full again.

'Here we go!' Scottie tipped hot pink froth from the saucepan into a Pyrex jug and, barely pausing for breath, slurped it straight from the jug.

Mesmerized, Irma gulped more wine, unconsciously keeping pace with Scottie. Soon all that was left was a drop or two of Chablis, and a small puddle of ice-cream.

'Your turn,' Scottie said, her lips moustached with pink.

Irma shook her head. She had gone much too far already and would have to pay for this.

'Don't you like strawberry? My oldest doesn't, either. Try the chocolate chip then.' Scottie took the second saucepan off the gas and dipped a spoon in, which she held to Irma's lips. 'Open up,' she coaxed. 'Careful – it's hot.'

Irma's mouth seemed to be opening of its own accord, as if Scottie was a puppet-master manipulating her strings. A few drops of hot brown lava trickled on to her tongue, mingled briefly with the sharp aftertaste of the wine, then slithered down her throat.

'Good girl! It'll build you up, this will. You're nothing but skin and bone.' Scottie hovered with a second spoonful, clucking with satisfaction as it too went down successfully.

Irma sat, transfixed, as Scottie picked up the third pan – the royal vanilla pecan. It had been Martin's favourite flavour once, long ago when . . .

Scottie put the spoon down and dipped her fingers into the saucepan. She held them out to Irma, white and warm and dripping. 'Suck,' she whispered.

Irma clamped her mouth shut, determined to break the spell. This must stop. Immediately.

But again Scottie took control, somehow easing her lips apart and slipping the ice-cream-coated fingers in. 'That's it,' she said as Irma sucked. 'Lovely, isn't it?'

A piece of nut took Irma by surprise – hard and crunchy amidst the sea of creamy richness. '*Enough*,' she tried to say, but another foamy mouthful prevented her from speaking.

'You're doing fine, love. Now let's mix the flavours up.' Scottie emptied the remains of the three cartons into one large pan and swirled the mixture round before putting it back on the gas. When it was hot, she tipped it into the jug, giggling as it overflowed and a whitish-pinkish-brownish pool spread across the worktop. 'Shut your eyes,' she ordered. 'You can taste better if you can't see. If you lose one of your senses, the others sort of sharpen up to compensate – you know, like a blind man who can hear a beech-nut falling on the M4.'

Try as she might to keep them open, Irma felt her eyelids inexorably closing. And through the clamour of the rain, she did indeed hear a tiny beech-nut floating to the ground. 'Must get on,' she murmured. 'Job to finish. It's late . . .'

'Din-dins first. You can't work on an empty stomach. Come on, open wide.'

The rim of the jug pressed against her lips as hot, sticky fluid streamed into her mouth. The sickly taste of strawberries mingled with the tang of chocolate and the musky sweetness of vanilla. The wine was only an echo now, a memory. Her whole body was filling up like a giant hot-water bottle, the frothy liquor turning her from iron-grey to pastel as it poured into her rigid limbs.

Never had she been so hot. The three gases were still blazing and their blue and orange fire was searing her mind, melting her will to resist. Scottie was leaning right over her, tipping the jug to give her the last sweet dregs. She could feel the girl's soft pillowy breasts squashed against her own more meagre ones. She didn't pull away.

The jug lost contact with her lips and droplets of warm ice-cream plopped on to her bare neck and slithered down inside her blouse. Opening her eyes, she saw the pointing fingers of the clock. 'Late,' she whimpered. 'Work to do. Should be back at—'

'You're tired,' said Scottie. 'Time for beddy-byes.'

The light was fading in the kitchen. The rain had diluted the colours and turned everything dim and murky. Yes, it must be time for bed if it was dark.

Soothing hands helped her to her feet, guided her upstairs and gently pushed the bedroom door open.

'Single beds?' Scottie's voice seemed to come from a distance.

Irma stared at the beige brocaded bedspreads, marooned from each other by a barren stretch of carpet. The room looked different, somehow. She rarely went there in the daytime, once she had made the beds and tidied up. Rain was fretting at the windows in a sullen rhythmic drone.

Scottie flung back the coverlet on the nearest bed. 'In you get,' she said.

'No, that's Martin's bed.'

'So?'

Martin had a moustache that pressed against his pillow. Moustaches were germ-traps, harbouring microbes from handkerchiefs and particles of food. She preferred her own space, anyway. People had their private smells and noises, even intimate secretions – best kept separate.

But Scottie had made a little nest in Martin's blankets and was plumping up the pillows. 'Come on now, don't fuss.'

Irma edged towards the bed. That too seemed different – smaller. She crawled in between the ice-blue sheets.

'Not in your clothes, silly. They'll get all creased.'

She hated undressing in front of strangers. Even with Martin, she always took her clothes off in the bathroom and came back in her dressing-gown.

'Here, let me help.' Scottie unbuttoned her blouse for her with swift and skilful hands. She was used to undressing children and putting them to bed. Irma lay passively and let her take the blouse off, shivering in the chilly room.

'Poor love, you're cold. I'll warm you up.' In a trice, Scottie had removed her jeans, revealing off-white pants with 'FRIDAY' embroidered on them, just above the crotch. Today was Monday, wasn't it? Irma felt more and more confused.

'Shove up a bit. You're hogging all the bed.' Scottie clambered in. She was still wearing her sweater, so her body felt warm and fuzzy at the top, whereas her bare legs were clammy-cold. A strand of her still-damp hair was trapped inside the sheet, trailing across Irma's neck like seaweed. She tried to move to the far side of the bed, but the wine-and-ice-cream cocktail suddenly surged into her throat. She slumped back against the pillow.

Scottie stroked her forehead. 'You're not well, are you? Working too hard, I expect. Just close your eyes and relax.'

She felt soft lips nuzzling her cheek. Other lips had been as soft as that. Years and years ago. Her little brother, wasn't it? His name began with an M – M for moustache, except he didn't have one then, just wispy blond down velveting his upper lip. He was embarrassed when she touched it with her finger. He had bitten the finger, hard, and when she cried, he kissed it better, hard. She'd had to pay for it. His hands had been stained with paint, she remembered. Always been good at art, her little brother.

There was a finger in her mouth now. Tasted of chocolate. Chocolate was forbidden. They had locked up all the sweets as a punishment; made them sleep on different floors. Frightening in the attic, cold in bed alone. Not now, though. Closing her eyes, she groped towards the heat.

Lying naked on her back, she listened to the silence. The rain must have stopped – but when? Painfully, like an invalid after a dangerous fever, she squinted through her eyelids and saw a mocking beam of sunlight rainbowing the sill.

Her little brother had grown into a man, a man with a moustache. He was here in the bedroom, frowning from the chest of drawers in his silver photo-frame. The pin-stripes were plumb-lines for his spine; he had just a single eye and that was narrowed. The photo had been taken at a wedding: six bridesmaids and a four-tier cake. They had stayed the night at a smart hotel with an enormous white bed just like another wedding cake. It had seemed a desecration to cut into the immaculate white-iced coverlet and disturb the sugared flounces of the pillows. She had lain stiff and lumpen like a slab of dried-out marzipan while the man in the photo (whose breath smelt sweet like dead carnations) hacked into her with his cake knife. In the morning, he'd ordered kippers for breakfast and the smell had made her retch.

She sniffed her fingers. They still smelt of fish. Somebody was in bed with her – a plump girl with big bosoms, fast asleep and breathing in little snorty gasps. A trail of dribble had snailed across the pillowcase.

Irma eased a foot out of bed and made contact with the floor. Their clothes lay scattered on the carpet, beside a jumble of blankets. She reached for her skirt. It had two accusing stains on the front. Her tights were snarled up with her knickers, one leg inside out; her bra dangled from the headboard. Her blouse was creased; her shoes nowhere to be seen.

She pushed the dishevelled clothing into the linen basket and rammed the lid back, hard. Scottie's clothes she folded in a pile. Then she put on her dressing-gown and stole guiltily downstairs.

Even halfway down, she could feel the heat surging from the kitchen. All three gases were still full on and everything was melting. The butter was an oily yellow pool in its glass dish; a pale, congealing crust clung to all the crannies of the hob where the ice-cream had boiled over. The upturned wine bottle was dribbling, like the girl upstairs, and the draining-board was littered with dirty saucepans and sticky spoons and jugs. The clock hands made a perfect vertical – six o'clock – and Martin's dinner still only a raw package in the fridge.

She crept into the sitting-room. Two rubber boots lay abandoned on their sides, their scarlet mouths almost touching, a muddy brown secretion seeping from their soles. She made a detour round them, to her desk. Rain had trickled through the crack again and soaked her sheets of paper. *'Our heavy industrial model produces approximately 240 gallons of foam-compound, which is pre-mixed in the extinguisher body in the ratio of . . .'*

The ink had run, smudging the words, while the crimson from a coloured folder had bled into the page beneath. No one ever told you about the mess a fire could make – foam and water everywhere, strangers invading your house, your life and work disrupted.

She mopped up the water and put her papers in order. Martin would be home in an hour, expecting to see the brochure finished. Hastily she refilled her fountain pen. (She never used a ballpoint –

cheap, slatternly things that defiled your writing.) *'The easy-control trigger action and quick-release safety catch are simple enough for a child to operate . . .'*

'Child,' she wrote again. Five letters, fifteen loaves. The word was decomposing, running into a rivulet of Waterman's Blue. The tear trickled down the paper, blurring her neat sketch of a lever-type extinguisher mounted on a two-wheeled trolley. She was extinguishing her work, pumping out great rhythmic sobs that rolled through her body like waves. All at once she recognized the rhythm.

She rushed to the door and banged on it with her fists. They had locked her in again. 'I didn't *do* it!' she shouted. 'He wasn't even there that night. He stayed with Ricky Barnes. It was raining really hard, so . . .' They couldn't hear. They were downstairs playing bridge, with the wireless on. 'You've got to believe me. I didn't even see him till . . .' The rain was lashing at the tiny attic window. Terrifying locked in there: dark shapes under dust-sheets, things that creaked and flapped. 'It's not fair! He started it. He got into my bed. I tried to push him off me, but . . .' Tears streaming down her cheeks, she went on hammering at the door. The rain made fun of her, echoing the noise as it beat against the pane. 'I don't care what you say, I didn't do it . . .'

' *'Course* you didn't, love.' Scottie was kneeling beside her, an arm around her shoulders. 'All better now. All over.'

Irma clung to her, aware of rough brown towelling beneath her fingers. 'Take that *off*,' she hissed. 'It's Martin's.'

'Hush, love. It's all right now.'

Suddenly the doorbell shrilled. She froze. 'That's him. He's here! He'll see you.'

The bell rang again. She tried to think coherently. Of course it wasn't Martin. He wouldn't ring – he had a key. Besides, he never got home till seven. She tugged at Scottie's sleeve. 'If it's the man selling brushes, tell him I'm not in. I'm busy – understand? Get rid of him, OK?'

Scottie nodded and disappeared. Closing the door, Irma returned to her desk. She had an urgent assignment to finish.

'Smoke can suffocate, before the flames even appear . . .' She made her up-strokes ramrod-straight, rounded her o's meticulously; her whole attention focused on the letters. *'Recent research has demonstrated that in the average fire, you have only four minutes to*

escape . . .' The last e looped into an l – a flame. She quenched it with blotting paper. She could hear voices at the front door: Scottie's and a deeper voice – a man. She must shut them out and concentrate on quick-release wall brackets, anti-corrosive coatings. But the pen fell from her fingers as footsteps tramped across the hall, coming nearer, nearer, until they were right outside the door. Where could she hide? Frantically she darted behind her desk and crouched down by the window, as hulking feet clumped into the room.

'Funny,' Scottie said. 'She *was* in here. I saw her close the door.'

Irma held her breath and peered round the edge of the desk, to be confronted by two heavy black shoes with toecaps, and attached to them a pair of navy serge legs.

So it wasn't Martin. Not her Martin, anyway. But suddenly she was eye to eye with Scottie, who had spotted her and was tripping over the far-too-long brown dressing-gown in her haste to reach the desk.

Angrily Irma stood up. The first thing she saw was the helmet. The man was holding it upside down, like a bucket. He was in his shirt-sleeves and she noticed the black epaulettes, each with a metal number on it, and a small silver button embossed with a crown. Behind him was a scrawny-looking woman, similarly dressed in navy serge slacks and white shirt, and wearing a black hat with a black and white checked band.

The man spoke first. 'Good evening, Mrs Groves. It *is* Mrs Groves, isn't it?'

She didn't answer but, regardless, he continued. 'I'm PC Gary Bennett and this is WPC Joyce Mills. We're here concerning—'

Scottie elbowed him aside. 'Let *me* tell her. It . . . it'll be a shock. Give her time.'

Irma stared coldly at the three of them. 'What's the matter? I haven't time to stop. I'm working to a deadline.' It wasn't just the brochure but Martin's dinner too. She would have to resort to the freezer and defrost the Dover sole. At least fish was low in fat.

The policeman had both hands round his helmet now and looked as if he wanted to squeeze it to death. 'Forgive us intruding like this, but it's about your . . . your husband, ma'am. First, though, could you confirm that you *are* Mrs Martin Groves.'

Scottie was snivelling uncontrollably. 'It's M. . . Marty, love. He . . . he's . . .'

The policeman cleared his throat. 'I'm afraid we have bad news.

There's been an accident.'

'Accident?' Irma repeated. 'What kind of accident?'

'A fire, ma'am – in the building where your husband works.'

Briskly she returned to her desk. 'No,' she said, 'you're mistaken.' She screwed up the tear-stained pages and threw them into the waste-paper basket, then opened a packet of fresh white virgin paper.

'I'm sorry, Mrs Groves, there's no mistake.' The scrawny woman had come over now. Her face was contorted into a peculiar sort of grimace, as if she was about to cry, like Scottie. 'Unfortunately your husband was trapped. You see, he was on the sixth floor, furthest from the fire escape, and there was only a tiny window.'

Irma's patience was running out. 'Would you please *go*. You're standing in my light.' How could anyone work with these continual interruptions? – strangers bursting in and inventing ludicrous stories, tramping in their dirty shoes across her pale cream carpet. She settled herself more firmly in her chair.

'I realize it must be an awful shock, ma'am.' The woman's voice was maddeningly kind. 'Perhaps your friend here could make a cup of tea.'

'She's *not* my friend,' Irma muttered. Scottie was still sniffling, wiping her nose on the sleeve of Martin's dressing-gown. Now *that* would have to be laundered, along with the sheets and blankets.

' 'Course. How many sugars, love?'

'I don't take sugar. And I don't want tea.' This work was vitally important. It could save lives and homes, give people time to escape. She picked up a freshly sharpened pencil and ruled a wide margin down the top sheet of paper. It was the little details that mattered – generous margins, good quality pens, the proper tools for the job.

'*Power, performance, satisfaction,*' she wrote. '*Yours with our impressive range of fire extinguishers. Spring into action with a forty-foot jet of water pumping from your nozzle at heroic speed . . . A touch of your thumb and the jet is transformed into a drenching spray.*' Her pen leapt in wild blue arcs across the page. '*Or change to pre-mix foam and shoot off 200 gallons in under ninety seconds. Watch it vanquish roof-high flames . . .*'

The serge legs hovered by her chair. 'I don't think you quite under-stand, Mrs Groves.' The policeman turned to Scottie, who was shuf-fling from foot to foot, chewing a strand of her hair. 'Has she any relatives – someone living near? A sister, perhaps, or. . . ?'

Irma waved him away. '*Choose from pistol-shaped squeeze-grip nozzle, complete with initial drop-in pressure charge, or powerful spray-gun action . . . Discharge time only 100 seconds and easily recharged . . . Ideal for use on delicate equipment.*'

And now the policewoman had the effrontery to put a hand on her shoulder. 'I know it must be hard to take it in, Mrs Groves, but if you could just stop writing for a moment . . .'

Irma pushed the hand off. Of course she couldn't stop. She was working brilliantly. The words were streaming on to the page almost faster than her pen could form them. '*High-pressure black rubber hose, twenty foot long, with turn-off cock and horn . . . solid hot-brass pressing-head . . . telescopic applicator . . .*'

Scottie stumbled over to the desk and tried to wrest the pen from her. 'Stop!' she entreated. '*Please.* You don't know what you're doing.'

Irma moved round to the far end of the desk, where she continued to write standing up. Impossible to stop. She had got into the rhythm now, and didn't even have to think. It was as simple, as inevitable, as breathing. '*After discharge, the head can be re-screwed to a full body and is ready for immediate use again, as many times as . . .*'

'Mrs Groves, I really feel it might be best if—'

'Leave me alone,' she demanded, starting a crisp new sheet of paper. '*Swivelling head emits violent jet of foam . . . double-purpose nozzle with total discharge . . . penetrates areas normally inaccessible . . .*'

The rhythm was impelling her, flooding through her body. She was merely the instrument, the receptacle. She *had* to go on – could no more stop than the rain could stop, or the darkness, or the fire. And if only that stupid little Scottie would clear off, the whole thing would be finished by the time Marty got home, and they could go out and celebrate with a six-course Chinese meal and then come back and work on their collage together.

Virgin in the Gym

Annie cowered in the doorway, assaulted by violent noise. The thud of feet on treadmills vied with relentless music booming from speakers round the walls. And some of the exercise-machines themselves contributed to the din, issuing commands in shrill robotic voices: 'Begin!' 'Change stations!' 'Stop and take your pulse!' The machines were uniformly black, crouching in menacing rows, doubled and quadrupled in the mirrors. Some of them had names, lettered in white across their flanks – all with the prefix 'life'. Life Cycle, Life Stepper, Life Rower, Life Cross Trainer. Death would be more fitting, surely – death resulting from slow torture.

And yet the victims seemed willing enough as they stepped, pedalled, pumped at full pelt. It was she who was the alien, her pink, plump, saggy flesh at odds with the rock-hard, deep-bronzed muscles of the true devotees here. And her old grey sweat-pants and dowdy T-shirt spelled sartorial disaster amid the multi-coloured, figure-defining Lycra. Not that anyone would notice her or her clothes. They were intent only on themselves, worshippers at the shrine of personal performance targets.

If she crept out now, she could stop off on the way home, buy the Sunday papers and retreat ignominiously to bed. Except she would probably end up crying all day, as she had done the last two Sundays, wondering where Steve was – worse, *knowing* where he was.

'Hi, Annie! Are you OK?'

She turned to see Tyler, the fitness instructor who had shown her round the gym. An 'initiation', he'd called it, although she could remember little of what he'd said, so intimidated was she by the intricacies of the hardware. Could anyone understand those batteries of

219

flashing dials and complex controls without a degree in computer science?

'Yes, I'm fine,' she lied, following him into the main body of the gym. He would expect her to make a start, put the initiation into practice. 'I'm just getting my bearings,' she said, shocked at her reflection in the mirrors. It was biceps that were meant to bulge, not bellies. But every time Steve disappeared, she would resort to comfort-eating, as if by wolfing down custard creams or croissants she could devour the man himself, trap him in her stomach to prevent him sneaking off again.

'Sure. Take your time.' Tyler gave his foxy smile. He was small but solidly built, with crew-cut sandy hair and a freckling of ginger fuzz on his legs. 'Just call me if you need me, OK?'

She nodded, moving hurriedly out of his range of vision into the Stretching Area. (She had been alarmed to find there were even machines for stretching – black again, and complicated.) Anatomical drawings on the wall depicted all manner of muscles she was sure she didn't possess. If she had managed to exist for thirty-seven years without gluteals or abductors, why bother about them now?

She caught the eye of a man on one of the machines and gave a nervous smile. The smile went unacknowledged – he was too busy honing his already impressive quadriceps. It was a sort of religion, presumably, this striving for physical (rather than spiritual) perfection, and resisting all distractions along the way. Instead of hymns and plainchant, the aggressive music whipped worshippers into line, spurring them on to ever greater heights with its insistent, punitive beat. And the fitness-instructor-priests, clad in vestments of red T-shirts and black shorts, preached a gospel of self-denial and constant effort, to overcome the evil of flab. The Reverend Tyler was nowhere in sight, thank the Lord. She had already noted his zeal in converting unbelievers.

She drifted to the Weights Area – perhaps the most daunting of all. The weightlifters' faces were contorted into grimaces of pure agony as they raised huge dumb-bells above their heads, every muscle straining, singlets dark with sweat. Their groans and grunts reminded her of Steve in bed, his little gasps and moans followed by a final 'Aaaaaagh!' sounding more like pain than pleasure. First exercise as religion, now exercise as sex – self-absorption, extreme physical exertion, flushed faces, heaving bodies. In fact, one of the most muscly of the weightlifters actually resembled a gigantic phallus, his whole gleaming body engorged and veined with blood. She had a sudden vision of Steve again, naked in Helen's bed, transformed into a vast tumescent penis.

With a shudder she returned to the treadmills. Only a couple of them were in use, yet the frenetic pounding of the two pairs of feet seemed to trample her brain to sludge. She had always been a quiet type, tiptoeing and whispering her way through life, but here you were programmed (like the music) to wham and thwack and thud.

'Aren't you going to make a start, Annie?'

She jumped: Tyler had crept up unawares. 'Er, yes,' she said, 'of course. But could you please go over the instructions for the tread-mill?' That at least seemed fairly straightforward: just walking on a moving platform – or running, if you were as fit as these two. She stepped on to the machine furthest away from them to give herself a chance of hearing Tyler.

'Remember, you enter your weight first, in pounds. A hundred and fifty, wasn't it?'

She flushed at this public proclamation, but there were no secrets in the gym. As well as weighing and measuring her, Tyler had calculated her body-fat index – a source of profound embarrassment.

'On your next visit I'll show you how to key in your own programme, but we'll start you on the manual controls today. It's simpler, and it means you can stop whenever you want.'

'Like *now*,' she muttered under her breath. Luckily the other two had just finished and were sauntering past with towels slung round their necks.

'These buttons control the speed. And the ones below raise or lower the gradient . . .'

Her mind strayed to Steve once more – still in bed with Helen, calculating the obnoxious woman's body-fat index, measuring her breasts . . .

'And if you'd like some entertainment, this is our cardio-theatre.' Tyler indicated the banks of TV screens mounted on the wall. 'There's a choice of twenty channels, and you can have either sub-titles or headphones.'

'Neither, thanks.' She would need all her wits to cope with the treadmill controls. The music was bad enough, although it didn't seem to bother Tyler – he simply raised his voice above it.

'In that case, press the Start button . . . No, don't cling to the bar like that. It's OK, you won't overbalance. Now turn up the speed a little . . . Good. And again. Keep pressing the right-hand button. And use the mirror to keep an eye on your posture. Head up! Shoulders down! . . . That's it. You're getting the hang of it now.'

Encouraged, she lengthened her stride, even increased the speed a bit more.

'Brilliant!' he smiled, giving her the thumbs-up sign. 'I'll be back in a while to check on how you're doing.'

As soon as he'd gone she stopped looking in the mirror and fixed her gaze instead on one of the silent television screens. Some sort of game-show was in progress; the contestants (all gratifyingly over-weight) were falling about and laughing as they performed ridiculous stunts.

The diversion was short-lived, however, because someone was approaching the next treadmill. My God, she thought, *Helen*! She stared at the long, tanned legs, the girlish waist, the sensuous, full-lipped mouth. She had spent many a night imagining Helen – then hacking her to pieces with an axe. The dismembered corpse had sometimes been an English rose, with blue eyes and perfect skin, other times a redhead, green-eyed and elfin-faced, and occasionally a foreigner, exotic with high cheekbones and a cascade of raven hair falling seductively over her shoulders. But this surely was the defini-tive Helen, combining elements of all three: blue-eyed, auburn-haired and with, yes, high cheekbones and a cover-girl complexion. And impeccably turned out, of course, in a shimmering purple leotard that clung to her pert little breasts. No wonder Steve was besotted. He'd been coming home later and later each night, pleading pressure of work – work that even stretched to Sundays, in the shape of mysteri-ous clients who were free only at weekends. And like a fool she had believed him, until she discovered Helen's letter in his wallet, at which point she'd resorted to murder. So how come Helen was still here, unscathed and as large as life?

She was watching her so intently she almost lost her footing. Helen didn't notice – her mind was on the treadmill, keying in some compli-cated programme. And as soon as she began to move, the easy, flow-ing rhythm of her feet became a further unspoken insult. Annie was the old carthorse, soon to be put out to grass, superseded by a lively thoroughbred filly. The filly broke into an effortless trot, graceful and high-stepping, while the broken-winded carthorse struggled to keep up. And yet the filly's very proximity acted as a spur. Each echoed the other's breathing, and their thudding hooves began to merge into a single steady beat.

The filly started to canter. The carthorse also quickened her pace. Bulk had certain advantages: strength, persistence, stamina. And a glance at the dials confirmed that she too was approaching a canter, galvanized by the power of Helen's feet. Their drumming pulse was acting like a stimulant, invigorating her tired, ungainly body, while the filly's rapid breathing seemed in turn to energise her lungs. The weight was slipping off her, pound by exultant pound, until she was nearly as lithe and slim as her rival. Then, with a final surge, she broke into a gallop – a young thoroughbred herself at last, sound in lung and limb. Sweat was pouring off her, and that, too, was a release, allowing her bitterness and jealousy to flow away, flow out.

Nothing else existed now save the rhythm of her feet, the thumping of her heart, startled from its torpor, the momentum of her legs, dynamic and untiring. Her face was flushed, her breath came in laboured gasps, but that was how Steve loved her – panting-hot and wild.

All the other exercisers vanished into nothing. Even Helen faded to a phantom, a mirage. She alone was left, running on and on in triumph.

'A Diet Sprite, please. . . . No, that's it. Nothing else.' Who wanted biscuits or chocolate, let alone a heavy meal?

Finding a free table, she sat sipping her drink luxuriously. The long shower had left her cool and refreshed, although her cheeks still glowed, she noticed. Even here in the café there were mirrors round the walls, but now, instead of avoiding them, she revelled in the image they reflected: clingy Lycra leotard and tights – in shimmering purple, of course. And no longer ancient tennis shoes, but Nike Air Max trainers.

'Hi! Mind if I join you?'

She eyed the man with distaste. He must be fifty at least, yet his close-cropped hair looked too blond to be natural, and his skimpy shorts revealed more than was decent. Without waiting for an answer, he plonked himself in the chair beside her. 'Are you new? I'm sure I'd have remembered you if I'd seen you around before.'

'No, you haven't,' she said curtly. 'This is my first time.'

'Well, if there's anything you want to know, just ask. I've been a member here for yonks. I'm Kevin, by the way.'

She didn't respond. She was concentrating on holding in her stomach while she flexed her gluteals.

'And what's your name?' He pressed on regardless.

'*Helen*,' she said, with a quick intake of breath.

'Great to meet you, Helen. Can I get you another drink?'

Abruptly she stood up, smoothing her tautly silken thighs. Did he really imagine that a woman like Helen would be grateful for his attentions? 'Sorry – haven't time. I'm due for Cardio-Tone in five minutes, and then a session on the weights.'